THE WOMAN WHO GOT HER LIFE BACK

A GIBSON

B
Boldwood

First published in Great Britain in 2025 by Boldwood Books Ltd.

Copyright © Fiona Gibson, 2025

Cover Design by Jane Dixon-Smith

Cover Images: Shutterstock

The moral right of Fiona Gibson to be identified as the author of this work has been asserted in accordance with the Copyright, Designs and Patents Act 1988.

All rights reserved. No part of this book may be reproduced in any form or by any electronic or mechanical means, including information storage and retrieval systems, without written permission from the author, except for the use of brief quotations in a book review. This book is a work of fiction and, except in the case of historical fact, any resemblance to actual persons, living or dead, is purely coincidental.

Every effort has been made to obtain the necessary permissions with reference to copyright material, both illustrative and quoted. We apologise for any omissions in this respect and will be pleased to make the appropriate acknowledgements in any future edition.

A CIP catalogue record for this book is available from the British Library.

Paperback ISBN 978-1-83617-225-3

Large Print ISBN 978-1-83617-226-0

Hardback ISBN 978-1-83617-224-6

Ebook ISBN 978-1-83617-227-7

Kindle ISBN 978-1-83617-228-4

Audio CD ISBN 978-1-83617-219-2

MP3 CD ISBN 978-1-83617-220-8

Digital audio download ISBN 978-1-83617-221-5

This book is printed on certified sustainable paper. Boldwood Books is dedicated to putting sustainability at the heart of our business. For more information please visit https://www.boldwoodbooks.com/about-us/sustainability/

Boldwood Books Ltd, 23 Bowerdean Street, London, SW6 3TN

www.boldwoodbooks.com

For Belinda Jones
A shining star

PROLOGUE

Spasms of pain are zapping across Celia's feet. She is trying on shoes and they don't have the ones she likes in her size. Although she is actually a six, with no small degree of effort, she's managed to cram her trotters into a five. *They'll be fine*, she tells herself as she hobbles around the shop.

They *look* great, which is what matters.

It's not as if she'll be walking far.

Mostly, she'll be sitting down.

'They look amazing on you,' the sales assistant enthuses. 'They're a real statement shoe, but *so* comfy to wear.'

'I love them,' Celia announces as, within the shoes, tiny people seem to be stabbing at her insteps with knives.

'Are they for something special?'

'Yes, my oldest friend's wedding.'

'Oh, they're perfect for that. So gorgeous and fun!' As much fun as sticking your feet into a fire – but they *are* gorgeous, Celia decides. And for Amanda's wedding she'll need all the help she can get.

Although several years have passed since she's seen her

friend, Celia knows it'll be an extravagant do, populated by glossy people from Amanda's media world in London. Currently, Celia's world is centred around the houseplant hospital she runs from her Glasgow flat. Nurturing drooping aspidistras and desiccated begonias back to full health: at forty-three, *this* is her comfort zone. Not being an unpartnered guest at a glittering social event, as Geoff, Celia's husband, has refused to go.

'Oh, no, that's not my thing,' he announced.

'What d'you mean, it's not your thing?' Celia asked in a panic.

He shrugged. 'You'll have a lot more fun on your own.'

Why do people do this? Pretend they're doing you a favour by not going with you? 'You have to come,' she protested. 'I won't know anyone.'

'You'll know Amanda, won't you?'

She blinked at him. 'I think Amanda might be a bit busy being the *bride*, Geoff. C'mon, we can make a weekend of it. It'll be fun—'

'Ugh, London.' He shuddered. 'All those crowds. So expensive...'

Celia started to protest that they could simply stroll around, taking it all in. That wouldn't cost much, would it? And they could visit Kew Gardens with its incredible, rare plant collections, unrivalled anywhere in the world! What she'd give to see those. She didn't mention that Kew isn't free to visit, although when she'd checked, she'd noted that entry was cheaper after 4 p.m. If she literally *galloped* from the various gardens and glasshouses to the famous pagoda, would she manage to see it all?

These things matter to Geoff. Saving money, that is. If Celia buys these shoes that are currently crushing her poor feet, she won't admit how much they cost. They are glossy red with a

Mary Jane-type strap and a chunky heel; a bit seventies, she thinks. Her mum had a pair just like them, and Celia remembers pulling them on in her bedroom when she and Amanda were kids. Celia loved those times: the two of them holed up in her bedroom with their favourite music blaring out from her tinny stereo. Whenever they dressed up and danced together, she would almost be able to block out the racket from the party raging on downstairs.

At around eleven years old, Celia and Amanda had invented a game. The 'yes game', they called it. Whenever one of them thought of something fun or a bit crazy to do, the other had to say yes. They created elaborate costumes, devised dance routines and roamed their neighbourhood dressed up as eccentric characters. Celia was naturally shy: 'A little mouse,' said Joyce, her mother, not entirely affectionately. Yet somehow, being around her best friend brought her out of herself. It was as if Amanda saw Celia differently to how the rest of the world seemed to view her. As the perfect partner in what could only be a thrilling future for both of them.

'Best friends forever,' Amanda would always say.

How lucky I am, Celia had thought. Despite what was happening at home, she truly believed that. But then, at eighteen, Celia's life veered off in a dramatically different direction – and there was no going back after that.

These days, there is barely any contact at all between Celia and Amanda. In fact, Celia was surprised to be invited to the wedding and had decided to decline, politely, until Geoff insisted that she went. 'I'll pay for your train fare and a hotel,' he announced out of the blue.

'Are you sure?' Celia reeled in shock. This from the man who regards buying a sandwich as a crazed extravagance! *How much do the ingredients cost, Celia? 15p?*

'It'll be good for you,' he insisted. 'You seem like you need a break.'

Still, he refused to go with her, and for weeks Celia has been dreading it. Amanda is a TV presenter; her husband-to-be, an actor. What will she talk about to people from those worlds? The best position, light-wise, for an ailing yucca? How to rescue a crispy Boston fern?

Yet something about these beautiful red shoes whisks her back to being in her childhood bedroom, with the friend she loved so much – when, for that short time, as they danced in her room, it felt to Celia as if anything was possible. And now, on this drizzly January afternoon, Celia tells herself that finding these shoes is a sign. A sign that she *can* do this; that she *can* travel to London alone and chat to beautiful strangers and not feel upset that Geoff has refused to come.

'So, the fives are okay for you?' the sales assistant prompts her.

'They're a little bit tight,' Celia concedes, her toes smashed agonisingly together, 'but I'm sure they'll stretch.'

'Oh, they definitely will. Honestly, you look fabulous in them. They were made for you.'

They just need wearing in, Celia assures herself as she leaves the shop.

On the morning of Amanda's wedding, Geoff comes to Glasgow Central Station to see her off. Having virtually shovelled her onto the 7.35 train, he waves briefly from the platform. But before it's even started to pull away, he's shot off like a whippet out of the trap.

Strange, Celia thinks. *Where's he off to in such a hurry?*

Later that night, after the wedding, she steps into her bleak little hotel room, peels off her new shoes and stares down at her traumatised feet. Her left heel is blistered, her toes pink and swollen like angry little sausages. She wonders if they'll ever recover.

What was the point of all that? she thinks as she tugs off the shift dress that clung uncomfortably to her stomach and hips. It was sweet of Amanda to invite her, but Celia suspects it was due to a sense of obligation – and nostalgia, perhaps. It's been twenty-five years since they've felt close.

No, it was *Geoff* who'd desperately wanted Celia to go. Something about this seems a little off. She doesn't quite know why she feels so uneasy – but there's one thing Celia does know.

Shoes never 'stretch' in the way you'd want them to.

You can't make them fit, just by loving them.

And you should always listen to your heart.

1

FOUR MONTHS LATER

Caustic wine shoots the wrong way down Celia's throat.

'Are you all *right*?' squawks Bernie, her sister-in-law, who requested this family Zoom. The Blooms are not especially close. Their Zoom calls always feel like something of an obligation, and today's was arranged to tie up lingering matters concerning Geoff and Bernie's deceased father's estate.

'I'm fine,' Celia manages, when her splutters have subsided. This particular vintage could melt chewing-gum off the pavement but she has another swig anyway. She and Geoff are stationed side by side, as if called in for questioning, at the kitchen table of their Glasgow flat. In their Grade II-listed former rectory in Somerset, Bernie and Lindor are entwined on a swampy, deep green velvet sofa that seems to be threatening to suck them right in.

Celia drains her glass. In fact, it wasn't the viciousness of the wine that caused the embarrassing choking episode. Rather, it's what her sister-in-law just said. 'Bernie, did I hear you right?' she says. 'D'you really mean you want us to have it?'

'Yes, we've talked it over and we'd *love* that.' As the elder sibling, Bernie has always assumed superiority in the family. She flicks her long, layered, dark brown hair and beams from the laptop screen.

'Well, that's amazing, Sis,' Geoff exclaims. 'If you're absolutely sure?'

'No, that doesn't sound fair at all,' Celia says quickly, shooting him a quick look.

'No, it is,' Bernie insists. 'It makes perfect sense. You guys are near enough to use it. *We* never would...' She glances at Lindor, who tweaks his pretentious, pointy little beard and murmurs in agreement.

The item in question is a rancid static caravan slowly rotting into the ground on the south Ayrshire coast. When their father died in September, everything was divided equally between his son and daughter, according to the will. It all seemed very simple – until Bernie's shock proposal today: that Geoff and Celia take the thing on.

Celia is fully aware of the state of it. On her insistence, shortly after her father-in-law's funeral, she and Geoff had driven over to check up on the place. He'd been reluctant, and she'd assumed he simply didn't want to bother himself with it. Perhaps, she wondered, he was hoping it would miraculously evaporate into the air, or tumble down the steep hillside and into the sea. However, her conscience had been niggling. What if it had been broken into, or there were issues with the site managers and they wanted it taken away? It's not that Celia had nurtured any particular fondness towards her father-in-law. Duncan was a belligerent old man and his attitude towards women left a lot to be desired. Once she'd overheard him announcing to Geoff that she had 'a fine rack on her' – and she'd caught him leering at her extremely functional M&S bra on the radiator. But still, she always found it hard to settle if things weren't done properly and rules adhered to. 'We can't just pretend it's not there,' she'd insisted. 'And Bernie's not going to do anything about it, is she?'

When Geoff's mum had still been around, the caravan had been reasonably cheerful. But she'd passed away several years before and Duncan had spent his final weeks in hospital, railing against vegetarians, lefties and 'all those bloody minorities. Like women!'

'Women aren't actually a minority, Duncan,' Celia had explained at his bedside, and Geoff had glared at her.

'Dad's ill,' he had hissed. 'He doesn't need lecturing.'

They had arrived at the caravan park on a bright, crisp winter's day. While the place was beautifully kept, the other mobile homes immaculate, Ailsa View stood out as the kind you'd hurry past in case you happened to glimpse something terrible at a grimy window. The kind where you'd think, *Bet there's a pervy old man in there, masturbating in a filthy string vest.*

After no small degree of wrangling, Geoff had managed to unlock the door. Celia had gagged as the smell belched out: stale smoke and burger fat with undertones of chemical toilet and lingering farts. She had peered around in the gloom, taking in the scuffed interior walls, the grimy grey carpet and fitted seat covers mottled with stains. What on earth were they going to do with this, now that Duncan had passed away?

'Well, it's half Bernie's,' Geoff had replied, 'so whatever we do has to be a joint decision.'

And here she is, sinewy arms draped all over Lindor, clearly relieved to have absolved herself from any responsibility for the wreck. 'This really is so kind of you,' Celia says, 'but honestly, I don't think we'll use it.'

'Oh, but you *will*,' Lindor drawls, as if he knows the first thing about their holiday habits. In fact, for the past two years

Celia and Geoff haven't gone anywhere together at all. They *could* go places. They are empty nesters now, and while they're certainly not rich, they could afford an annual package holiday. But it's all golf for Geoff these days. Golf socials and weekends and even holidays to the Algarve with the lads from work. The Bakery Boys, they call themselves, conveying the image that it's all kneading dough and crimping pastry edges. In fact, their workplace is a faceless production plant churning out thousands of pies, pasties and sausage rolls daily: the epicentre of processed meats and saturated fat.

Geoff is proud to have risen through the ranks to the lofty position of Production Manager, and *Where would you have been without him, Celia?* – that's a favourite line of her mother's. That, and *Look how hard he works and what he's done for you! I hope you make him a nice packed lunch?*

A packed lunch? When will her mum realise it's not 1953, and that there's no shortage of readily available pastry goods at the factory? Yet somewhere, deep in her core, Celia clings on to the belief that actually, she *should* be grateful for Geoff having stepped into her life.

After all, she had messed up big time and had no one to blame but herself. *You should be grateful, girl. A lot of men wouldn't have taken you on.* And now she and Geoff are basically being gifted a caravan, which would send her mother into a spin of delight. But it's like inheriting a dog, Celia decides, when you've had no say in the matter. And not a well-trained dog who's easy to love, but one with 'issues' – aggressive and prone to gnawing the furniture, with bowel troubles.

Having refilled her glass, Celia looks at her husband. 'I hate to say this, Geoff, but I think Ailsa View has come to the end of its natural life.'

He affects a dramatic double take, as if she has just imparted terrible news – *I'm sorry, but the kindest option is to put it to sleep.*

'I don't think so,' he exclaims.

'Your parents *loved* that caravan. It's so full of memories of them,' drawls Lindor, who's clearly an authority on the matter despite having never set foot in Scotland, let alone in proximity to the mouldering heap. It's always amused Celia to imagine the moment when he decided to rename himself after a spherical chocolate truffle, Lindor-von-whatever-the-heck-he's-called, supposedly with aristocratic Austrian heritage, when occasionally a northern English accent sneaks out and she suspects he's from Hull.

However, she isn't amused now. Four months ago, Celia felt as if she were being basically *exiled* to London for Amanda's wedding – albeit for just one night – and that feeling of things being weird and out of kilter engulfs her again.

'All those wonderful holidays they had,' Lindor warbles on, 'by the seaside. All those happy, happy times—'

'And we will too,' Geoff announces. 'Won't we, Celia?'

Feeling defeated, she nods.

'And we'll raise a glass to you two *and* to Mum and Dad,' Geoff concludes, 'every time we go there.'

'Great!' Unable to mask her relief, Bernie sweeps a hand through her chestnut mane and bares large, square-cut teeth.

And that, seemingly, is that.

2

'Hey, Enzo?' Laura starts. 'Can I ask a favour?'

'Yeah, sure.' He pours a coffee while gripping his phone.

'Just a little thing. Mathilde's a bit het up about it. Would you mind looking after—' The call cuts out. Her phone must have died and Enzo lets out a sigh.

Laura is the mother of their nine-year-old daughter, Mathilde. Enzo has a great deal of admiration for his ex-partner. She is smart and ambitious and a fantastic mum. As a travel PR, she is also brilliant at chaperoning journalists and influencers on press trips all over the world. However, while Laura manages her professional life with remarkable flair, she is less hot on details when it comes to her own domestic arrangements. Hence previous panicky requests for Enzo to take care of various pets when she's been going away on a trip.

Exhibit A: Magnus, the ill-tempered tabby, who clearly found his temporary accommodation lacking.

B: The hamster, Fluff – 'you won't even notice he's there,' Laura insisted – who kept Enzo up from dusk until dawn every night as he scampered in his wheel.

And C: Fin, the goldfish, who had the audacity to fucking die on him!

What is it this time?

Only a plant, as it turns out, when he arrives at Laura's flat. Spike the cactus whom Mathilde was worried about leaving alone for ten days. 'That's no problem,' Enzo says, relieved. It's like thinking you have a cancerous growth and being told it's only a boil.

A cactus won't tear at the sofa and protest-pee on Enzo's pillow. It won't escape during the night – Mathilde swore she hadn't left Fluff's cage door open – and finally be found trying to burrow its way to the core of Enzo's mattress. The cat has already been dispatched to a friend's, the hamster is long deceased and the goldfish was never replaced.

'You do know cacti are indestructible though,' he says.

'Yes, but it's the longest I'll have been away,' Laura says firmly. She has already explained that, on top of the planned New York trip, she has been asked to cover a sick colleague's Alaskan tour. 'You'll just feel better with him being with you at Dad's, won't you?' she asks. Spike's pronouns have always been he/him.

'Yeah.' Perched on a kitchen stool at the worktop, Mathilde swivels round from her intricate drawing. 'He shouldn't be left alone all that time.'

'You know, Mathilde, cacti are desert plants,' Enzo remarks. 'They live for decades – hundreds of years, some of them. They hardly need any water or anything at all. They actually hold their water stores inside their—'

'Daddy's mansplaining,' Laura cuts in with an eye roll. 'Yes, we know that, Enzo. Thank you. But just in case, okay? You don't mind, do you?'

'Of course not. It's not a problem at all.'

'Great.' She adjusts her neat blonde ponytail and swills out her mug at the sink. Enzo and Laura are on good terms. They always have been, apart from that hellish period five years ago when she'd had an affair with some guy who'd resurfaced from her university days. She had confessed, saying it was just a crazy mistake. But things were never the same after that. Their once happy and easy-going relationship felt like a broken vase that they'd tried, clumsily, to glue back together. Now the cracks were all they could see.

Months of bickering followed until, tearfully, Laura decided that they weren't doing Mathilde any favours by doggedly staying together. They'd be better parents – better *friends* – if he moved out.

Enzo was prepared for it to be awful and depressing but weirdly, it wasn't. He rented a flat a few streets away, and once they had settled into the new shape of things, a different kind of relationship emerged. They had become friends. Proper friends who hung out and shared in-jokes and sent each other silly memes. Although Laura has had a couple of relationships over the years, and Enzo too has dated occasionally, she is currently single and they still spend significant amounts of time together as a family. Some summers, Laura had even joined them for a few days at Enzo's parents' thatched cottage close to Brittany's south coast.

Enzo and his sister had grown up in that house. One of the benefits of being a teacher – like Enzo – are the long holidays, which allowed him and Mathilde to spend a whole month with her beloved grandparents every summer. Enzo enjoys working at a big urban state secondary school – never a dull moment there – where he is Monsieur Fontaine and teaches French. Yet sometimes he misses being in nature. Tending an overgrown hedge, or digging away at the earth with his father, always brought a sense of calmness that he had never experienced in the classroom.

Then Enzo's father had died suddenly of a heart attack in the very garden he'd loved so much. And pretty soon it became clear that his mother wasn't coping, that things were changing at the family home. The ramshackle but always welcoming house took on a smell – an odour of not coping – and Enzo's sister Valérie called with the startling news that their mum had taken to wandering through the village with her top half on, all ready for church (best blouse, smart jacket), but only tights on below. As if, part way through dressing, she had lost interest. On a hastily arranged visit, Enzo had seen that their mum was struggling to cope, and that the house was beginning to fray at the seams.

As time went on, he was on hand as much as possible but it was his sister – whom Laura fondly refers to as Sainte Valérie – who insisted that they respect their mother's wishes and arrange a rota of carers instead of moving her into a home. She passed away a year or so later in her favourite chair with the garden view.

Feeling somewhat helpless and guilty at living so far away in Glasgow, Enzo insisted on taking responsibility for the clearing of the family home. He hadn't imagined that, at seven years old, Mathilde would want to come with him. 'It'll be too sad, darling,' he told her, 'with Mamie and Papi not there any more. I don't want you to see it like that.'

Laura agreed. 'Better to remember it how it was, sweetheart,' she said. But Mathilde had insisted on coming, and as she and her father had wrapped and packed up her grandparents' possessions, her constant chatter had stopped him from wallowing too much.

'Can we take Spike home with us?' she'd asked when everything was done. She had always been fascinated by her grandparents' tall, spikey cactus which occasionally sprouted vivid pink blooms.

'I don't think we're allowed to take live plants out of France,' Enzo explained.

'Please, Daddy. Please. I want to look after him!'

'No, we could be in trouble, honey. And what if the customs people confiscated him?'

Enzo did look into it, briefly. But it seemed that it would be possible only with the correct documentation, and by the time he had driven his parents' ancient furniture to various antiques sellers in a hired van, he was in no frame of mind for wading through the paperwork necessary in order to import what was, in fact, a very ordinary cactus. If Mathilde really wanted one, he'd buy her one in Asda. They could call him Spike Two.

That afternoon he called Laura, and naturally Mathilde wanted to chat to her mum. 'Mathilde says you're trying to palm her off with a supermarket cactus,' Laura reprimanded him.

'No, I'm not,' he protested. 'But it *is* only a plant.'

'You and your cold heart! I've looked it up,' she breezed on. 'To bring it to the UK, all you need is a phytosanitary certificate—'

'Laura, I don't have the time or—'

'It's the only thing she wants from her grandparents' house,' she retorted. 'To remember them by.' With his ex-partner and daughter railing against him, Enzo was relieved when he had to break off to let in the house clearance men, who had come to take away the last of his parents' things. And when that was done, he looked around the empty house in which he'd spent his entire childhood.

The garden was already running wild, the herb pots shrouded in weeds. The fig tree had been damaged in a storm and had to be severely cut back. Enzo rubbed at his wet eyes, determined not to get upset in front of Mathilde. Then he took her by the hand and locked the front door for one final time.

Spike! He'd forgotten to rehome him with his sister or a neighbour in the village. Too late now. He must have been thrown into a box or, more likely, slung somewhere in the overgrown garden by the rough-handed house clearance guys. To Enzo's relief, Mathilde seemed to have forgotten all about him.

She seemed in oddly high spirits as they stopped off at Valérie's for sweet, buttery *gâteau breton*, and then hugged goodbye and drove onwards to the Roscoff ferry. They watched a movie on the crossing, and Enzo kept checking his daughter's face, expecting her big brown eyes to be moist, her mouth crumpled into a frown. She still seemed eerily fine. Happy, even. And the whole drive back to Scotland she chattered away, and they played I spy, slipping effortlessly between English and French.

Back in Glasgow they pulled up outside Enzo's flat and started to carry in their bags and the boxes containing a few choice items from his parents' house. The hand-embroidered white tablecloth that had only ever appeared on special occasions. A set of branded Orangina tumblers and the ceramic storage jars – marked *farine*, *sucre*, *sel* – that Laura had always admired, which Valérie had been happy for him to take.

There were some of his dad's favourite leather-bound novels, silver cutlery in a velvet-lined box, and a small oil painting of the beach at Le Pouldu where Enzo and Valérie had played as children. Boxes of memories that they unpacked at the kitchen table, and pored over. Still Mathilde seemed fine as she lifted her lilac backpack onto the table and unzipped it. Out came a colouring book, a bunch of crumpled T-shirts and a see-through pouch of hair accessories. And her furry dog pyjama case, lovingly named Hector, that she'd had for years.

'Daddy?'

'Uh-huh?' Enzo glanced round.

'Look.'

She unzipped Hector's stomach and peeled the opening apart. Enzo strolled over and saw immediately that it wasn't pyjamas in there. Unless nightwear had suddenly become dusky green and covered in spikes?

'Mathilde!' he exclaimed. 'I told you. I said we couldn't bring him home!'

'Nobody found him, did they?' She regarded him levelly.

'No, but they *could* have.'

'But they didn't.'

'Yes, but...' Sensing himself being pulled into an endless loop, Enzo sighed heavily, carefully lifted Spike from the pyjama case and tried to assume the demeanour of... what, exactly? What was appropriate here? At school, with the kids, he knew how to handle pretty much any situation. There was jovial Monsieur Fontaine, let's-get-serious Monsieur Fontaine and, *very* occasionally, this-is-unacceptable-behaviour Monsieur Fontaine – because you can't let the kids run the show. However, Mathilde wasn't a pupil. She was his daughter and she had just witnessed the dismantling of her grandparents' home. So what did it matter that she'd smuggled Spike into Scotland?

Now, as he and Mathilde get ready to leave, he catches Laura's eye, understanding the silent message being transmitted: *I know it's a bit silly asking you to cactus-sit, but thanks for going with it.* Then, looking relieved, she hugs Enzo, and Mathilde, and wishes her a brilliant time on the school trip to Scarborough. It'll be her first trip away without at least one of her parents. From beach games and fairground rides to a visit to a castle, as far as Enzo can gather, an enormous amount of activities have been scheduled for the four-day trip.

'Remember every detail, darling,' Laura insists. 'I want to hear everything about it!'

'I will, Mum. Good luck on your trip!'

'Yeah, hope it goes well,' Enzo says, and off they set, to spend a chilled Sunday afternoon at his place before he needs to think about revving up for school in the morning. He's thinking tacos and a movie and, of course, agreeing on a suitable spot for Spike for the duration of his stay. Mathilde has her backpack, and Enzo is carrying the cactus extremely carefully in his red ceramic pot as they walk; it seemed like the safest option, rather than risk him being knocked around in a carrier bag. Obviously, Spike's wellbeing is of the upmost importance – and that's fine by him.

At least it's not a goldfish, Enzo muses. There's no way he wants a repeat of that.

3

On top of her houseplant hospital, Celia has a second job. She works part-time at Elegance, a local boutique catering mainly to mature wedding guests, particularly the mothers of brides and grooms. There's nothing she can't tell you about fascinators and obscure designer labels never encountered beyond this kind of shop ('Exclusive high-class fashions from Italy').

On this crisp and sunny May morning, Celia is up with the lark, as is her habit on a shop day when she has to appear, well, *elegant*. Or as close a proximation as she can possibly manage to fudge together. This means her shoulder-length light brown hair, with its habit of frizzing, must be washed and blow-dried and given a good old frying with straighteners so ancient that the manufacturer no longer exists. 'Your medieval waffle irons,' as Terri, her close friend from the flat upstairs, laughingly refers to them. Celia must also wear light 'classic' make-up, plus smart trousers and heels and what her mother would term 'a nice blouse', and her nails must be neatly filed and polished, and on no account clogged with soil.

That's her shop persona. It's also her visiting-mum persona

as once a week – it's all Celia can bear – she drops by after work to passive smoke in her mother's overheated living room and to watch the soaps together. However, right now, at 7.27 a.m., Celia is focussed on what she regards as the most important – and certainly the most *enjoyable* – part of her day.

This involves checking on the numerous houseplants currently under her expert care. Geoff has already left for work and Celia is glad about this. She treasures having the flat to herself and being able to potter without interference or criticism. And so, clad in baggy-kneed tracksuit bottoms and an ancient sweatshirt, she tackles the business of watering, misting and gently wiping down leaves with her own home-blended leaf care oil.

The Baxters' Kentia palm, she is pleased to note, has perked up dramatically since she gently freed it from its original pot. A droopy poinsettia with a severe case of root mould is still looking rather sorry for itself, but it's early days and Celia explained to its owner that its treatment plan might span a couple of weeks.

On the nursery shelves she checks over spider plant babies which are already thriving, and repots one of her own begonias. All the while she chats soothingly, believing absolutely that this is a crucial part of a plant's care. She regards herself as part doctor, part nurse, and her bedside manner is impeccable.

Geoff, who encounters nature only on golf courses, has a strong aversion to Celia's 'jungle' taking over the flat. And so most of this activity happens in the plant room, a smallish spare bedroom which she and Terri fitted out with floor-to-ceiling shelving, working smoothly together with drills and screwdrivers (although admittedly, since Celia's son Logan moved out, several 'overspill' plants have begun to colonise his bedroom). As a business, her hospital has been thriving for several years –

although her love of plants grew from seeds planted decades ago.

Celia's parents were no gardeners and as a child, it pained her to look out and see the overgrown borders and weed-infested flagstones scattered with rain-mushed cigarette butts. The old cooker that had been shoved out there, which was now mottled with rust, caused an ache in her gut.

Celia took over a small corner of a border, digging it over and discovering what looked like actual plants – rather than weeds – in different parts of the garden. Using library books to identify them, she would rehome them in her patch where they had room to flourish and grow.

Soon she was acquiring seeds, cuttings and even small plants, with roots attached, from the park. A fervent abider of rules, she wasn't entirely sure whether this would be classed as stealing and preferred not to dwell on it too much. While her parents barely registered what their only child was up to, kindly neighbours festooned her with tips and more plants, encouraging her to cultivate yet more of the otherwise unloved back garden of 67 Bute Road.

'You're doing a great job there, Celia,' Mrs Blakely announced, peering over the fence. 'Good on you, girl. Your mum and dad are very lucky to have a kid like you.' She looked a bit pained when she said that. Emotional, even. Celia couldn't understand why.

Gradually, it wasn't just Celia's lupins and lavender that blossomed, but her belief in herself. Achieving decent test results at school didn't come easily to her and she had to work extremely hard. But out here in her garden she *could* make things happen, and it wasn't even that difficult.

She grew several ivy varieties in pots on the ancient cooker.

Soon they began to trail over, shrouding the rusting appliance with verdant leaves. Celia had taught herself to use the lawnmower – all that digging had made her physically strong – and created an actual lawn.

From the outside at least, it almost looked like a house where a normal family might live.

* * *

With her shop persona in place, Celia has arrived at Elegance, although it's not quite time to open up. As she rearranges the jewellery in the window, she remembers the horror of stepping into Amanda's wedding reception all by herself, back in January. The vast room was filled with sparkling chandeliers. Beautiful people were all chatting and laughing over the tinkle of light jazz being played on a grand piano. Celia wasn't checking into her hotel until later that night, and was horribly conscious of her scuffed suitcase. To make matters worse, at some point during her journey, one of its wheels had broken.

Celia looked around in panic, hoping to spot Amanda. Unable to locate her, she hauled the malfunctioning wheelie case through the crowds as if leading a misbehaving toddler to the toilets. Aware of stickiness in her armpits, she pulled off her blazer and bundled it on top of her case. What should she do now? Drink copiously? Hide here in this corner – or in the loos – until it was all over? At the very least she should remove the wretched acrylic cardigan that was making her sweat like a horse. However, to Celia, the prospect of exposing her arms was akin to baring her bottom, and as she made the decision to remain covered up, Amanda fluttered towards her in a full-length cream silk slip.

'Darling! You made it!' She hugged her tightly.

''Course I did!' Celia grinned. 'Wouldn't have missed this for the world.'

'Oh, that's so great. I did wonder, when you didn't RSVP—'

'I'm so sorry. I thought I had,' she fibbed. She had put off replying, willing the pipes to crack or the kitchen ceiling to fall in. Any domestic emergency would have served as an excuse – and her husband's generous gesture had come very late in the day.

'Where's Geoff?' Amanda's nostrils quivered as if she were trying to locate the source of a bad smell.

'He couldn't come. Something came up and he's really sorry. He sends his love.'

'Ah, that's a shame,' Amanda said quickly. 'Anyway, you look fabulous.'

'Oh, no. But *you* do.' For a moment Celia absorbed the vision of her oldest friend. Her fine blonde hair was piled up beautifully with tiny white flowers threaded through it, and a sparkly choker glinted around her long slender neck.

She sensed then that Amanda was keen to get away from her. 'You must meet Jasper,' she announced. 'You'll love him!'

'I'm sure I will. And congratulations!' Celia babbled a little belatedly.

'Thanks. Never thought it would happen, but here I am!' And then Amanda merged back into the crowds, leaving Celia quite alone.

It was almost impossible to believe how close they'd been, back in the day. How they'd spread a faded satin bedspread on Celia's lawn, and had 'banquets' of whatever they'd been able to plunder from their respective homes. How they'd shared secrets and chattered late into the night. At one point the girls had acquired a two-person tent, dragged from a skip and without any poles or pegs. They had erected it somehow, using branches carted home from the park, and took to camping out all night.

Celia loved her garden. Not just because it was hers to care for, but also for what it gave her in return.

She had a place of her own now. A place where she belonged, and which soothed her. It made sense then for Celia to plan a future involving being outdoors and helping things to grow.

The thing with gardening, she read in a library book once, *is that plants actually want to flourish. All we have to do is give them their best chance.* Celia pictured her future self then, not as a weed struggling through a pavement crack, merely surviving, but rather thriving as she stretched up towards the sun. She mapped out a plan to go to college to study horticulture and garden design. She felt sure that, if she focussed hard enough, she could get there. But then, with the end of school in sight, Celia's world took a very different course.

One sunny spring afternoon she crouched down in the park in the shady area where crocuses grew. *There are hundreds,* she told herself. *No one will miss one or two.*

Should she take a yellow, a purple or a white? Celia's dad had left some years before, and there'd been a fight the previous night, between her mum and a boyfriend who'd only just come on to the scene. A slammed front door; his car revving loudly and him driving away.

Celia was trying not to think about all of this as, poised with the trowel she always carried in her coat pocket, she started to dig.

'Hey, what're you up to?'

'Oh!' She sprang up, her heart banging as if she were about to be dragged off to jail.

'I wasn't, I mean I—' Her cheeks were flaming.

The man smirked. 'Yeah, well, if *everyone* went around digging up plants, there'd be none left in the park, would there? And then how would it look?'

She had no idea if he was teasing or not. But that's how it started, with Celia and this man; twenty-seven (so he said) to her tender eighteen. As Amanda made plans for a thrilling new life in London that wouldn't include her, he swept Celia off her feet.

Only when it was all over and he'd disappeared from her life, from Glasgow – from *the Earth*, so it seemed – did Celia realise that something was different. That there was no going back to how things had been before.

Determinedly, she adopted the approach she had always relied on whenever there'd been a late-night party, or a fight, downstairs. *If I ignore it for long enough, it'll stop.*

She kept herself busy in her garden, and if there was ever a fleeting thought of *Shouldn't I have had a period by now?*, that too was pushed away, buried deep into the loamy earth.

It was her mother who'd noticed her changing body and made her do a test. Who was this boyfriend? Celia never had boyfriends! 'She's gone and got herself pregnant,' her mum told all and sundry – as if she'd done it all by herself. Well done, Celia. A medical first!

She yearned for a friend to spill it all out to, but it was too late for that. Amanda was on the verge of moving away, and Celia rarely saw her anyway, especially after she told her she was having a baby. She suspected she was actually *afraid* to come near her, as if unplanned pregnancies were contagious.

The baby arrived and Celia no longer cared about how it had happened or that Amanda was 400 miles away. A few letters were exchanged – letters! How quaint! – but these soon petered out and Celia told herself she didn't need anyone any more. Not now that she had this perfect little thing nestling in her arms, *needing* her – his blue eyes wide and round, focussed fully on her, his mouth a perfect pink bud. Her baby was the most beautiful thing she had ever seen in her life.

Celia felt that, somehow, this was her destiny. That she was complete. Never mind cuttings and seedlings and thinning out. All of that was forgotten as she looked after her son, immersed in a bubble of feeds and sleeps and cuddles. In her childhood bedroom, she didn't even mind the night wakes or nappies or any of that. She had grown this tiny person who loved and needed her absolutely.

With remarkable speed, the weeds re-colonised her lawn and herbaceous borders, but Celia didn't care. There would be no horticulture course now; no future in creating beautiful gardens. Because at nineteen she had her hands full with baby Logan – and then along came Geoffrey Bloom. Ordinary Geoff, whom she'd never really noticed at school. Later he'd have to remind her that he'd been in her maths class. But back then he'd turned up at her house, saying, rather shyly, 'I heard you'd had a baby?' And he'd handed her a bunch of peach carnations from the petrol station at the end of her street.

Never mind that she hadn't *swooned* like a heroine in one of her mum's romance novels. He was obviously keen, and happy to go for walks with her and the baby in his buggy (Celia wouldn't have left a guinea pig in her mother's care). And gradually, Geoff grew on Celia and she decided she liked him very much. Compared to the person who had come before him, there were two major points in his favour.

One: he was her age. Still a boy, really – not a man.

And two: he was normal! Compared to the only other person she'd slept with – not to mention her home life – Geoff was ordinariness personified. And these same age plus normality aspects elevated him to perfect boyfriend status and soon, with a little help from his ever-generous mum, he and Celia managed to scrape together enough money to rent a tiny one-bedroomed flat.

'Lovely Geoffrey,' her mother would croon to her friends. 'Celia's so lucky that he took her on.' As if she were a lame old horse – useful only for colossal vet's bills.

Geoff knew what had happened with Celia and the man she'd met in the park. However, as soon as she'd told him, he politely asked her not to speak of it ever again. He wouldn't even say his name. Whenever it was unavoidable, it was just The Person. Obviously, The Person wasn't named on Logan's birth certificate. Celia would no more have put 'Santa Claus' in the 'father' part and it was left blank.

From that point on it was always assumed that Geoff was Logan's dad, and in all but the actual conception part, he was. They were a proper family of three and in time, as Celia started working locally, they managed to buy the slightly run-down tenement flat in which they still live. Terri has told her off whenever she has mentioned being 'rescued' by Geoff ('No, honey – you rescued *yourself*.'). But without him, where would she have been?

Celia told herself she was lucky and, in those early years, Geoff seemed to care for her and made her feel safe. But now something is happening and she can't put her finger on what it is. It's not just the way he shovels down the dinners she cooks without comment or thanks. It's not even those frequent weekends away and golfing holidays with the Bakery Boys. There's something else, she can sense it: his dad's caravan, for one thing. And his refusal to discuss what they'll do with it.

Not my problem, Celia tells herself as she opens up the shop.

She has a son she adores and she presides over Glasgow's only houseplant hospital. And if Celia focusses hard enough, and goes through the motions of running her neat and orderly life, then she can almost believe that everything is going to be all right.

4

Amanda stares at Jasper in disbelief. 'Is that all you can say?' she splutters.

'What, that you'll get something else?' He turns away from her in the bright and airy bedroom of their east London flat. He's checking his hair in the mirror now; never mind that Amanda is upset and wants to talk things through. There's a daub of rust-coloured paint in it, she notices. When they met, Jasper was an actor but ever since he's been 'waiting for the right part', he has pivoted. Pivoted towards his *art*.

'You're talking as if I've left a scarf on the train,' she retorts.

He frowns. 'It's just a job, babe. And jobs come and go. We both know that.'

'Yes, but they want someone younger. That's what's so hard to take.' In truth, *all* of it is hard to take. Presenting *Look for a Lifestyle* has been, if not Amanda's most prestigious, then her steadiest job in years, with the added bonus of copious free outfits, plus complimentary cuts and colours at John Frieda. Jasper's earnings are minimal and, still with a hefty mortgage on her light-filled Bethnal Green flat, they certainly need the money.

'There's loads of work for people like you,' he says, clearly tiring of the subject already. 'You just have to hang in there.'

'Well, thanks for that.'

He spins – *pivots* – towards her and his eyebrows shoot up. 'I'm sorry, darling. I really am. But what else d'you want me to say?'

'Nothing,' she says quickly as her eyes well up. 'I'm fine. Really. I knew this would happen at some point.'

'Yeah, and look at it this way. You've had a good run!' He reaches for her hand, and as she snatches hers away, he makes that irritating huffy noise. A sort of *whinny*, like a horse, accompanied by a toss of the bouncy dark hair that he's so proud of and is always tweaking. She almost expects him to stamp a hoof.

Although there's a significant age gap – at thirty-three, Jasper is a decade younger – Amanda had been under the illusion that Jasper was a proper grown-up when they first got together. He'd charmed her, bombarding her with messages and flowers, and she'd been swept away by his chiselled looks. And how wonderfully *youthful* he made her feel! No longer edging through her forties, worried about her future on TV, but on a par with her boyfriend and his beautiful friends with their boundless energy and perky bodies and peachy skin.

'I'm going to the gym,' she announces.

'Great! Enjoy yourself. See you later.'

She glares at him, aware of a sharp tang of distaste, then grabs her gym bag from the hallway and leaves the flat. Yet as soon as she's outside in the cool morning air, she decides she can't face Reformer Pilates today.

Instead, she marches briskly to the park, picking up a coffee on the way, with the intention of finding a bench and just sitting there, away from Jasper, with the time and headspace to think. That team meeting they had yesterday, when they talked about 'shaking things up' with the morning show – she had no idea they were planning to *shake her off* it.

'They said they want to keep things fresh,' admitted Ollie, her agent, when he called her first thing this morning. 'It's a bugger, but there you go. So sorry, darling.'

She was aware that her contract had ended. However, she'd reassured herself that they would renew automatically as they always had these past few years. Now Amanda realises that she is clearly *not* fresh. At forty-three she has hit that 'tricky in-between stage', according to Ollie. Too old to be young, yet not old enough to join the bevvy of glamorous silver-haired women currently whipping up a storm in the fashion world.

What does an *in-between person* do next?

It was raining earlier and it's unseasonably chilly for May. Amanda wishes she'd put on a jacket. As it is, she's come out in a fine-knit sweater, yoga pants and Birkenstocks and all the benches are damp. With a shiver, she pulls out her phone and flicks dolefully through her contacts as she walks, wondering who she can call.

Once upon a time she had so many friends in London that she'd established a system in order to see them in groups. Although it was never as satisfying as a one-to-one, she'd reassure herself: *That's a batch of five who've seen me.* She had fallen into that way of thinking; that, in granting friends a few hours of her company, she had ticked several boxes and therefore no one would think her rude or up herself. As something of a celebrity, Amanda has always prided herself on remaining unaffected and lovely to work with; true to her down-to-earth Glaswegian roots. However, as time went on, Amanda started to find these group gatherings trickier to arrange. 'Who else is coming?' someone would ask, and she'd rattle off a few names. 'Oh, right. D'you know, I think I'll leave it this time?'

There became more I-think-I'll-leave-its and Amanda wondered if her friends had started to *mind* being batched. If, in fact, it felt insulting. Yet, with so many people in her life, how could she possibly spend time with everyone individually? And, crucially, where have all those people gone? At some point over the past eighteen months or so – since she met Jasper, actually – Amanda has started to realise that, in a city of over eight million people, she is actually bloody lonely. Lonely and jobless – although of course the latter is only a temporary state of affairs. She is confident that Ollie will call again soon, with good news this time. She just has to hold her nerve.

Having finished her coffee, she drops the cup into a bin. Without thinking where she's heading, she has emerged from the other side of the huge, sprawling park and is now in Hackney. Twenty-five years ago, this was where she first landed when she'd moved to London. She'd been desperate to get here, and was thrilled to gain a place on a fashion journalism course. She'd left her devoted and devastated parents ('Look after yourself in that London!') and her so-called best friend who clearly wasn't her best friend any more.

Once upon a time, Amanda and Celia had shared everything. Clothes, shoes, secrets and dreams: there was almost nothing that hadn't flowed freely between them. All those nights they'd spent dressing up and dancing, up in Celia's bedroom while her mum had those crazy parties! All the garden picnics and camp-outs, the nights spent chatting until dawn.

They were still close as teenagers until suddenly Celia had become guarded, scurrying off to meet someone Amanda didn't know. 'Just a boy,' was all she'd tell her. 'Just someone I met.'

Then, just before Amanda left Glasgow, news came through

that Celia was pregnant. She hadn't even told her herself. Amanda's mum had heard it through local gossip, and wasn't it shocking? 'Poor Celia!' she said. 'That sweet girl. My heart breaks for her.' Amanda was doubly glad she was moving away.

She switched her focus to her own future. However, the aunt she was lodging with in London seemed to be under the impression that she was a *child*, and not a fully grown woman who knew everything at the age of eighteen. Outrageously, she even tried to impose a curfew on her. All hell would break loose whenever Amanda tottered in after a few drinks with her new, party-loving crowd.

She moved out of her aunt's and into a riotous house-share in Dalston, and from there she never looked back. These were *real* friends whom she could rely on. Not strange ones obsessed with gardening like an old person. Amanda's new crowd did not spend their Saturday afternoons dragging a decrepit lawnmower up and down. Instead, they all clustered around a giant table in the pub.

Visits home to Glasgow were rare and brief, occasional meet-ups with Celia more of an obligation than a pleasure. For one thing, she'd got together with Geoff Bloom from school and Amanda had no idea what to say about that. Obviously, he wasn't Celia's son's father and there was still no information forthcoming about that – who the guy was, whether he was sending her money or any of that. Celia had become this closed book, and that made being with her feel rather pointless and sad.

Plus, she always had her little boy with her. Weird, fearful Logan, forever sucking on a blanket and clinging tightly to his mum, as if Amanda was planning to rip him from her arms and throw him into the back of a van. She knew enough about children to realise that you couldn't leave them unattended, but what about Geoff? Couldn't he have looked after Logan for an hour or two? As it was, she had to watch Celia wiping his nose and bum – so many emissions pouring out of the kid! – while wondering how quickly she could get away.

Now, as Amanda stops to buy a second takeaway coffee (she'll be over-caffeinated, but fuck it), she remembers the one time the three of them – Celia, Geoff and Logan – came down here on a trip. Geoff had moaned about the prices of everything and the fact that the city was 'busy' and 'very big'. What had he expected? That London would turn out to be a little village with Postman Pat trundling about?

They'd stayed in some dreadful hotel that reeked of fried bacon, paid for by Geoff's work. 'Neither of you have changed a bit!' Amanda exclaimed when she met up with them in the bar. In fact, Celia had. She looked exhausted, Amanda thought. But Geoff still wore his sandy hair in that terrible side parting, plus those aviator sunglasses she associated with perverts. She'd caught him looking down at her breasts. Do men think it's undetectable when they do that? Don't they think women have *eyes*?

'What d'you do again, Geoff?' Amanda had asked.

'I'm in pastry,' he'd replied. 'Savoury bakes. Pies, sausage rolls and all that.'

'Mmm!' Her stomach turned. Meanwhile, Celia looked stiff and uncomfortable, and the adolescent Logan had sat there fiddling with a Rubik's cube, pale as a seashell. *If you held him up to the light, you'd see through him*, Amanda thought.

What had Celia ever seen in him? Not Logan – she guessed everyone loved their kids – but this plain potato-faced man with fleshy pink ears whom she'd decided to marry (fortunately it had been a tiny do and no invitation had come her way). Geoff was a way out, she supposed. An emergency exit from that terrible family, if you could even call it a family – Mum addled with drink, Dad having run off to live with some woman in Wales. No wonder Celia grew up odd, filling her bedroom with cuttings and plants instead of posters of pop stars and copious make-up.

That's it, Amanda had decided after their London visit. Some friendships have a sell-by date. Because when you only have 'the old days' to hold you together, is there really any point? Amanda almost hadn't invited Celia to her wedding. Years had passed with no real contact between them, and she certainly didn't want Geoff there, bragging about innovations on the sausage roll production line. But then, when the guest list was finalised and she realised that Jasper would be inviting his entire boarding school year group, she realised it was somewhat… *unbalanced*. As if Amanda didn't have any history at all. And one night, after a few cocktails with her colleagues, she'd discovered (to some surprise) that she still had Celia's email address. Fuelled by several negronis, she typed:

Hey Celia hope all's good! Exciting news – I'm getting married! To the lovely Jasper. We'd love you, Geoff and Logan to be there…

She stopped. Did she really want the strange, whey-faced adolescent at her reception? She retyped:

We'd love you and Geoff to be there to celebrate with us. No presents! Details below. Hope you can make it.
   Love Amanda xxx

Soft rain is falling and a cool wind ripples her long, fine blonde hair. She should have brought a hat – her ears are chilled – and as she starts to make her way home, it hits her.

Her beautiful flat that she'd been so excited to buy. She'd adored it before Jasper moved in, but she doesn't any more. She doesn't want to go back – not with Jasper there, pouting and sulking and preening his hair. She pictures her wedding – the glitterballs and her gorgeous silk dress, all the champagne and kisses and well-wishers. And Celia. She pictures Celia staggering in, miraculously without Geoff, but dragging a battered wheelie case with a busted wheel. Celia, her oldest friend, wearing a flowery dress with a cheap blazer and an old cardigan (so many layers!) and shoes that were quite startling, really. Glossy red shoes that didn't go with the outfit at all. Amanda's heart had twisted. It was hateful of her to even think it, but Celia really couldn't carry off shoes like that.

Amanda meant to text her to say thank you for coming, and for the gift. That ugly beige vase that she had no intention of ever displaying, and which Jasper is currently using to store his dirty brushes in.

She could scrub it down and take it to a charity shop or just leave it where it is, in his 'studio', full of filthy water and splattered with paint. That's not the main issue, currently. What to do about Jasper? *That's* what's churning in her mind as she finally turns back towards home.

And right now, Amanda has no answer to that.

5

If Terri's day off coincides with one of Celia's shop days, she often pops into the boutique to see her. 'What the heck does he want that for?' she asks, having arrived armed with what Celia thinks of as 'luxury coffees' (i.e. takeaway coffees). On this somewhat slow-moving Monday morning, Celia is delighted to see her.

'Honestly,' she replies, 'it's a complete mystery to me.' The pair are poring over pictures of the decrepit caravan that Celia took on her last visit there.

'D'you think he's still grieving, and this is his way of hanging on to a part of his dad?' Terri suggests.

'Maybe.' Celia exhales. After all, only seven months have passed since her father-in-law passed away, and she's aware that Geoff misses him deeply. 'I've tried to broach it but got nowhere,' she adds. 'You know what he's like. So stubborn and unwilling to discuss anything.'

Terri nods, continuing to scroll through the caravan pictures as Celia attends to customers. Two friends, whom she would put at late sixties, are in search of outfits for a wedding. 'How about this?' Celia plucks an elegant dusky blue dress from the rail. 'It's lovely with this embroidered detail under the bustline...' Elegance is a 'bustline' kind of shop. There is much trying on and debating, and happily a couple of purchases too.

Once they've gone, Celia perches next to her friend on the chaise longue and sips her coffee. Geoff's frugality has seeped into Celia's psyche over the years, and she regards a cafe-made Americano as a rare treat. 'So, your favourite boy's coming home on Friday,' she says with a smile.

'Logan? Already?' Terri beams. She has always been extremely fond of Celia's son.

'Yep, exams are over so that's him back for the summer.'

'Can't wait to see him,' she enthuses. 'Does he know you've been landed with that shitty old caravan?' A psychiatric nurse at a high security hospital, Terri is never one to mince words. The day they moved into the flat below hers, she was at the door in a tight pink top and skinny jeans, welcoming them with a towering coconut cake. Logan, who'd just turned four, was delighted. However, Celia had caught Geoff's slight lip curl at Terri's short choppy blonde hair, dark roots showing, and the big gold hoop earrings and neon nails. As soon as she'd gone, he had hurried to Chubb-lock the front door as if she might burst back in.

'I hope she's not going to make a habit of that,' he had announced. *I hope she is,* Celia had thought.

'No, I haven't told him yet,' she says. 'He hates talking on the phone and I didn't want to get into it all by text.'

'Yeah, I get that.' Still clutching Celia's phone, Terri zooms in on an interior shot. 'Y'know, we could transform this place. Give it a really deep clean – get right down to the bones of it...'

'Oh, I don't think so,' Celia says briskly. 'Honestly, I'm hoping he'll just get rid of it.'

'He won't though, will he?' Terri grimaces. 'Be realistic.'

Another customer comes in and Celia jumps up, fixing on her bright and helpful shop-lady face. However, as she and the elderly woman discuss separates and fitted jackets, she is aware of Terri still scrolling and hatching a plan. The customer leaves, and Terri hands Celia her phone.

'Right – I'll tell you what we're going to do,' she announces. 'We're going to transform it into a proper little holiday home.'

'What?' Celia exclaims.

'You and me – and Logan too, if he'll help us. I've got tons of fabric at home. I could make curtains, cushion covers, cheer the place up… It'll be unrecognisable by the time we've finished.' Celia is still struggling to picture it as anything other than a mouldering heap. 'Wouldn't that be great, to have a little place on the coast?' Terri goes on, dark eyes glinting. 'I mean, *we* could use it. You and me – any time we're free over the summer.'

'What – go away together, you mean?' Celia brightens. Having been flung into motherhood at nineteen, and gotten together with Geoff that same year, girls' holidays have never felt like an option for her. She skipped those typical friend-acquiring stages – the student flat-shares, the office gang – and her small cluster of school gate friends have long since scattered away. As for the caravan, the thought of being trapped in it with Geoff has hardly been enticing to her. But with Terri, and the place all spruced up? That's a different matter.

'D'you really think we could make it habitable?' she asks.

'Definitely. The thing is, you just have to see its potential.' Terri plucks a pink fascinator from its stand and positions it on her head.

'Gorgeous!' Celia laughs.

She checks her reflection in the full-length mirror, affecting a pout. Sometimes Celia is reminded how lucky she is that Terri lives upstairs. Ten years older, and certainly wiser, she has always had her back. 'So when can we start?' her friend asks.

Celia considers this. 'It'll be a lot easier to tackle with Geoff out of the way.'

'Definitely.' Terri nods.

'He's heading up north for golf this weekend. They normally set off on a Friday night to get the whole day in...'

'Saturday, then? I'm free.'

Celia finishes her coffee and smiles. 'You *really* want to scrub out a disgusting caravan on your day off?'

Terri whips off the fascinator and places it back on its stand in the window. 'Can't wait to get my hands on it. What's that thing your old friend does? That thing on morning TV?'

Celia chuckles. Although they have never met, Terri is aware of Amanda's glittering career. 'It's a makeover thing. *Look for a Lifestyle*, it's called...'

'That's what we'll do, then. We'll give the old heap a total makeover. It won't know what's hit it.' Then Celia leaves Terri to attend to a mother and her grown-up daughter who are bubbling with chatter about their forthcoming cruise, and the kind of outfits they'll need to see them through it. 'A holiday of a lifetime,' Celia enthuses, aware that her affluent customers often have several 'holidays of a lifetime' every year.

Yet now Celia is also filled with a sense of excitement and anticipation. She certainly feels entirely differently about being gifted her father-in-law's rank old mobile home.

With the prospect of weekends away with Terri, it could turn out to be pretty wonderful after all.

6

Enzo is a pack-the-night-before man. A few basics flung into a case and that's it. Not Mathilde who adores clothes and, at nine years old, has developed her own very particular, somewhat eccentric style with no input from him or even her mother (Laura is a classic dresser and Enzo throws on whatever is clean and to hand).

In contrast, Mathilde mixes eye-popping patterns with fluffy things and shimmery things and bright tights. The effect, he has to admit, is quite wonderful. But it also requires an extraordinary amount of thought and planning, and she has spent every spare moment of the past few days preparing for the school trip to Scarborough, packing and re-packing her rucksack more times than he can count.

Enzo hopes he's a good dad and he certainly tries his best. But does a forty-two-year-old teacher have any opinion on whether the mushroom-patterned top should be substituted for the silver sweater, and if clothes should be folded or rolled? He does not! He can feign enthusiasm for Mathilde's new wash-bag made from recycled sea plastics, and *of course* he's happy that a tree is planted for every order. But he remembers his own school trip to the Pyrenees, when they'd slept under canvas on hard, rocky ground and his socks had entirely disintegrated inside his boots. On the last day he'd stolen a fork from the kitchen crew to drag through his matted hair. It had been the best week of his life.

Finally, Scarborough Day has arrived. On a normal school day when Enzo has Mathilde, he'll drop her off at her school's breakfast club before driving farther out to the secondary school where he works. However, on this drizzly Tuesday morning, Mathilde's best friend's mum has offered to drop off the girls at the coach.

For his morning to run smoothly, Enzo must have his wits about him. His plan is to dispatch Mathilde at Honey's and make a speedy getaway. However, as he feared, Saska, her mother, has other ideas and he is virtually hauled by the collar into her kitchen where a coffee is pressed into his hands and her exuberant labradoodle zooms in on his crotch.

The girls whoop and hug and clatter upstairs to Honey's room. 'Is Mathilde excited?' Saska asks. 'Honey's been counting the days.'

'Oh, yes. She's been talking about nothing else.' Enzo sips scalding coffee from a rough-hewn ceramic vessel, devoid of handle and looking like some ancient object discovered by archaeologists. He recognises it as Saska's own work.

'So they're back on Saturday afternoon,' she goes on as Enzo tries to gently steer the salivating hound away from his genitals.

'Yes, that's right.'

'Which means you'll be free for litter pick in the morning?'

'Saturday morning?' Enzo tries to appear as if he'd remembered. 'Yes, I hope so. I really do. If I can, I'll definitely be there.'

'I know you enjoy it, Enzo.' She grins and tosses back a mane of crinkly russet hair.

'Er... yeah! Sure. I really do.' In fact, he is not averse to joining the regular crew, donning a hi-vis tabard and spending an hour or so filling bin bags with rubbish. When he first moved to Scotland with Laura – they'd met on a walking holiday in the Dordogne – he was keen to settle into life here in Glasgow and do his bit for the local neighbourhood. And after he and Laura split up, on the weekends Mathilde was at her mum's, he was sometimes grateful for this community enterprise just to get him out of the flat on a Saturday morning. Snapping at litter with a little grabber device – heck, after a brief and dismal foray into online dating, he'd found himself almost looking forward to it. One time he'd discovered a mixtape of nineties indie tracks, complete with hand-illustrated card insert, lying in the gutter. Never mind that he didn't own a tape player. It had still been the highlight of his week. However, in recent times, he's been conscious of Saska's laser beam spearing into his forehead whenever they see each other out and about.

Enzo, Enzo, hiiii! Could I interest you in— It's as if the very sight of him triggers a 'Poor hapless male!' alert in her and she feels compelled to muscle in. As if, left to his own devices, he'd wither and die alone in his little flat.

He places the mug on her worktop, momentarily impressed that it can remain upright despite its convex bottom, and readies himself for escape.

'The thing is... Digby, leave Enzo alone!' Saska touches his arm. 'It's not just a normal litter pick this week.'

'Oh, isn't it?' He frowns.

'No, I'm planning a little... *thing* afterwards.'

'Right!' Of course she is. Saska has a hand in everything around here: amateur dramatics, an improvisational band *(Come along! Anything goes! You can play a cheese grater if you want to!*) and not only the weekly litter pick, but the numerous social activities she manages to bolt on to it. Litter pick coffee mornings, litter pick picnics, and even a pickers' Christmas lunch in the pub where she'd manhandled Enzo into the vacant seat next to a startled woman in a tie-dyed shawl.

'Sit next to Claire,' she'd ordered him. 'She's on her own like you!'

'We're starting litter pick singles,' she announces. Does this mean what Enzo thinks it means? 'Just a casual thing over coffee, back here after we've done all the hard work,' she adds. 'A chance to mingle and chat in a relaxed environment...'

'That sounds *great*.' Enzo makes for the hallway and calls upstairs to his daughter.

'What is it, Dad?' Mathilde has appeared on the landing.

'I need to get off to work, love. Come and give me a hug because I'm not going to see you till Saturday!' He's not proud of using his daughter as a diversion, but needs must.

She hurries down towards him and they hug. 'Bye, darling,' he says. 'Have a great time and remember to keep your diary, won't you? Me and Mum want to hear all about it.'

Mathilde is vibrating with excitement. 'I will. And look after Spike!'

''Course I will. Don't you worry about that.' He opens the door and steps outside. 'Thanks, Saska,' he adds as she and Digby follow him out. 'I really appreciate—'

'No worries at all.' She shoos the dog back indoors. 'So, with litter pick singles? You will come along, won't you, Enzo? It's so hard to get men to come to these social things, I never understand why...'

'I'll try,' he says, realising he'll have to conjure up an excuse, and also that Digby must have drooled on the front of his trousers. If he cranks up his car's heating, will the wet patch have evaporated by the time he gets to school?

'If it works out, we'll make it a regular event,' Saska adds.

'Great!' On the pavement now, Enzo is less than three metres from the sanctuary of his car.

'There's that common ground, isn't there? A shared community spirit?'

'Yes, absolutely.' He fishes out his key and unlocks the car, hoping the beep and brief flash of lights will signify to Saska that very shortly he'll have a class of thirty-two first years, not *waiting* for him exactly (most have zero interest in learning French) but to whom he is contractually obliged to present himself.

'See you on Saturday then.' She beams at him. 'Litter pick at nine-thirty sharp, okay?'

'Of course.' Enzo forces a smile, relaxing only when he has driven away.

However, by the time Saturday rolls around, it's not Saska's litter pick – or the 'singles-mingle' or whatever it's called – that's burning at the forefront of Enzo's mind.

It's Mathilde's beloved cactus. Because at some point – without him actually *doing* anything – he seems to have killed it stone dead.

7

'You know what your academic career's like, Logan?' Terri says from the driver's seat of her ancient Mini. 'It's like those horse films my dad used to love.'

'You mean Westerns?' Logan mumbles from the back seat. At 7.40 a.m. Celia suspects he is not yet fully awake.

'Yeah, the ones that go on for ever and ever.' Terri grins.

'They just *feel* that way,' Celia says with a smile, glancing back fondly at her son. It was lovely to bring him home yesterday from his student house in Stirling. She fussed around him, and he hung out with her in the kitchen well past midnight, drinking his preferred hibiscus tea and chatting about this and that in the easy way the two of them have together. They have always slotted together quite happily as a pair. And if other people think he's odd, then sod them, Celia has always thought. The moment she first held him was the first time she'd ever felt truly right with the world. She had family now. She had *grown* him. Nothing would ever change that.

Now his six-foot-two frame is folded up like a piece of camping furniture among bulging sacks of fabric and Terri's sewing machine, plus cans of paint in a variety of hues, and boxes piled with cleaning products. 'The kind of film where you feel you're gonna *die* right there on the sofa,' Terri continues, clearly relishing the theme. 'And you'll be carried out and still there'll be horses clip-clopping all over the plains...'

'I've only got a year to go, Terri,' Logan says mildly.

'Yeah, you *say* that,' she teases. In fact, Terri does have a valid point. At twenty-four, Logan has done an admirable job of stretching out the student life stage for longer than Celia had anticipated. Courses have been started and abandoned, and she'd begun to despair that he would ever find his pathway until he landed upon his current field of interest. She's had to battle with Geoff to allow him to continue, albeit with minimal financial support from the two of them these days. Logan is adept at shoestring living and not averse to bar work and holiday jobs.

'Mycology,' Terri muses. 'Thought you'd have covered everything about mushrooms in your first year. I mean, what is there to learn?'

'A *huge* amount, actually,' Logan says, indulging her.

'You should've met that guy I was dating.' Terri chuckles, glancing over at Celia. 'Remember Pete-with-the-feet?'

'Oh yes.'

'Seemed normal, y'know? Polite, clean underwear, not like the one who'd turn his boxers inside out to get a second day's wear...' Celia laughs and looks back again to see her son trying to disappear into his polo neck sweater. 'But a terrible case of fungal feet,' Terri continues cheerfully. 'Rotting, they were. You could've given *them* an inspection, Logan.'

'Not on the curriculum.' He snorts.

'Oh, I know what it is,' she announces, taking a bend in the road rather too quickly. 'It's magic mushrooms, isn't it? Bet that's it, eh, Loge? That's why you're so keen!'

'It's *mycology*,' Celia says with emphasis. 'It's a proper, serious subject, Terri.'

'And it's not just mushrooms,' Logan retorts. 'It's all kinds of fungi and yeasts.'

Terri laughs, and Celia enjoys their exchange; the way her son and her friend also slot back together so easily. Sometimes she feels that Terri understands Logan better than Geoff does. 'Sorry I'm rushing off, son,' he'd said last night as Logan unpacked his tattered textbooks and a toothbrush that looked as if it had been gnawed by a dog. 'It's just, this golf thing was booked ages ago and the guys are intent on getting out on the course first thing.'

'No worries, Dad,' Logan said.

'I'll take some time off while you're home,' he went on. 'We could do a fishing trip to Loch Fyne, if you like?'

'Yeah, great.' Both Celia and Logan know that this is unlikely to happen. Geoff has been a good dad, all things considered – being plunged into fatherhood as a teenager, as Celia was. *Taking them on.* However, his involvement in the nitty-gritty of Logan's life has been minimal, apart from securing him an annual summer job at Prime Pastry Products (PPP) since he's been old enough to work. This year, even that has come to an abrupt halt. Cost-cutting, apparently. Geoff refused to go into it any further than that.

As they near the coast, Celia reflects on how lucky she is to have a son who, while not ecstatic about the prospect, has at least agreed to help with the caravan makeover today. 'What'll you want me to do?' he asks.

'Whatever we tell you,' Celia replies with a smile.

'Manual labour, basically,' Terri adds, and he laughs dryly in acknowledgement that he's simply not built that way. In fact, although extremely smart academically, Logan has the air of a young man perpetually baffled by everyday life. By nine he had the periodic table firmly stamped on his brain, yet was incapable of removing a yoghurt pot lid without splatting his jumper. His clothes are moth-eaten, knitwear unravelling, faded T-shirts hanging from his bony frame. His tousled dark hair is forever flopping into his clear blue eyes, and his skin is translucently pale. Although Celia adores every cell in his body, she also worries about him, lost in a world of fungal spores.

The conversation veers towards Logan's plans for the summer – or rather his lack of any so far, given the fact that there's no job for him at PPP. 'You didn't think of staying in Stirling for the summer?' Terri asks.

'No, I'm subletting my room for a few weeks,' he explains.

'Just needed to be home for a bit?'

Logan nods. 'It's nice, yeah.'

Celia's heart swells at this. That fact that he still chose to come home, despite the lack of guaranteed holiday work. The trio slips into an easy silence, and Celia turns on the music: Candi Staton, 'Young Hearts Run Free'. Terri's car is old enough to have a CD player and the artefact currently blaring out is always referred to as 'The Pink CD', being pink – or 'that bloody CD' if it's Geoff talking. The seventies disco compilation is actually Celia's and came free with a box of cereal or something. She can't quite remember.

'Oh, I love this song,' Celia announces, ignoring Logan's protests as Terri starts to sing.

'Oh my God,' he cries as 'Boogie Nights' follows, and the two women belt out the disco classic together. They are laughing and Celia's heart is filled with happiness. She no longer doubts that the three of them will be able to transform the caravan. Celia is not averse to physical graft, and she knows that Logan will lope around, taking orders from Terri, who'll assume charge of the creative side of things. She makes virtually all of her own clothes, for cost reasons – Celia often hears her sewing machine whirring late into the night. When Logan was little and requiring a fancy-dress outfit with zero warning, Terri would save the day. Yet Geoff would barely acknowledge the fact. He'd come home to find Logan teetering on a kitchen chair, and Terri with pins clamped between her lips, fitting an elaborate costume around him. Be it a dragon, a bear or even a building – he once asked, 'Can I be the Houses of Parliament, Terri?' – there was nothing their friend couldn't pull out of the hat.

'Hey, Geoff!' she'd greet him. 'How're things at Sausage Roll Central?'

Superficially, Geoff takes her irreverent attitude in good humour. 'Fine, thanks, Terri. All good!' he'd reply. Yet Celia is relieved that Geoff set off for his golf trip last night. She doesn't want to involve him in Project Caravan – at least, not yet. He'd be bound to have opinions and most likely trample all over their plans. She would rather present the makeover as a fait accompli.

'Next right,' she says, and Terri slows down, cursing the temperamental gears as she takes the junction.

Celia turns off the music and glances back. 'Not a word to Dad about this, okay, love?'

'All right, Mum.'

'He'll be amazed,' Terri enthuses. 'You've got to film it, the first time he sees it—'

'Oh, I will!' Celia grins as the caravan site comes into view, and they turn in through the gateway, spotting the sea glittering beneath the pale morning sky. The narrow lane snakes between rows of immaculate static caravans, and tubs are brimming with cheery tulips and daffodils all fluttering in the breeze.

'Oh, this is lovely,' Terri announces. 'Much nicer than I imagined.'

She's right, Celia decides; it really is a beautiful spot and she's feeling so much more positive about it now. To their left, a woman is watering her hanging baskets and a young couple are strolling towards them with a honey-coloured spaniel on a lead. The woman's peaked cap blows off in the light wind and, laughing, she retrieves it.

Beyond the park, a path zigzags its way down the hillside towards the pebbly cove. Today the sea is choppy, the steeply sided island of Ailsa Craig a smudged silhouette on the horizon. Celia has brought a picnic, with a flask of tea, so they can happily work all day, plus her swimsuit in case there's time for a dip. As a child there'd be occasional trips to the seaside with Amanda's mum and dad: a nice, normal family who'd all jump into the sea, and then tuck into piping-hot fish and chips afterwards, shrouded in huge luxurious beach towels.

Perhaps today they'll also walk to the next beach where there are often seals, apparently. But before that, there's much work to be done. They plan to strip out the dingy soft furnishings, scrub the place until it's gleaming and paint the interior a clean, fresh white. Then Terri will run up cheery new curtains and cushion covers. It'll be amazing when it's done, Celia thinks, glancing happily at her friend. She can't wait to get started.

'So which one is it?' Terri asks.

Logan leans forward, pointing between them. 'It's that one, isn't it, Mum? The one right at the end there?'

'That's right. I'm surprised you remember. Y'know, last time you were here, you must've been about ten?' Logan nods. Back then Geoff's parents had just bought Ailsa View, and there followed a flurry of family day trips. Betty was a kind and loving granny, a baker of cakes and maker of deliciously creamy rice pudding, cooked on the caravan's tiny stove. And Celia and Logan had paddled in the sea and scoured the beach for fossils and agates; geology was his passion at the time. Rock specimens were gathered and stored in a shoebox that he'd divided into separate compartments. But then Grandma Betty died and the invitations dried up.

'It looks terrible,' he murmurs as they approach.

'Yeah. Lots for you to study in there, Loge,' Terri remarks with a smile. 'A massive array of fungal spores, I'd imagine.'

He nods. 'Bet there are.'

'Brought your microscope?'

'Aw, I forgot! You should've said.'

Terri chuckles and parks up, and is the first to jump out of the car. 'Let's get to it, then!' she calls back. Logan unfolds himself and clambers out, rotating his shoulders and stretching out his arms. He glances back at his mother. 'Come on then, Mum!' he says.

Celia nods. It's all she can do. Because something is wrong on this beautiful spring morning. Something she can't make sense of at all.

That's not our car parked there, she tells herself.

It just looks very much like it.

And it has the same number plate—W*ait, it has the same number plate?*

'That's our car,' she announces out loud, over the steady thud of her heart. And now Terri is saying something, and Logan too as his dark hair is blown across his face by the wind. They are both looking at Celia, and Terri is gesticulating for her to get out of the car.

'Come on,' she calls out. 'Let's get started!'

But Celia is still rooted to the passenger seat, still telling herself that this can't be happening. Not when, minutes ago, they were singing along to 'Boogie Nights'. Not when Geoff headed off yesterday to pick up Malcolm and Davie and drive them up to the north-east coast for golf.

Celia gets it now. Her heart seems to freeze as everything slips into place.

She might be the idiot who's believed in all these 'golf trips with the Bakery Boys'. But she's not a complete fool because there's one thing she understands very clearly.

A person cannot be in two places at once.

8

'Mum, what's our car doing here?'

As Celia climbs out of Terri's Mini she feels the sharp wind hitting her cheek. She can also hear the rhythmic surge of the sea and taste salt on her tongue. So it would seem that her senses are in fully working order. But they can't be – not properly – because somehow her world has stopped.

Geoff didn't drive up north yesterday with Malcolm and Davie. He came here, to his parents' static caravan instead. Perhaps golf is happening here and she misunderstood? Celia looks around wildly, taking in the wooden site office and the tiny shop, supplier of tinned spaghetti and Cup a Soups, almost hoping to spot Geoff in his navy-blue top with the quarter zip, swinging a club.

'I don't know, Logan,' she replies.

Terri frowns. 'Is there any *reason* why Geoff would be here?'

'I'm not sure,' Celia murmurs. 'I can't think...'

'D'you think Dad's decided to do the place out to surprise *us*?' Logan is a man now. A fully grown man of six-foot-two. Yet sometimes his innocence snags at Celia's heart.

'I really don't think so, love,' she replies. 'No, I can't imagine that.'

'Well, should we just go home or—' Terri breaks off, tension flickering in her dark eyes. Celia sees that she has registered it too: what's going on here. What *has* been going on for God knows how long.

'Something must've happened,' Celia says quickly.

'Yeah,' Logan says. 'Maybe the site owner called him and he's had to come over and check on something?' Celia catches Logan scrutinising her face, as if he wants to believe this. She swallows hard, propelled back to when he was her little boy who loved going to the park with her, or to the cinema – or even for a trundle around Morrison's, so long as they were together.

And all those tricky questions he asked:

Why is there war?

Will you and Daddy ever die?

And – the most difficult of all – *Are you in love with Daddy?*

'Of course I am, sweetheart!' Weren't they happy as a family? And wasn't she lucky that Geoff had 'taken her on'?

'Mum,' Logan says, more firmly now, 'are we going in, or what?'

Celia nods. Her mouth is dry, her heart banging hard. A gull observes them from the roof of the caravan, and she notices whitish poo streaked across a window. 'Please,' she says firmly, 'both of you, go and wait in Terri's car.'

Logan stares at her, frowning. 'Why?'

'Just do what I say, love. Please.'

Terri touches her arm. 'Sweetheart, I don't think you should go in if—'

'Both of you,' Celia commands, waving them away. 'Sit and wait in the car, just for a minute, all right?' To signal that there will be no further debate, she turns away and crosses the square patch of neatly mown grass towards Ailsa View.

Even in her agitated state she carefully steps around a patch of pale-yellow primroses. Glancing back, she sees Terri and Logan climbing into the front seats of Terri's car. Logan pulls a *what-the-hell-are-you-doing?* face, and she merely shakes her head.

Celia isn't what you'd call a brave person. Whenever the fairground came to town, she favoured the teacup ride over the chair-o-plane and has never sampled recreational drugs of any kind. A sip of Red Bull once made her fear she was having a heart attack. A single puff on a cigarette and she nearly passed out.

Yet now, conscious as she is of Logan and Terri watching through the windscreen, something seems to surge up in her. As if her son and best friend are installed not in Terri's ropey old Mini, but plush cinema seats. And she is no longer real-life Celia Bloom, tender of plants and seller of peplum jackets and fascinators, but in a movie here on this windblown campsite on the coast.

She is *playing a part*. She can feel it, beaming into the back of her head – the combined unwavering gaze of Logan and Terri – and it's propelling her towards the scuffed door of her in-laws' caravan.

Oddly unafraid, she feels in her jeans pocket for the key. It took some finding – this single Yale key with a paper label attached, in her mother-in-law's handwriting: *Caravan spare*. She hadn't been able to find the main key on the sailing boat key ring. As the caravan makeover was meant to be a surprise, she hadn't quizzed Geoff about its whereabouts. But now, even before Celia tries the door, she knows she needn't have bothered rummaging through the jumble of cables and redundant remote controls in the kitchen drawer for any key at all.

Because of course Ailsa View is unlocked.

It's unlocked because Geoff isn't golfing up north with Malcolm and Davie.

He is *here*.

Quietly, she depresses the handle and pushes the door open. A dank mustiness seeps into her nostrils as she steps inside.

In the murky gloomy of Ailsa View, there is no view of anything as the flimsy grey curtains are drawn. Celia waits for her eyes to adjust to the gloom in the main living space. And as they do, and the familiar shapes of fitted seating and cheap melamine cupboards come into focus, she is aware of her other senses sharpening too.

Everything is shimmeringly vivid to her. She can smell spores in the air. She can feel them clinging to her face and hair and knows she will take them home with her when this is done. When her life has turned on its head and there is no going back to what it was before.

Her with a baby as well, Celia heard her mother telling a friend on the phone. *He's a saint, I tell you! A living saint!*

She can taste dankness at the back of her throat. And she can hear something too. A soft sigh which could have just been the wind. Outside the caravan, something rattles tinnily. She pictures Logan and Terri waiting anxiously in the car and wonders briefly if she has got this wrong. And then, as another sound fills her head, she knows she hasn't – and now everything makes sense.

Why Geoff was delighted to be gifted this caravan by his sister. Why he was so keen for Celia to attend Amanda's wedding in London that he threw money at her to make her go.

The hotel! The train ticket! Did she really think he'd booked and paid for all of that out of the goodness of his heart?

The noises grow louder. There's a gasp and a squeal. Then rhythmic thumping as if someone is whacking a hefty gardening manual against the thin partition wall.

'Oh, oh, *OHHH!*'

Now it's Celia's heart that's thumping – also rhythmically, although not quite in time with the commotion in the bedroom. No, her heartbeat is faster. It's actually racing. She's amazed they can't hear it battering against her ribs. But then they're lost, aren't they? Lost in the moment. Is this what it's like, she wonders, when sex is passionate? Celia's mind shoots her back to that other time she was lied to, when she was eighteen years old. How different her life would have been if she'd had proper sex education. Or Google! Why hadn't Google existed in 1994? Celia has actually *googled* Google to find out when it came out. And what about contraception? She'd murmured something about it – whether it would 'be okay' – and he'd said, 'Yes, don't worry, I'm infertile.'

Celia had never heard the term before. Only 'fertile', connected to soil and growth and making beautiful things happen. And it did, in the form of her baby boy, and of course she adored him from the moment she first saw his little face. But still she was lied to and no one will take her for a fool ever again.

It's like a switch in her. No one seems to hear her footsteps on the grubby carpet as she treads carefully through the dingy room. No one registers her presence as she stands there at the open bedroom door, her vision filled by her husband's naked hairy backside in front of her. She might have struggled to remember him from her maths class, when he'd turned up at her house with a bunch of carnations from the petrol station. But she'd recognise that arse anywhere – she could pick it out in a police line-up – even before he spins around and sees her standing there.

'Celia! For fuck's sake!'

His lady companion – who'd been on all fours, Geoff's hands clamped to her hips – flumps face down onto the bed as if shot.

'What are you doing here?' he yells.

'Well, that's nice,' Celia shoots back. 'That's very nice, Geoff.'

'Oh my God,' the woman cries, and there's a flurry of sheets as she scrambles up to a seating position and tries to cover herself.

Rod-straight dark hair, thin face with concave cheeks, looks significantly younger – early thirties, maybe? As Celia is registering all this, Geoff stumbles naked off the bed and snatches at clothes from the floor. While feeding one leg into his boxers he seems to be addressing both women at once. 'Yes, I know. I know what I said! I'm sorry! Celia, wait. Hang on. It's not what you think...'

The woman is gulping noisily and Celia thinks, *why is SHE crying?* Is it shame or embarrassment, or had Geoff lied that Ailsa View was more at the luxury end of the mobile home scale? Had he promised her a hot tub?

She also realises that she *knows* her from somewhere. At least, they have met before in a very different situation to this one. For one thing, Celia is pretty sure the woman was wearing clothes.

'Celia,' she starts, wiping at her face. 'I'm so sorry—' But the rest fades away as where they've met comes to her.

This woman works with Geoff at PPP. At least, she's connected to the company somehow because she was doing the rounds of the conference room, handing out samples when they launched their haggis-en-croute. It was their attempt to go upmarket and attract 'a more discerning customer.' Celia had taken one just to be polite and had to spit it out into a napkin – thick, oily pastry with a clump of grainy, pungent meat buried within. Whose idea had that been? Geoff's, as it turned out.

Bile rises in Celia's throat as she turns away from the bedroom and stomps through the caravan towards the door. As she steps outside, the wind whips at her hair. Despite what she's just witnessed, it's a relief to be able to breathe again. No one has followed her out.

Spotting her, Terri and Logan leap out of the car and hurry towards her. Terri is hugging her now as Celia spills it all out.

No, her friend tells her, she's not the idiot. Not one bit – and she mustn't think like that. 'How could this possibly be your fault?'

'Of course it's not, Mum,' Logan cries.

But really, Celia thinks: the way Geoff had bounded off, when he'd shovelled her onto that London-bound train? The way he's been with her all of these weeks, months – *years?*

She should have known.

9

If Spike's not actually dead then he's chronically unwell. What the heck has Enzo done?

Nothing! He's done nothing! He's hardly even looked at him!

Although he's alone in his flat, Enzo finds himself leaping to the defensive, pacing around the table and rubbing distractedly at his face.

He gave Spike some water, but only a dribble! To a cactus, was that akin to being waterboarded? Has he drowned the poor thing?

Enzo exhales forcefully and examines him more carefully now. Spike is certainly no longer the proudly erect, spikey baguette that Enzo had carried so carefully from Laura's place. Now he's flopped over and shrivelled in his pot on the living room table. It's as if every droplet of moisture has been sucked out of him during the night.

Enzo opens the venetian blind and hovers, trying to will Spike back to peak health through the combination of bright morning sunlight and the power of his mind.

Don't panic. Maybe this is what cacti do in the night.

Yeah, that's it, he decides. *They wilt in order to conserve their energy stores. They do this when no one's looking so they won't be mocked. Isn't nature amazing?* Yet at the same time he knows he's kidding himself, just as he had when Laura had left Mathilde's goldfish in his care. When he'd tried to convince himself that the orangey sliver floating on its side was merely 'resting.'

What is it about him and his ability to let things die? Two years, Spike has resided at Laura's and nothing untoward has happened. Yet now, at 9.15 on this bright and breezy Saturday morning, Enzo is downing his second coffee and flipping open his laptop because Mathilde is due home from Scarborough this afternoon. So he needs a solution – and fast.

Already showered and dressed, he's also aware that the community litter pick kicks off outside the library in precisely fifteen minutes. Saska insists on a prompt start as if overseeing an Olympic event rather than a raggedy group guilt-tripped into cleaning the streets. It wouldn't surprise him if she turned up with a starter gun. Although he'd planned to help – clearly, he'll have no time for that now – Enzo had already concocted an excuse as to why he'd be unable to join litter pick singles at Saska's later this morning. Polite but firm, he decided: *Sorry, a pile of work to get through.* That's the best approach. Give her an inch and you'll be picking at Bombay mix from a distinctly turd-like ceramic coil pot.

Now Enzo couldn't care less about litter pick singles or even the litter pick itself. *Fuck community spirit*, he decides, now clicking into action and googling 'droopy cactus' and poring over the confusing array of information about positioning and ambient temperature and specialist feeds. Has Spike been starved while Mathilde's been away? Admittedly, Enzo hasn't paid him an awful lot of attention. Has he been starved of love?

Darling, I'm sorry, but plants don't live forever.

Hadn't he said, that day he picked up Mathilde from her mum's, that cacti actually *did*?

His mobile rings and his heart jerks. Mathilde, still more than 200 miles away in Scarborough, knows what he's done! Never mind that she doesn't have a phone. Teachers do, don't they? She's somehow cottoned on to what's happened and begged to borrow one of theirs.

Enzo grabs his phone. It's Saska. He lets it ring out and immediately she texts.

> We're ready for you!

At 9.32 he is now two minutes late to start cleansing the neighbourhood. Enzo grew up in the Breton countryside where even the nearest town was sleepy, coming to life only on Tuesdays – market day – when the narrow streets filled with stalls piled with gnarly loaves and fat, glossy cherries, and glistening roasted chickens. He'd found the country stifling and had yearned for city life. So he'd moved to Nantes to study and messed around a bit, until he'd finally managed to haul himself together and establish a proper career. He'd taught in schools there for a few years, and then there'd been that walking holiday in the Dordogne and that had changed everything.

Enzo had planned to do it alone but he'd met Laura, also a solo traveller, and he realised he never wanted to be alone again. For a while they'd lived on Brittany's south coast but she missed Glasgow, the city in which she'd grown up. And although Enzo was a keen walker, and a lover of the wildest of landscapes, he'd always felt more suited to urban life.

You can be anything you like in a big city, he thought. *Your every move isn't commented upon. You are FREE.*

He was wrong, he realises as Saska texts again:

> Slept in, naughty man?! We're coming for you!

He looks down from his second-floor window and sees the litter pick gang approaching in their hi-vis yellow vests, bin liners attached to hoops, pickers snap-snapping. Claire-with-the-shawl glances up and he springs away from the window.

He turns back to his phone. *Sorry, something's come up,* he replies. But as he sets it down on the table – face down, as if that'll halt further communications – his doorbell rings.

10

Amanda stares at the vegetable rack in her sleek and spacious kitchen. Last time she looked, there were lots of lovely vegetables sitting there. Plump organic vegetables, bought at immense cost from east London's most Instagrammable greengrocer.

Where are they now? Not here, clearly! Amanda is no cook, but since she acquired a top-of-the-range air fryer she's been feeding the beast with as much foodstuff as it can possibly handle. She had planned to roast vegetables for lunch, drizzled with a tahini dressing and sprinkled with seeds. Now all that remains in the rack is a single withered potato the size of a thumb.

In her soft black cami, yoga pants and fluffy mules, she marches through to her guest room. At least, it *used* to be her guest room: beautifully designed, the walls a subtle pink called Calamine Rose, the bed made up with a multitude of plump pillows and unnecessary cushions and an embroidered bedspread from Anthropologie. Sometimes, during her lengthy spells as a single woman, Amanda would go in there just to sit and inhale the calm and beauty of a room barely used, yet

The Woman Who Got Her Spark Back 67

always ready. Her *guest room*. It made her feel so grown-up and sorted; the perfect hostess.

However, since Jasper's career pivot, it hasn't been Amanda's guest room. Now it's his art studio and it looks like shit.

Jasper doesn't appear to have noticed her standing there in the doorway, fixing him with a furious glare. He is clearly busy, 'in the flow' as he puts it, sitting cross-legged on the bare wooden floor which she had stripped by a handsome muscular guy with his thrumming sander and painted a soft white.

'Jasper.'

'Hmm?' He doesn't even bother looking up.

'What are you doing?' Amanda snaps.

'Printing?' *Obviously*, his tone implies.

'What d'you mean, printing?' Her gaze skims the small paint-daubed objects scattered all around him. They're vegetables, she realises. Chunks of sweet potato and carrot and butternut squash. *Her* vegetables from Roots & Fruits!

He grabs a piece of something – organic beetroot, is it? Does he know how much these things cost? – and presses it firmly onto the large sheet of white paper on the floor. 'I'm changing direction,' he says.

'Oh, and which direction is that?' An *out-of-my-life* direction? She can only hope.

'Remember potato printing?' Jasper glances up briefly. 'I'm using that simple technique but in a much freer way, without any set plan. I'm going on instinct, letting the vegetables *speak* to me—'

'You're potato printing?' Amanda exclaims. 'What are you, five?'

'Yeah, well, I thought you'd say that. I predicted it.' He assumes a hurt expression.

'So what are they saying, then?'

'Who?'

'The vegetables,' she says sharply. 'What are they telling you?'

He blows out air, as if confirming to himself that of course she doesn't get it – and why would she? She's just a silly, fluffy-headed TV presenter. Not a fine artist like him.

'I'm not getting into this with you,' he growls.

'C'mon,' she says, 'I want to know what that piece of beetroot's saying. "Hey, Jasper! Amanda bought me because I support gut health and can lower blood pressure and she's been awfully stressed lately, in case you haven't noticed"—'

'No need to be facetious,' he cuts in. 'Y'know, I actually thought you might be interested to know why I'm doing this.'

'Tell me, then.' When it comes to Jasper's art, Amanda would be more interested in watching butter melt.

'I'm changing my style because they didn't want it, basically!' he says with some force.

Confused now, she pushes away her fair tousled hair and looks down at him.

'I don't understand. Who didn't want what?'

'The painting I donated to that charity thing. The one that's in their exhibition?'

Amanda remembers now, vaguely. It's a local exhibition with a charity raffle that Jasper had somehow got wind of. He'd barrelled right in there, brandishing a hideous abstract painting the size of a dining table, announcing that he'd like to donate it out of the goodness of his heart. Jasper is moderately recognisable – about as much as Amanda is these days – having played one of the lesser police officers in a popular TV drama. She suspected the exhibition organisers only agreed to take the 'work' so they could put 'Including an original painting by a local celebrity' on their marketing material.

'D'you mean someone's won it?' she asks.

'That's right,' he replies.

'But...' She frowns. 'They don't actually *want* it?'

'Well, they said they can't accommodate it,' he mumbles.

Her gaze skims the canvases stacked up against every wall in her once beautiful room. The violent splatters of brown and mustard bring to mind the one and only time Amanda has had the misfortune to witness a baby's nappy being changed. Celia tackling Logan's bottom as if it were no more arduous than cleansing her face.

'Maybe it's too big for their house?' she offers.

'It's not that big!'

'Well, not everyone's home can take, uh... such a *statement piece.*'

'You mean you hated it, don't you?' He stares up at her.

'I didn't say that.' Now she registers a daub of oily paint on a gauzy curtain – it looks as if someone has rubbed a kebab on it – and Celia's wedding present vase jammed with dirty brushes on the floor. Yet more filthy receptacles of brushes and palette knives are crammed on the mid-century dressing table that Amanda had shipped back from Copenhagen at immense expense.

Finding it all too upsetting to look at, she steps out of the room, closing the door quietly behind her. *This must be what it's like to have a teenager*, she reflects, making her way back to the kitchen. Perhaps it's a good thing she's not a mother because how does anyone have the patience?

Now Jasper has sloped after her and flings open the fridge with unnecessary force. She hates the way he does this, yanking hard on the door of the brushed steel appliance as if it's some ancient casket, gummed together for decades with barnacles. Despite trying to ignore him, she can't help glaring over as he extracts a triangle of Laughing Cow cheese from the fridge. In their early days together, she'd taken him to her favourite Japanese and Vietnamese restaurants. That was before she realised he prefers to eat like a child. Crisps, chocolate, spreadable cheese: it's one endless kid's packed lunch around here.

Now, as if to further crank up her irritation, Jasper places the foil triangle on the worktop, stabs at it with the bread knife and squeezes it, like a spot, onto a cracker. 'D'you have to do that?' she asks.

He turns and frowns. 'What?'

'There's a little red tab on each triangle. You pull the tab and it opens the foil—'

'Are you telling me how to open cheese?'

Amanda senses her heart quickening. Lust, that's what it was when they'd first locked eyes over cocktails in an intimate basement bar. Hours later he'd pushed her up against the wall in his faceless flat close to London Bridge and she'd orgasmed like never before in her life.

He crunches the cracker noisily and a fragment shoots out of his mouth. *Calm down*, she tells herself firmly. *Getting mad at him won't help.* 'Maybe,' she starts, 'you could offer them something else?'

'What, the raffle winner, you mean?' he asks, spraying more crumbs.

'Yes. Why not?'

He shrugs. 'Like... what?'

'Um... like a potato print?'

'Oh, very funny!'

'I'm serious! Isn't that your new direction?'

'You just don't get it, do you?' he thunders.

'Get what?' she asks, genuinely confused.

'How hurtful this is. How humiliating!'

She steps back, shocked by his outburst. 'I think you're taking this a bit personally, Jasper…'

'But it *is* personal. It's like, I've given them a piece of my work – of *myself* – and they don't fucking want it!'

She stares at him, thinking, *which piece of yourself might that be?* They can have *all* of him for all she cares. Take the chump off her hands. But she can't admit this, can she? That less than five months after their glittering wedding, she actually wants out? Their ill-tempered exchange continues, and all the while Amanda is berating herself for allowing her libido to override her common sense, when it came to marrying him. She couldn't believe it when he proposed; that this beautiful man would want to spend the rest of his life with her. She felt like the luckiest woman in London then. But she doesn't feel lucky now.

'I'm going out,' he barks at her.

'Good! Go then!' The front door bangs and suddenly, without warning, Amanda's eyes flood with hot tears. She needs to speak to someone – to let it all out. Briefly, she thinks of calling her lovely mum. Amanda's parents left Glasgow many years ago, for a cottage on the Northumberland coast. They adore her, and of course they'd listen and console her and say it doesn't matter; everyone makes mistakes. But then what? They'd worry themselves senseless and she couldn't bear that. She also has an older brother, Gary. But he lives in Brisbane and although they get along well, they don't have that kind of relationship.

Amanda is crying heartily now, sitting on the kitchen floor next to the foil cheese wrapper that Jasper must have dropped. It's not his stupid paintings, or the way he manhandles her fridge, or the fact that Ollie hasn't called with any job offers. It's not even the realisation that Jasper's youth and beauty haven't rubbed off on her (quite the contrary; now she feels *old*), or the fact that she is not in love with him. It's the realisation that there is no one in London she feels she can call – not one friend whom she knows will be there for her.

Perhaps that's her fault. The result of all that *batching*. But then it occurs to her that there *is* someone – and didn't she travel all the way from Glasgow for her wedding? Surely she'll be willing to listen and won't judge her?

Amanda wipes more hot tears from her face, grateful now that Jasper stormed out. Then, having coughed away the roughness from her throat, she wipes her nose on her sleeve and calls her oldest friend.

11

'Amanda! Hi!' Celia is gripping her phone. She almost didn't answer it – she and Terri and Logan have only just arrived back at her flat – but something niggled at her. *Why is Amanda calling? She never calls. Something terrible must have happened.*

'Hey, Celia,' Amanda starts. 'How are things? Is this a good time?'

'Erm, uh... it's not the *greatest* time, actually...'

'Oh, you're at work, right?'

'Actually, I'm just—'

'Still at that florist's?'

'No, um, they shut down.' *About ten years ago.* Celia is standing in the middle of her kitchen. Terri is mouthing, 'Just hang up!' and Logan looks baffled as to why his mother is even conducting a phone conversation right now.

'Aw, shame. So what're you up to now?' Amanda asks.

Apart from catching Geoff doing it doggy style with another woman in a rancid caravan? 'I, um... I work at another shop. A boutique in—'

'Oh, cool! A little independent place?'

'Uh, yes.'

'So you're in fashion too!'

'I... I suppose so,' Celia says, keen to wrap up this call because she needs to sit down, ingest strong alcohol and try to wrap her head around what has happened today. The unlocked caravan. Geoff's hairy backside. It feels like she imagined it all. 'So, are *you* okay?' she asks quickly.

'Um, yeah! I'm good. Crazy busy, y'know. Just the usual. Work-work-work, too much to juggle, but that's just life, eh!' Celia frowns, still confused as to why Amanda has called her when they haven't spoken on the phone since something like 2006. 'So lovely to see you at our wedding,' she goes on. 'Shame we didn't get to chat properly. So anyway, how're you?'

Haven't they done this bit already? 'Good. Great!'

'So, any news? You must have news!'

Celia opens her mouth to speak but nothing comes out.

'How's your dad?'

'Still in Wales, I think.' *He hardly ever replies to my texts so your guess is as good as mine.*

'And your mum?'

Drunk, probably. 'She's great!'

'And Laurence?'

Celia is too taken aback to remind her that her son is called Logan, and now Terri is gesticulating to her to get off the phone. 'He's fine.'

'Still into his Rubik's cube?'

'No, he's doing mycology.'

'Biology? Ah, amazing! How old is he now? Fifteen? I'm terrible, I lose track...'

'He's twenty-four,' Celia replies, but already Amanda is babbling over her.

'Crazy, isn't it? How time flies? Oh, and thanks for the

wedding present. That beautiful vase. I meant to message to say we *love* it...'

Terri is trying to talk to Celia now. 'Say you're busy,' she commands.

'Oh, d'you have a customer?' Amanda asks.

'A customer?'

'In your shop.'

'No, no. I'm at home—'

'I thought you were at work?'

'No,' Celia says forcefully. A small silence hovers. 'In fact, I really can't talk right now, Amanda,' she blurts out as tears spring suddenly into her eyes.

'Oh God, Celia. I'm sorry. Are you... okay?'

'I'm not, I'm afraid. This, uh, *thing's* happened with Geoff and I'm going to have to—'

'Has he had an accident?'

Why is Amanda asking her all this stuff? Why is she having to explain?

'No, it's more of a personal thing and I have to go, I'm sorry...' With a gulp she finishes the call abruptly.

Now Terri presses a mug of tea into Celia's hands – she'd prefer wine, but accepts it – and enfolds her in a hug, and Logan pats her shoulder ineffectually. He means well, though, and Celia is relieved at least to be off the bloody phone and at home, where she feels safe, with the people she feels closest to.

No pink CD was blaring on the drive home from the caravan site. Young hearts were not running free. There was no ribbing Logan about his course, calling him 'Mushroom Man', or joking about him boiling up fungi for hallucinogenic tea.

'He's in there with a woman,' Celia had announced to her son and best friend after she'd blundered out of the caravan.

Logan stared at her. 'What d'you mean? What're they doing?'

Christ, did she have to spell it out? Draw a diagram? 'He's having sex with someone,' she cried, in case he'd been under the illusion that they'd been icing cupcakes or doing a crossword together, and that had silenced him for the whole journey home.

Now he is hunched mutely by the cooker. 'You know you can stay with me for as long as you want,' Terri says. 'Both of you, I mean. If Geoff comes back here.'

'Will he, though?' Logan exclaims. 'I mean, will he dare, after what he's done?'

'I don't know, love. I don't know anything right now.' Celia shakes her head as Terri waves a plate of custard creams in front of her. Her skin feels tender, as if lightly scoured, from all the salty crying. The doorbell rings and Celia flinches.

'I'll get it,' Terri announces, but Celia shakes her head.

'No, just leave it. It might be him.'

'I'll tell him to fuck off then.'

'If it was Dad, wouldn't he just... *come in*?' Logan ventures.

'He's scared, maybe,' Terri suggests as the bell rings again.

'Just leave it, Mum,' Logan says. 'Whoever it is, they'll soon go away.'

Celia, who has spent the past hour crying at her kitchen table, doesn't care whether they go away or stand there waiting until Christmas. She can barely think. But then the bell ding-dongs yet again and it occurs to her that perhaps it's Geoff's lover, come to have it out with her. Is she going to suggest a *duel*?

With Terri at her heels, she marches through to answer the door and flings it open aggressively. 'Hello?'

'Hi! Are you Celia?' The woman is very tall and skinny with a large quantity of crinkly reddish hair tumbling over her shoulders. This is definitely not haggis-en-croute woman and the man at her side is *not* Geoff. Her husband is a sandy-haired two-timing shitbag whom she could happily cosh with her secateurs, and this is just a normal, pleasant-looking man, with wavy, dark brown hair and a hint of stubble around his jaw, clutching a cactus in a pot. Even in her highly emotional state, Celia registers a *trichocereus* requiring urgent re-potting in a mixture comprising 50 per cent inorganic material such as pumice and perlite and decomposed granite.

'Er, yes. Yes, I'm Celia.' She tries to calm her galloping thoughts.

'And this is the houseplant hospital?' the man asks brightly.

'That's right,' Celia starts. 'But actually, today's a bit—'

'Not right now,' Terri announces loudly, having arrived at Celia's side. 'We're at capacity. All hospital beds are full.'

'Oh.' The man's expression falls. 'Could we, erm… just ask for a bit of advice then, please?'

'Not today,' Terri snaps, and Celia sees him flinch.

The woman steps forward. 'But I thought you did *doorstep consultations*?' she says, as if Celia has somehow been misleading the public.

'I'm sorry,' she starts, shaking her head. 'I can't—'

'We're not doing anything today,' Terri declares, arms folded.

Celia catches the woman throwing her husband an exasperated look. She wants to help, and in any other circumstances she'd be happy to dispense advice for free right here, as she often does. She hates to see a plant looking sorry for itself when the correct care would put things right.

'It's just… it's really important to us, isn't it, Enzo?' The woman's eyes widen plaintively as she places a hand on his arm. She turns back to Celia. 'The kids are back from their school trip this afternoon. Mathilde's going to be *so* upset…'

'Oh, is she?' She should help, Celia thinks. This is a *child's* cactus. She knows how attached she'd become to her own plants in the garden she created as a young girl.

'Yes, it belonged to her grandparents,' the woman adds, 'and they've gone now. Passed away. It was all Mathilde wanted when their house was cleared.'

Something twists at Celia's heart. 'So it's an heirloom plant?'

'Well, sort of,' Enzo starts, looking a little uneasy now.

'Yes, exactly,' his wife says quickly.

'I don't think there's much hope for it,' announces Terri, as if she knows the first thing about plants. She virtually murdered a *xanthosoma* until Celia stepped in.

'You mean... it's a lost cause?' Enzo's face falls. He has kind eyes, Celia decides – and a trustworthy face. A slight accent too, she's noticed. Perhaps he's French? She glances at Terri, grateful that's she's here for her, as she has been all these years. But this is her houseplant hospital and her life.

'*Nothing's* a lost cause,' she says.

'Really?' Enzo smiles and she sees a glimmer of hope in his eyes. But just as Celia is about to examine the poor cactus, Terri shakes her head firmly.

'We can't deal with this now.'

Of course she's right. 'I'm sorry,' Celia starts. 'This isn't the best time. Give me a call in the week and leave me a voicemail. You'll find me under houseplant hospital, Celia Bloom—'

'In the week isn't any good to us,' the woman announces, dark eyes flashing. 'We need you to do something *now*—'

'I'm sorry, I—' Celia starts.

'Isn't this supposed to be a hospital? Don't you take emergency admissions?'

'D'you *mind*?' Terri snaps, and Celia catches the man grimacing, as if distinctly uncomfortable with his wife's pushiness.

'I'm sorry,' she says, catching his eye. 'If I could, I'd help you, but I can't right now.'

'Oh, no problem at all.' His cheeks flush. 'Thanks anyway. We should've called rather than just turning up like this.'

'That would be better,' she says.

He nods, and although Celia is relieved to close the door, she still feels a pang of regret because obviously that sorry-looking cactus is extremely important to their child. She also hates being rude to anyone. She simply can't bear it.

Still, hopefully they'll call and, when she's not quite so demented, she'll do whatever she can to put things right.

12

Mathilde, darling, I have something to tell you.

No, that won't do. She'll think someone's died.

Someone *has* died! Enzo reminds himself. He and Saska have just left Celia's house and he's still cringing about how strident she was there.

Listen, sweetheart, something's happened to Spike. I'm sorry, but sometimes things die and he had a good, long, happy life, and we should cherish that... No, that's terrible. Mathilde is a smart kid and won't tolerate being patronised.

We'll get you a new one. We'll go out together and you can choose any cactus you like. Enzo continues in this vein, running through his lines as if rehearsing a play. Now he pictures his audience of one pinging a hard sweet at his head, as happened when he was roped into performing in the teacher pantomime. Meanwhile Saska, who likes things to go according to her plans, is ranting on about the 'misrepresenting of services' they'd just witnessed.

'Claire said she's really good,' she announces. 'A plant genius, she said. Completely rescued her maidenhair fern when it had gone all brown and crispy. It wouldn't have taken much, would it, for her to at least offer us a bit of advice?'

'Well, we did just turn up unannounced,' Enzo reasons. 'She actually looked upset, did you notice? Like she'd been crying?'

'And that other woman?' Saska goes on, ignoring this. 'The forceful one? Basically shooing us away!'

'We don't know what they were dealing with, do we?' Exasperated, Enzo glances at her. He wishes he hadn't answered the door when she'd buzzed, and involved her in this Spike situation. But then Saska is the kind of person who makes things happen, and it had seemed hopeful that Celia could make everything all right.

As there's no chance of that happening, he thanks Saska for her help, and carries Spike back into his flat, figuring that he still has time to fix things if he gets a move on.

Alone this time, he sets off, crossing his leafy street of creamy sandstone tenement flats and striding towards the main shopping area of his neighbourhood. Once offering little more than vape shops and a scattering of decrepit old barbers, it's now the hub of Glasgow's hipster Southside. The main street is awash with Italian cannoli, New York bagels and French patisseries. Enzo's mouth waters at the sight of a window filled with honey-soaked Syrian baklawa shaped like little nests. If he weren't on a mission, he'd buy some for Mathilde coming home later as they're her favourites. But the queue is long and so, inhaling the aroma of baking and excellent coffee, he marches onwards to where the bustling street meets the park.

Here, he remembers, there's a plant shop. He's passed it with Mathilde and they'd marvelled at how cool it looked, all exposed red brick and leafy greenery, with young people coming out brandishing all manner of plants for their shared flats. Students buying houseplants? He wouldn't have had a clue what to do with one at twenty years old. Hasn't a clue what to do with one now, clearly, at forty-two. So a substitute Spike must be found.

Enzo isn't exactly a fashion man or a follower of trends. Mathilde has teased him for not knowing what chia pudding is. But he does know that cacti are – or were? – 'having a moment', and even if that moment has passed, surely he can find the right kind somewhere. As challenges go, he cannot believe that this one is insurmountable. After all, he has managed to haul an extremely rabbly bunch of first years through the conjugation of the twenty most common irregular verbs.

Already, Enzo is feeling more hopeful. He steps into the shop, registering a couple of young women in baggy jeans and T-shirts debating whether to go for the big bushy thing or the spindly twiggy one.

'Hi, can I help?' A smiley pink-cheeked woman, her fringe secured back from her forehead with a glittery clip, is clutching a tray of miniature cacti—*Yes-there-are-cacti-here!*

'Erm, I'm actually after a cactus,' he announces.

'You've come to the right place.' She beams at him.

'D'you, uh, have any bigger varieties?' Four hours he has now until the coach pulls up outside Mathilde's school. Four hours in which to locate an acceptable substitute, get it potted in Spike's pot and redeem himself.

'A bigger cactus? Hang on a sec...' More studenty types wander in, clutching coffees, discussing 'which one Marla would go for' and whether that trailing plant would 'work on our fireplace?' When Enzo was a student, the only thing growing in his apartment was fuzzy mould in coffee cups. What's happening to young people? Not the kids he teaches – they're not yet in the plant-buying demographic – but these twentysomethings cooing over greenery. They seem so much more sorted than he was as they browse the plants in this beautifully arranged shop ('curated', that would be the word).

Now the smiley woman is showing Enzo a selection of cacti on a shelf. 'There are lovely ones here,' she enthuses, lurching into another language. Not that Enzo isn't multilingual – as well as being fluent in English, he also speaks Italian and Spanish and he knows a little Greek. But the language she's speaking isn't one that's in modern usage. 'So we have the *echinocereus rigidissimus*, that's the in thing right now, the kids are wild for these – and the *epiphyllum anguliger* looks good anywhere. And this is a favourite of mine, the *rebutia minuscula*. Isn't it a darling?'

'Er, yes. It is.' But it's not what he wants! On she goes, as if advising him on accessories, while Enzo stares at the spiky orbs and fuzzy sausages and a spine-free variety with zig-zag-edged leaves. Right now a spike-free cactus seems as useful as a wheelless bicycle.

The woman looks at him expectantly. 'Anything you like?'

He fishes his phone from his pocket and brings up his photo of the collapsed Spike. 'I'm actually looking for one like this. I mean, before I killed it, obviously.'

'Oh dear, that does look bad.' She peers at the photo and presses her lips together. 'I'm afraid I can't help you with that.' She looks genuinely regretful, like a doctor who has just imparted bad news. 'I find that people are going more for the compact little spherical varieties right now,' she adds.

And so, as if informed that the cut of his jeans is all wrong, Enzo thanks her and edges past a bunch of hipster girls admiring a tiny garden in a glass dome, and he mooches home.

* * *

It's only a plant, he reminds himself later as he smiles and nods in recognition to several mums and dads who are making their way to school. Even his parents weren't that bothered about it. Hardly gave the thing a second glance, as far as he could make out. One visit, Mathilde exclaimed, '*Regarde, le cactus fleurit!*' Her grandparents hadn't even noticed the exuberant pink blooms. '*Ah, c'est joli,*' his mum had said with a shrug. Besides, Mathilde will be too full of tales of the Scarborough trip to be worried about anything else. She mightn't even care, Enzo tells himself.

Outside the school, parents have gathered in clusters. He spots Saska in the distance, chattering loudly with a group of women, and deliberately hangs back. Although she's promised not to mention Spike's demise to Honey or Mathilde, he's had quite enough interaction with her for one day.

The vision of deceased Spike shimmers into Enzo's brain. Then the coach appears around the corner, and his chest seems to compress as if it's being sat on as it pulls up to a halt.

The doors open and a teacher steps down, calling out, 'Okay, everyone! Nice and slowly, no pushing please…' And out they come, chatting excitedly as if four days together haven't quite been enough.

Enzo senses himself tensing as Mathilde's friend Mo jumps out, then the curly blonde-headed friend whose name he can never remember. Several more follow, and now here come Honey and Mathilde. The pair are so engrossed in chatting that it takes his daughter a moment to pause and look around. Then she spots him and a smile lights up her face.

'Dad!' She hurries towards him and squeezes him in a hug.

'Hi, darling! Did you have a good time?'

'It was amazing!'

'Great. I've missed you. It's been so quiet around here!'

She laughs and he smiles and takes her hand. 'Can Honey come home with us?' she asks.

'Oh, love, you've just had a whole four days together. I think she'll want some time with her mum.'

'Aw, okay.' Her face falls briefly then brightens again as she starts to rattle off the many, many highlights of the trip. The fairground. Races on the beach. A sandcastle contest which she and Honey won. She stops suddenly. 'I didn't say bye to Honey!'

'Let's just get home,' he says. The sooner it's dealt with, the better, he reckons. Do it quickly, like ripping a plaster off a wound.

He senses her looking up at him as they fall into step. 'You're being weird, Dad.'

'Am I?' He forces a chuckle. 'Maybe I'm weird all the time and you'd just forgotten.'

She smiles, and they fall into a comfortable silence for a few moments until a voice calls out behind them. 'Enzo! Enzo!'

He swings round to see Saska clutching Honey's rucksack, and her daughter pelting towards them. 'Mum says it's okay!' Honey announces.

Enzo and Mathilde stop. 'Hey, Honey,' Enzo says. 'What's okay?'

'Mathilde can stay over tonight with us. Keep the holiday going!' Honey's eyes are bright, her reddish hair springing around her flushed cheeks.

'I think everyone probably wants a quiet night tonight,' Enzo starts, turning to Mathilde. 'We'll get your stuff unpacked, maybe watch a movie together. I've got pizzas in...'

'Please, Dad,' Mathilde implores.

'Honestly, it's fine.' Saska smiles. 'The girls can do movie-and-pizza at our place. You don't have any plans, do you?'

'Er, no,' Enzo replies. 'Not especially—'

'Great,' Saska enthuses. And so Mathilde pulls off her bulging rucksack and thrusts it at him to take home. Saska assures them that they are awash with spare pyjamas and toothbrushes, and off they go.

Enzo marches towards home feeling a little deflated now. Despite the Spike situation, he'd been looking forward to Mathilde coming back today. Now he faces the prospect of an evening alone that he hadn't bargained for. Occasionally, without him noticing it sneaking up on him, Enzo finds himself feeling a little lonely these days. He has friends, of course – from school, and the five-a-side team he plays with now and then, although he fears that his footballing days will be over soon. He has dad-friends too, whom he's met through Mathilde, and many of the women in school gate circles are friendly and invite him to things. Drinks, barbecues; in the warmer months there's no shortage of those. Yet still certain gaps can appear on a quiet evening or a yawning weekend afternoon when Mathilde is at her mum's, and his friends are occupied with their own families.

Sometimes Enzo even finds himself wondering if – and specifically how – he will ever meet anyone. Despite copious badgering from friends, he has refused to involve himself further in online dating after a soul-sapping foray a year or so ago. The women he met were either clearly not interested, or they had nothing in common, or there simply wasn't enough of that thing – that elusive 'thing' – to keep things going.

Would real life dating be better? He was willing to give it a go, and so one of his five-a-side mates arranged for him to meet Janetta, Brown Owl of the local Brownie pack (Enzo had been unfamiliar with the title before then). She'd ripped open a crisp packet and laid it flat on the pub table, and crunched away while detailing the trouble she was having with her painful ankles. Neither suggested meeting up again and Enzo assumed that would be the end of it. However, at around that time, Mathilde announced that she wanted to join the Brownies. How about Cubs instead? he suggested. He was pretty sure girls could be Cubs now! Nope, it had to be Brownies – so Enzo would literally drop her off and run.

'Brown Owl has a twinkle for you,' Laura teased him, followed by a flirtatious hoot: Twit-twoo! 'You should give the apps another go,' she added. However, the thought of swiping appals him. Plus, as a teacher, he fears that a pupil's parent (or worse, an older pupil) might spot his profile and then it'd all come out at school. Monsieur Fontaine's on Tinder! He shudders at the thought.

'Not Tinder, silly,' Laura ribbed him. 'You need an over-forties site.'

'Why aren't *you* on an over-forties site?' he teased.

She spluttered at the thought. 'I'm not ready for that.'

'It's all right for me, though?' They laughed, and in fact Enzo knows that Laura has enough on her plate, with Mathilde and her job and a wide circle of friends. 'But you do know that's how people do things now,' she added. 'Have done for about twenty years, in fact.'

Not us, though, he thought; *we met climbing a hill.* This triggered a rare pang of sadness and he changed the subject.

Almost home now, he decides to stop off at the supermarket for some treats for Mathilde. It's not that he spoils her or treads on eggshells around her. She is self-assured and strong-minded, a happy girl most of the time – brimming with enthusiasm for life. But, given the cactus situation, he wants to make her homecoming tomorrow as enjoyable as it can possibly be.

With that thought in mind, he roams the aisles, filling a basket with her favourite things, as if that will make it all right:

Cheestrings and Coco Pops which her mother wouldn't approve of – but then Laura is in New York right now and needs must.

And then he spots it. An oasis in the desert at the end of the biscuit aisle. Enzo virtually gallops towards the table filled with cacti and quickly assesses the many varieties on sale. There are sizeable globes and tiny orbs, and crinkly ones and another with a showy orange flower on top.

He doesn't really register any of these. Because there is one, single, tall, erect, spine-covered baguette.

In his excitement, Enzo grabs the thing as if it were as innocuous as a cucumber and the spikes pierce his hand. 'Ow!' he yelps. But the pain subsides instantly and it's in his basket now, propped upright between a box of chocolate biscuits and the contraband cereal, and he virtually skips to the checkout with glee in his heart.

Enzo doesn't particularly enjoy supermarket shopping normally. But these places are great, he decides now. The sheer variety of the goods on offer!

'You know there are some that are in flower?' The woman at the till smiles as he unloads his purchases. 'They're lovely, those ones.'

'This one's fine, thanks,' he says, and as it glides along slowly on the conveyor belt Enzo feels like the happiest man on earth.

13

On this damp and drizzly Monday morning, Celia wonders how she could possibly have failed to realise that Geoff was having an affair. Now she thinks that someone must have crept into their bedroom while she was sleeping and tapped the top off her head – like you do with a boiled egg – and scooped out her brain and replaced it with potting compost.

Because really the signs were obvious. As she unlocks the front door of Elegance and lets herself in, she finds herself running through them in her mind.

First up, there was that morning Geoff saw her off on her London-bound train. She thinks of it now as 'The Pret Incident'. Occasionally, when she's alone in town, Celia does something rebellious and pretty wild.

She buys herself a Pret a Manger sandwich.

It doesn't matter that Geoff is unlikely to ever find out. That delicious sense of naughtiness isn't diminished one bit. It feels doubly naughty if there's a window seat free, where she can perch brazenly, daring one of his 'spies' – a colleague or a golf pal – to spot her as she relishes her illicit snack.

At thirteen-hours-twenty-six, subject seen consuming outrageously priced chicken and avocado in soft wholegrain plus small additional item, possible Love Bar.

However, on the morning of her departure for Amanda's wedding, it wasn't Celia who'd splashed out on an outrageously priced falafel wrap from Pret, but Geoff. 'Here. This'll keep you going,' he announced, pressing the paper bag into her hands.

'Thank you!' She'd have been no more shocked if he'd handed her an entire lobster as a journey snack.

'No worries. Have a brilliant time!'

Now, of course, she knows that his burst of generosity was due to the fact that he was anticipating something of a 'brilliant time' too.

By the time she arrived at the wedding venue, one of her suitcase wheels had broken. She'd caught a couple smirking as she'd dragged it across the room and parked it in a corner, glaring at it as if it had disappointed her terribly today.

Sweaty and mortified, she'd then hidden in the loos where she'd tried to phone Geoff several times, just to be reassured by the familiarity of his voice. However, he hadn't picked up or returned her calls. Clearly, he'd been busy. Busy stuffing his haggis into that woman's *croute*.

Such an energetic performance, Celia reflects darkly as she clicks on the lights and flits around the shop, running a feather duster over the shelves. Quite unlike the kind of sex she and Geoff have been having for years now: a tweak here and a twiddle there as if he were adjusting the boiler settings to save 50p on the utility bill. Then on he'd climb and thrash about a bit. The usual routine. Until the last time they'd had sex, three or four weeks ago now. Instead of falling asleep instantly – as had been his habit – he clambered off her and reached for an item on his bedside table.

Glasses. He put his *glasses* on and then picked up a biro, plus the newspaper which he buys with actual money on Sundays because he enjoys the sudoku.

Sitting up in bed, he studied the half-done puzzle, jotting notes in the margin as if the sex had been an irksome interruption. Celia watched him raptly. *He's just relaxed,* she told herself. *Isn't it great that we're so comfortable together that he can switch so easily post-orgasm to the puzzle page?* But actually, that didn't make her feel any better.

How very stupid she was not to realise that he does in fact have feelings – *intense* feelings, judging from what she witnessed at the caravan – for someone else. As far as she could make out, there was no sudoku happening there.

Parked behind the shop counter, Celia checks the time. The morning is creeping on at a snail's pace due to an absence of customers, and now the shop is the cleanest it's been since Celia started working here some five years ago. She could catch up on emailing plant hospital customers but isn't sure she would be capable of making sense. Terri badgered her to call Ruth, her boss, to explain that she needs time off ('No one would expect you to be all smiley and enthusiastic about fascinators!'). But what would Celia have done at home? Yesterday the flat felt terribly claustrophobic. Logan had taken himself off to his room, and Celia found herself torn between desperately wanting Geoff to contact her, and never wishing to hear from him ever again. As it is, there's still no word and she's certainly not planning to contact *him.*

An extremely stylish older woman breezes into the shop with a cheery hello. They exchange pleasantries as she peruses the rails. 'Looking for anything special?' Celia asks, and she smiles.

'Just an anniversary.'

'Oh, is it yours?'

'Yes – our first, actually.' Her eyes seem to sparkle as Celia thinks, *her first!* She's probably seventy and she looks fantastic and so happy. 'The anniversary of our first date,' she adds.

'That's lovely!' Something seems to catch in Celia's throat. 'Are you going out to dinner?'

'He's actually booked a lovely hotel in the Highlands so we're staying over.'

'That sounds perfect,' Celia croaks.

The woman murmurs that yes, he's terribly thoughtful like that, and she gathers an armful of dresses in various size options and disappears into the changing room. They say 'room', but it's separated from the main shop area only by a heavy velvet curtain on a rail.

Soon the woman emerges, briefly, looking rather elegant in one of the frocks. 'Oh, that's lovely on you,' Celia enthuses. 'The colour's just right and it fits you perfectly…'

'You think so?'

Celia nods. *Imagine*, she thinks, *being newly in love like this woman clearly is*. Actually, she can't imagine, and emotions are welling up in her now and she wishes she'd taken Terri's advice and not come in. This having to be perky and enthusiastic – it's too much.

The woman disappears again and emerges in her own smart trousers and blouse, and hands Celia a dress. 'I'm going for this one.'

'That's the one you came out in?'

'Well, no.' She smiles awkwardly, running a hand over her silvery bob. 'It's the smaller size and it is a bit tight around the middle.' *Why buy it then?* Celia wants to cry because the woman is beautiful as she is. 'I've got time to slim into it,' she adds, and of course Celia accepts this because her job is just to sell clothes. Yet as soon as the woman has left with the size ten, she berates herself for not even trying to persuade her that she looked wonderful in the dress that actually fitted. And that the ten will never fit her, unless she eschews all food and has several ribs removed. Yet this happens all the time: customers picking their fantasy size over their actual size. And it never works – at least, hardly ever. Because outfits are returned, unworn and in mint condition, bar the faint whiff of failure and disappointment. All that hope – it's heartbreaking sometimes. Celia remembers those ridiculous ill-fitting red shoes she'd bought for Amanda's wedding and tries to push the thought from her mind.

Yet she can't – not today. What were Geoff and his lover doing while she was safely out of the way in London, being patronised by that old boor she'd been put next to at the table?

Celia remembers the man clearly. Short grey hair, neatly trimmed beard, wire-framed spectacles. His casual question about what was 'on her agenda' in London ('Er, no plans really!') led to him recommending she caught a performance at the Festival Hall. And *this* segued neatly into him railing against how people behaved at the last classical concert he attended. 'Clapping,' he spluttered. 'Clapping in time with the "beat".' He waggled his fingers to denote quotation marks.

'Really?' Celia tried to look suitably shocked. Having never been to a classical concert, she couldn't understand what was so bad about enjoying yourself.

'It was *Carmina Burana*,' he added.

'I'm not sure I know him,' she admitted.

He frowned at her. 'That's the *piece*. Not the composer...'

'Oh.' She sensed herself reddening and wished she could spirit herself home, to the flat where Geoff commandeered the central heating thermostat. Where he stopped short of keeping it at Baltic temperatures only because she insisted it would shock her plants.

Even *that* would have been better than feeling so lost at the wedding, the front of her shift dress smattered with oily marks from where the wrap's falafel filling had tumbled out on the train.

Geoff and Celia hadn't been gifted his parents' caravan at that point. He still would have had access to it, as he had keys. However, with Celia in London, and Logan not around either, he'd have been able to invite that woman to their flat.

This means they did it in our bed, Celia decides. Or in the living room – on the sofa where she sits watching *Gardener's World*. She pictures herself curled up there with a cup of tea, oblivious, while Monty Don demonstrated how to create a hawthorn hedge.

Because where else would they do it? Not her and Monty – although she does have feelings, proving that she's not entirely dead below the waist – but Geoff and his ladylove. Not in the plant room, surely? Geoff has always had an aversion to so much greenery 'taking over' their flat, and she can't imagine the rickety pull-out bed in there would stand up to too much vigorous thrashing. And surely he wouldn't have whisked her into Logan's room where Celia stores the shade-loving ferns?

Now the image she's conjured up, of Geoff bending that woman over the kitchen table – the table at which she and Logan used to play Jenga together, and where he'd do his homework dutifully – tips her over the edge. To her horror tears are coming, in a boutique for mature ladies, and they will not stop. She scurries to the changing room and draws the velvet curtain and flops down onto the stool. And she cries and cries, praying that no customers come in because she will be incapable of helping them, just as she couldn't help that nice man who'd shown up at her flat with the cactus.

Celia doesn't know how long she has been in there, crying her heart out over all the years lost with a man whom she doubts ever really loved her. Maybe he thought, with her having a baby, that she'd be grateful somehow.

Well, she was. She was extremely grateful. But now, as she hears the shop door opening, and the owner Ruth call out, 'Celia? Celia, love, are you there?', she feels as if her heart has shattered all over the changing room floor.

14

'Yes, Kelly, I *know* you're new to the team but we need to hit the ground running, all right?'

Amanda glares up from her seat on the train. It's been a very long time since she visited her home city of Glasgow, but she has always been extremely specific about her seat reservation. Although she only booked yesterday, she was relieved to be able to secure one in the quiet coach. 'We need the whole team on this,' the man announces, not merely flouting the rules but storming furiously up and down the aisle as he speaks.

Amanda inhales deeply and shuts her eyes as if that will make him go away. She likes to think she's a tolerant person. Throughout her younger years – her flat-sharing years – she'd put up with sinks heaped with stinky dishes and flatmates 'borrowing' her clothes. Then as her career took off, after she'd been plucked from obscurity in a club to present late-night TV, and then *better* TV, she'd put up with a different raft of things. Sure, there was good stuff: free clothes and holidays, and instead of living on cereal and toast, she now had a favourite booth in a restaurant with a little brass button that said *'Press for champagne'.*

However, along with the money and perks and model boyfriends came the relentless demands of having to look gorgeous all the time. Having constant blow-dries and manicures and her eyebrows laminated, plus a personal trainer yelling, 'Come on, Amanda! It's a win-win!' All of *that* she could tolerate – plus the strangers coming up to her in Tesco, wanting selfies and trailing after her while she bought pan scourers and tampons. Today she has even coped with not having a table seat but a substandard one with a silly tray. But this man in a pink shirt marching back and forth while shouting? It's too much and Amanda snaps.

'Excuse me!' Now she too is out of her seat. Phone Man gawps at her.

'Sorry,' he tells Kelly, quickly averting his gaze. 'Someone's trying to say something.'

'It's the quiet coach,' Amanda announces. 'Could you make your call somewhere else?'

He blows out air as if she had made an outrageous suggestion. 'Sorry,' he says again. 'Some woman's trying to talk to me here...' *Some mad woman*, his tone implies. Weirdly, no one else seems to be remotely disturbed by his display. *Is it me?* Amanda thinks wildly as she sits back down. *Am I the mad woman on the train?* Maybe she is. She hasn't thought out this trip exactly. She just knew she had to get away for a while, just to clear her head and figure out what to do. About her career, for one thing, but more urgently about her potato-printing, Laughing-Cow-triangle-stabbing husband. She glares around the carriage and shakes her head, teacher-style, at the seemingly unconcerned passengers. *Honestly, class, I'd have expected more from you.*

The whole of yesterday she'd wondered what to do because actually, Celia sounded as if she had a lot on her plate herself. Then it struck Amanda that this was the perfect time for a surprise visit. Whatever was happening for Celia – and she'd thought it better not to call back or text – then at least they could have some fun together.

Amanda hadn't got around to telling her *why* she'd called, and about her frustrations with Jasper. Better to chat face-to-face, she decides. Celia was always an excellent listener; so patient and thoughtful and wise. At least, she had been before she met that mysterious boy – Logan's real dad – and went all weird on her. That's another good reason for this visit, Amanda reflects. To put things right, and try to build a sense of closeness again because, obviously, at Amanda's wedding there'd barely been any time to chat.

The train is approaching Wigan. Maybe that arsehole will get off, she reasons. At least the pleasantly scented woman next to her has been engrossed in a book the whole journey so far. Amanda's spirits lift slightly as Phone Man quietens down and makes for the end of the carriage. However, it's only to check on his luggage and now he's back to his pacing and ostentatious ranting.

The woman next to her gives her a *what-can-you-do?* look and turns back to her book. Amanda used to travel first class but she's not that flush these days. Her mortgage is crippling and Jasper contributes not a bean, and she can sense her blood pressure rising. What can she do? Complain to the guard, or whatever they're called now? Is it 'colleagues'? There should be a cord she can pull in case of emergency/insufferable men. Why *isn't* there one? Where are the colleagues? Now a jovial woman is making her way along the carriage, checking tickets from Wigan – but of course Phone Man has stopped shouting into his phone now and sat back down across the aisle. So Amanda would feel silly complaining.

From her toffee leather cross-body bag she pulls out a small silver compact, flips it open and checks her face. She looks tired and wired and her skin is ashen. *Cortisol face. That's what it is.* Stress hormones have rushed to her head and dissipated her fillers; that's why her face is hanging like that. She snaps the compact shut, trying to calm herself with deep breathing and reminding herself to 'accept the things you cannot change,' as she keeps reading in every damn self-help book she happens to pick up.

Arseholes never get off at Wigan, she reflects. They go all the way to Glasgow Central and you can't change that.

However, the man's conversation has taken a more worrying tone, and it seems it's not Kelly he's yacking to now, but a friend with an interest in tittle-tattle. 'Yeah, mate, there's this woman here. Sure I've seen her on TV. I think it's her but she looks different in the flesh. Not what you'd expect. Kinda *older*...'

Up she leaps – the reading girl barely seems to notice – grabbing her phone and bag and stomping down the aisle, wondering whatever happened to her sparkly life, to those press-for-champagne days. Despite not being a quiet coach, the next carriage is virtually silent. Amanda finds not only a vacant seat but a table seat, with a charger socket and – result! – no one sitting beside her. Settling at the window, she checks out the middle-aged couple sitting opposite. Nice, well-dressed people in light knitwear who smile politely before turning back to their puzzle books as the train rattles north.

This is what Amanda needs. A spell of calmness and pleasant scenery for the rest of the journey to Scotland. As they speed through rolling Cumbrian countryside, she senses the cortisol retreating from her face and returning to wherever the heck it's meant to be. It's quite nice out there, Amanda reflects. All these fields and hills are having a settling effect on her brain and at forty-three, she has started to understand the point of nature. Maybe Celia will fancy a road trip up north, while she's staying? That would be lovely: some proper quality time together.

The train pulls into Carlisle. Soon Amanda will be back in Scotland. After decades in London her accent has been diluted to homeopathic levels. It's a tiny part of her now – a trace element. But it's still buried in there, brushing her vowels and inflections, and Glasgow is still in her heart. She's picturing cocktails tonight, and cosying up in Celia's spare room (she assumes she has one. Doesn't everyone?). Then hopefully tomorrow they can head somewhere *sans* Geoff. She's visualising the magnificence of Loch Lomond and a delightful waterside pub. She knows Celia has some little shop job but surely she'll be able to arrange a day off?

The arrival of a panting woman gripping a multitude of carrier bags snaps Amanda out of her reverie. Without asking if the seat is free, the woman lands heavily beside her and dumps her bags at her feet. There follows much rummaging in said bags and Amanda's nostrils flare. She has an aversion to carrier bags. She hasn't used one since 2006. Now the woman seems to find what she's been hunting for and the item extracted causes Amanda's heart to sink.

A cardboard food carton. This is plonked on the table and as it's opened, Amanda is engulfed by a powerful whiff of nuggets and fries. Hot food on a train! An automatic fine should be issued for this. The woman tears open a little red sachet with her pointy teeth, squirts ketchup all over her meal and proceeds to tuck in noisily with her fingers.

Amanda's stomach rolls and she senses her cortisol peaking

again, but she isn't up to a second train confrontation. Instead, with every audible chomp and slurp, she tells herself firmly to accept the things she cannot change as soon she is back home in Glasgow.

And then, she is sure of it, everything will be all right.

15

Celia has almost reached home, head bent against the fine rain, when she sees a taxi pulling up outside her block. With her anorak hood up she hurries past and lets herself into the flat, calling to Logan that she's back.

'Hey, Mum.'

He doesn't emerge from his room, which stings her a little. But then he probably needs time on his own to come to terms with stuff, just as she is having to do. She's tried to talk to him, and been rebuffed, and she's not going to force him if he really can't bear to discuss things right now.

Instead, she tugs off her wet jacket and then flinches when the doorbell rings.

Is that Geoff? Was that him pulling up in a taxi?

No, Geoff has the car. It was at the caravan site. Celia saw it with her own eyes. A houseplant customer, then? Has she forgotten an appointment? Maybe it's that pleasant man with the droopy cactus and the frankly rather rude wife. For a moment Celia freezes, wondering what to do.

Enzo, his name was. She remembers that now, although she doesn't think his wife's name was mentioned. Better deal with it, she decides, going to answer the door and reeling back at the vision before her.

'Hi, darling!'

'Amanda!' she exclaims. It's not just Amanda. It's Amanda with an enormous suitcase on Celia's doorstep. Is she hallucinating now? But no, the hug is real, virtually knocking the wind out of her as Amanda babbles an explanation.

'Thought I'd surprise you! Only decided to come up yesterday. Thought, if I mentioned it, then you'd start to plan, and I don't want to put you to any trouble...'

'Oh, it's, er... it's no trouble—'

'It *is* okay, isn't it? To surprise you like this?'

'Um, of course it is,' Celia fibs, wondering which parallel universe she's landed in as Amanda follows her in and Logan emerges, looking confused with hair all askew, from his room.

'Hi! You won't remember me,' Amanda gushes, forcing a hug on him too. 'It's been years since I saw you. I'm Amanda, Celia's best friend.'

* * *

If Amanda is amazed that Logan isn't a teenager called Laurence, then she conceals it very well. And now Terri has popped in after her shift, clicking straight into tea-making mode once introductions are over. In challenging times, the kettle is her go-to appliance.

'I remember you when you were in nappies, Logan,' Amanda announces, at which Logan cringes visibly, backing up against the fridge.

Terri shoots Celia a quick look. *Does she really?* her expression says. In fact, Celia remembers the couple of times Amanda had visited – at the tiny one-bedroomed flat, where they'd lived before this place – when Logan was still at the nappy stage. The bottom-cleaning business had clearly appalled her and she'd acted as if it had been quite rude of Logan not to hold it in until she'd gone.

'And look at you now,' she enthuses. 'You're a big, handsome man. So tall and grown-up! And *so* like your dad...'

Celia gasps, momentarily stunned, and Logan gawps at Amanda as if she has morphed into a bizarre amphibian. Doesn't she remember that Geoff isn't his biological father? Logan knows. Of course he does. Celia had told him, as soon as he was old enough to understand – that there was 'a relationship that didn't work out'. But of course Geoff was his real daddy and it made no difference at all, she assured him. *He loves us and that's all that matters.*

''S'cuse me,' Logan says quickly and zooms off to his room.

Perhaps realising her faux pas, Amanda switches tack. 'Anyway, it's lovely to be here, Celia. And your place looks great. So homely!'

'Er, thanks...' Celia catches her appraising the worn-out kitchen, the ancient fridge and antiquated cooker.

'So, are you up here visiting family?' Terri asks.

'Not really, no.' Amanda's smile seems to congeal, and no further information is supplied. *So why are you here?* Celia wants to cry out. Although she knows it's wrong, that perhaps she should be delighted by this surprise visit, she is already willing her to leave. After all, she was sent home early from work today and she is definitely not up to making polite chit-chat.

'So what do you do, Terri?' Amanda asks. Of course, Celia reflects, no one asks TV presenters what they 'do.'

'I'm a nurse,' she replies.

'Oh, what kind?'

'Psychiatric.'

'So you're a psychologist?'

'No, I'm a *nurse*,' Terri reiterates, 'in a psychiatric hospital.' Celia is conscious of her back teeth jamming together.

'Oh, right. You mean people with mental illnesses?'

'Well, it's a secure facility,' Terri starts.

'What does that mean?'

Terri regards her levelly. 'They can't go out.'

'You mean it's like jail?'

'It's a *hospital*,' she explains, flashing Celia another quick look, which has the effect of triggering a wave of shame in her. As if this is somehow her fault; that Amanda seems to have no idea how to behave beyond her fashiony circles. 'Our patients have secure care needs,' Terri adds firmly.

'Why's that?'

'Well, there are murderers...'

'Murderers!' Amanda exclaims with some glee. 'Wow. Any famous ones?'

Terri bites into a custard cream with a sharp snap. 'I can't talk about individual patients.'

'Oh, of course. No, I understand. But I really admire people like you.'

She's acting like she's on *Look for a Lifestyle*, Celia realises, picturing the last time she saw her on morning TV. Amanda was interviewing a woman – a firefighter, she remembers now – who'd come on to the show for a style makeover. *It's amazing, the kind of work you do, Linda. And you're obviously used to dressing practically and that's great! That's amazing! But shall we try a more flattering silhouette?* Celia couldn't understand what was wrong with Linda's silhouette.

Now Terri offers Amanda the plate of biscuits. She waves it away dismissively.

'No thanks. Aren't they terrifying?'

'I *like* custard creams,' Terri quips, and Amanda laughs.

'I mean the murderers.'

'Well, all jobs have their challenging parts, don't they?' Terri remarks.

'You're right,' Amanda agrees, nodding. 'We had difficult women on the show sometimes. Oh my God, so tricky!' Another boisterous laugh. 'Ones who'd suddenly refuse to wear this colour or that colour or a dress or a skirt. Nightmare!' As if that might be on par with the daily medical care of a convicted serial killer. 'Or they'd have a panic attack and refuse to be filmed. We always had a back-up person in reserve...'

'Well, that sounds wise.' Terri clonks down her mug on the table. 'But look, I'll let you two catch up.' She turns to Celia and gives her a quick hug. 'Anything you need – anything at all – just let me know, okay?'

Celia nods. 'Thanks so much, Terri. I will.'

'Lovely to meet you, Amanda,' Terri adds.

'You too!' Amanda grins, and Terri calls out to Logan through his closed bedroom door as she leaves.

'Bye, darling. You know where I am, okay?' *Don't worry*, is her silent addition. *That crazy woman will be gone soon.*

Now Amanda exhales forcefully as if relieved that all the niceties – being pleasant to civilians – are done, and she flops down onto a kitchen chair and exhales loudly. 'It really is so good to be here,' she announces.

Celia looks at her, still baffled as to why she's shown up like this, and where she plans to stay tonight. Not here, surely? Wouldn't she have checked if it was convenient? No, she must have popped in on her way to somewhere far more interesting. 'So... are things okay with you?' she ventures.

'What, with me?' Amanda frowns, seemingly taken aback by the question. 'Oh, yeah. Everything's great.'

'And married life's good, is it?'

'Yeah, it's, uh... it's fine!' She reaches for a custard cream from the plate and then pulls back as if remembering that she doesn't consume such low-rent snacks. 'Me and Jasper... Well, he's great. He's a funny thing, but hey!'

Celia blinks at her as she takes the seat opposite. Is something wrong, and that's why Amanda has shown up unannounced? Surely, if that were the case, she'd have plenty of people in London she could turn to? 'I just need a little bit of time away from it all, you know?' she adds, sweeping a hand through lustrous golden tresses.

Celia nods, although she *doesn't* know. 'What about your work?' she asks. 'How's that going?'

'Um, well, I've just lost *Look for a Lifestyle* but that's fine—'

'You're not doing that any more?' Celia exclaims.

'No, but that's perfectly okay,' Amanda insists. 'It had run its course for me, really. No point in flogging a thing after it's peaked.'

'No,' Celia murmurs. 'No, definitely not.' Had her marriage 'peaked'? The sudden thought overcomes her. Should she have done something before they hit that stage? If so, what? Now Amanda is telling her about Jasper giving up acting for painting, and getting a tiny splash of paint on her guest room curtain, and Celia is finding it impossible to figure out whether this is a significant marriage wobble or simply an amusing anecdote served up for her entertainment.

She can't imagine it's anything serious. It feels like only last week that Amanda's wedding guests were sniggering at Celia's busted wheelie case, and she was being patronised for not knowing anything about classical music. Yet on and on her old friend goes, babbling about this and that – how 'Ollie' (whoever Ollie might be) will come up with something because he's a 'darling' and 'manages everything amazingly.' Of course, Amanda is unaware of what happened to Celia just two days ago, which would certainly stop her mid-flow. Yet Celia can't bring herself to go into it all right now.

She just wants to be alone. Alone, tucked up in bed, knowing that Logan is close by and that the most vulnerable among her houseplant charges are perking up nicely. And then, just as happened in the shop today, her eyes fill with tears and she can't take it. She can't sit here being bombarded with all this information about Jasper's abstract art and something about him stabbing a cheese. What's that all about? She doesn't care, that's the thing – and clearly, Amanda doesn't either. She seems to have forgotten that Celia had abruptly cut off their phone call on Saturday. Isn't she even *slightly* curious as to what might be happening here?

Suddenly the tears spill over and a sob escapes.

Amanda stops abruptly. 'Celia!' She grasps for her hand across the table. 'What is it? What's wrong?'

She shakes her head. 'Just some stuff I've got going on. That's all.'

'Oh, darling, I've been ranting on. I'm so sorry…'

'No, *I'm* sorry,' Celia murmurs, pulling her hand away and getting up, hoping that will transmit the signal that it's time to leave. That this really isn't the time for cosy table chats. Amanda jumps up too and goes to hug Celia, but Celia shrinks away. 'I'm sorry, Amanda. It's lovely to see you. But I have to tell you, this really isn't a good time…'

'No, it *is*,' she exclaims, eyes wide. 'If there's some life stuff happening, we can talk about it.' *Life stuff?* Is that what this is? 'Don't worry about being on form for me or any of that,' Amanda continues. 'If something's going on...' She breaks off, glancing around the kitchen as if Geoff might leap out of a cupboard. 'Well then, obviously,' she adds, 'I've come at *exactly* the right time.'

16

'Aw, c'mon, Enzo,' says his friend Nina. 'Just the one. We all need a drink after that.'

Parents' evening is over at last. The final trickle of mums and dads have mooched off into the drizzle – either reassured that their child is doing as well as they've been claiming, or amazed that some positivity has emerged from their discussions tonight. (You can always tell those ones, Enzo believes. They virtually *bound* out of school). The trend these days is for the pupil to sit in on teacher meetings, which Enzo is fine with, although of course it means being extra-diplomatic. But even if the child isn't present, Enzo still tries to highlight the positive, however challenging the child might be.

'She's full of life and contributes so much to the class...' *By insisting on doing her friends' hair while I'm trying to convey the basics of the past perfect tense...* 'He's so interested in the world around him—' i.e., *his mates messing around* '—and I'd love to see him focus a little more.' *Because really, what is language about? Communication – and he never stops bloody talking.* 'But he's definitely making progress this term.'

'Oh, that's good.' The kid's mother smiled. 'Because he likes your lessons, Mr Fontaine.' *Funnily enough, I heard him call me a wanker yesterday.*

Now Enzo is looking forward to picking up Mathilde from her friend Mo's and settling in for a quiet evening. He pictures poor Spike, hidden away at the back of his wardrobe until he decides what to do with him. At least Mathilde hasn't cottoned on to the subterfuge (replacement Spike is standing proud) and so all seems happy at home.

However Nina, a chemistry teacher, is insisting that they head to the pub, as is her partner, Deputy Head Hayley and their other friend Zain, who teaches maths.

'Just the one, Enzo,' Hayley urges him.

'What, on a Monday night?'

'Yeah, why not? We've got an old friend staying and she's coming out to meet us. I'm sure you two would get along.'

Enzo looks at her in surprise and then chuckles. Now he gets it: a plan has been hatched and Nina and Hayley are keen to set him up. 'I really have to go,' he explains. 'Laura's away for work at the moment and Mathilde's staying with me.'

'Just come for ten minutes,' Nina says. 'Just to say hi!'

'Nina, no one goes to the pub for ten minutes,' Zain remarks with a smirk.

'Honestly, I can't come out tonight,' Enzo insists as they all leave the building together and make their way across the stark concrete playground towards the car park.

Theirs is a big urban school, built in the seventies and now distinctly ragged around the edges, which is precisely how Enzo feels right now. However, its results are consistently good. 'Punches above its weight,' is the consensus in the neighbourhood, and Enzo is proud of that. They might not be able to offer trips to China, a wide array of sporting activities and intensive tutoring in the run-up to exams, but they do their best and, for the most part, it's a happy school and the kids are brilliant.

That is, brilliant in terms of spirit and character, if not always willing to apply themselves and sit on their arses for more than five minutes. However, Enzo does understand that the classroom setting doesn't suit everyone. Mathilde far prefers music, dancing and art to maths and science.

He's about to head to his car when Nina stops him. 'How about Friday night, then? We're doing a bit of dinner at our place. Can you come along to that?'

'Laura's away,' he reminds her, and Nina grins.

'So when's she back? And aren't there such things as babysitters any more?'

He believes there are, but Enzo hasn't had cause to book one for years. 'Uh, she's back on Wednesday,' he admits.

'So you *are* free on Friday night?'

Free for 'a bit of dinner'? He's aware that, at her and Hayley's place, Nina has assumed the role of home cook – her unshakeable confidence far outweighing any culinary abilities. Last time they invited a bunch of them over, she proudly served up a prawn linguine so enthusiastically speckled with tiny dried red chillis that Zain's eyes streamed and Enzo lost the power of speech.

'You lot just aren't used to punchy flavours,' she retorted, as Zain's girlfriend Marianne gulped tap water from a pint glass.

'I'll need to check with Laura,' Enzo says, although he knows already that Mathilde will be at her mum's on Friday night. Of course, it's not Nina's cooking that's causing his hesitation but the prospect of meeting this friend of theirs. Because what if it's awkward? That Brown Owl scenario has left him wary of being set up, even in a relaxed group scenario which Nina insists is all they're planning.

'Just a nice casual night at our place,' she says with a smile. 'Say you'll come, Enzo. Seven-thirty?'

Would this be worse – or better – than Saska's litter pick singles? Is the entire world intent on setting him up? 'I'm not sure,' he starts and Hayley laughs.

"Course he's coming,' she announces. Then to Enzo, 'Her name's Kim, by the way. And you're going to love her, I promise.'

17

It turns out that Amanda *wasn't* en route to somewhere more interesting when she bowled up at Celia's flat. In fact, this is where she plans to stay tonight – 'If you're sure it's no trouble?'

'Of course not,' Celia manages. 'It's fine!' But first Amanda insists that they go out locally for a drink.

Being whisked off to the pub on a week night – on any night, in fact – is a new experience for Celia. 'So you actually caught him,' Amanda marvels, a shade too loudly at their corner table, 'in the caravan?'

'That's right,' Celia replies.

'Actually *doing* it? In the act?'

She nods and gulps her G&T, wishing her friend would dial down the glee just a little. As it is, it seems that Amanda is finding the caravan incident even more fascinating than Terri working with murderers.

'My God, what an arsehole. I'm sorry, Celia, but that's the shittiest thing I've ever heard. He's always creeped me out. Am I allowed to say that?'

Celia looks at her, startled, and takes another big sip of her

G&T. It's an extremely strong one – she can feel it surging through her veins – and she tries to figure out how she feels, hearing her husband being spoken of like that. Although Terri is extremely direct on most topics, she has always held back where Geoff is concerned. Celia understands this. You should never badmouth a friend's partner while they're still together.

And now, it seems, Celia is *not* with Geoff any more. At least, in the two days since she caught him, she still hasn't had a call or even a message, and has yet to fully comprehend what's happened. Of course, the possibility remains that he might come crawling back to her, and that she might choose to forgive him. But what would happen then? Would she ever be able to erase the image of his naked butt from her mind?

'Of course you're allowed to say that,' she tells Amanda, a little tipsy already, the gin having rushed to her head. 'You can say whatever you like.'

'Good,' Amanda says, pushing back her tumbling fair hair. People have recognised her in here, Celia notices. At least they have realised that she is *somebody*. The barman was flirty when Amanda went up for their drinks, and there was a ripple of excitement among the boisterous women installed around the big table.

How must it feel to have that happen? Celia wonders. Unless someone's yucca is ailing, or an orchid has developed a peculiar fungus, then she is accustomed to going through life barely noticed. As a child she sometimes wondered if her parents – who seemed to be either partying or fighting – actually remembered that she was there. Whenever Amanda happened to mention her favourite babysitter, who'd patiently paint her nails for her, Celia would listen, fascinated. Not because of the manicure aspect particularly, but because it seemed that Amanda was never left at home alone.

That suggested, Celia decided back then that Amanda needed to be looked after because she was *precious*. And following this logical thread, Celia could only ascertain that she herself was not precious at all.

However now, in the dimly lit pub, she *is* the focus of rapt interest and, as if a prize might be at stake, she is trying to respond quickly to her friend's rapid-fire questions.

'Did you have any idea that something was going on?'

'No. Not at all.'

'Weren't there any signs?'

Celia bites her lip. 'Well, he did buy me a falafel wrap…'

'What?'

She quickly summarises the incident before she caught the London train. 'And you thought that was weird?' Amanda asks, frowning.

'A bit, yes. When you know what he's like—'

'Yes, I *do* know.' Amanda shudders, and Celia leans forward, curious now.

'What d'you mean?'

Amanda pauses to sip her drink. 'I hate to say this, Celia, but Geoff's a tit-starer.'

'Is he?' She is genuinely astounded as Amanda nods gravely and takes another swig. If Geoff has even given her own breasts a cursory glance, then Celia has never noticed. She came to the conclusion many years ago that he didn't like them very much, but then she remembers overhearing his father's inappropriate comment. 'His dad once said I had a great rack,' she murmurs, as if piecing clues together.

'There you are, then! He's passed it down.'

Is creepiness hereditary, Celia wonders, like eye colour, or the shape of a nose? Is there a boob-staring gene? 'Yes, he must have.' She nods.

'Has he ever done this before?'

'Stared at boobs?'

'Slept with anyone else.'

'Oh.' Celia's cheeks flame. 'I've no idea. Maybe?' How is she supposed to know?

'What about Logan? What does he think about all this?'

Before they came out, Celia had tapped lightly on her son's closed bedroom door and called his name, anxious to check up on him. But his gruff response suggested that he did not wish to be checked up on at all. 'Well, he's shocked of course,' she replies.

'Did he see it too?'

'See *what*?'

'Them doing it.'

Celia shudders at the thought and drains her glass. 'God, no.'

'Well, that's good.' Amanda nods sagely as if she understands the first thing about the effects of parental adultery on a grown-up child. 'You know, you've got to *own* this, Celia,' she adds.

'What d'you mean?'

'I mean you have to take charge of the thing rather than it taking charge of you.'

'Take charge of what?' Geoff's wandering penis? It seems like even he can't control that, and he's *attached* to the thing.

'The situation,' Amanda says with some force. 'You can't fall apart when terrible things happen, Celia. You have to put on a brave face to show you're coping, and before you know it, you really are. And you'll be stronger for it, you know. You *will* survive.'

So she's going all Gloria Gaynor on her now. 'Of course I will,' Celia says quietly, but in truth she doesn't quite believe it.

Amanda squeezes her hand. 'You're so, so brave. I hope you realise that.'

Is she? It doesn't feel that way. But the strong alcohol, and simply being away from the flat, in the cosiest of pubs – Celia rarely goes out at night – have taken the edge off a little, and when Amanda suggests another drink, she readily agrees.

Unused to fielding so many questions, she tries to switch the focus to Amanda's life in London as they have a second, and then a third G&T. 'So are you and Jasper really okay?' she ventures.

'Oh, yes, we're *fine*. Like I said, I just need a little break.' Amanda seems reluctant to delve into it any further, and the conversation switches back to Celia's situation as finally they make their way home.

'It might turn out for the best,' Amanda announces loudly as Celia lets them in. 'You'll be better off without him, you know—' She breaks off as Celia mimes a shushing motion, index finger pressed to her lips.

'What is it?'

'Logan,' Celia mouths, eyes wide. Christ, they're standing right outside his room. Has Amanda forgotten that he exists?

'Oh, right.' She grimaces. Then, lowering her volume only by a notch, 'So, what shall we do tomorrow?'

'Tomorrow?' Celia tugs off her shabby jacket and hangs it on a hook in the hall. What's the best way to ask, 'How long are you staying?' without seeming rude? She knows better than to bark, 'When are you going home?' But still it's tricky, and despite being grateful for the impromptu night out, Celia is still rattled by Amanda's sudden arrival. 'I'm not sure,' she replies warily.

'We should do something nice to cheer you up,' Amanda decides. 'Something lovely and treaty – *that's* what you need. Just the two of us together.'

Celia looks at her, trying to form an appropriate expression, but her facial muscles won't behave and the challenge overwhelms her. Instead, she tries to gather her faculties together in preparation for wrestling with the clunky second-hand pull-out bed. It's currently swathed in an ancient blanket and heaped with pots and tools in her plant room.

It has occurred to her that Amanda could share her double bed, but that feels like a step too far and Celia needs her space. No, this is where Amanda will have to sleep tonight.

Celia had bought the bed for sleepovers many years ago, in the hope that Logan might wish to have friends staying over from time to time. Like the other kids, she thought. *Like the kids who have sleepovers.* He had a small group of friends from the school chess club, but Terri suggested that sleepovers were more of a girl thing really, and that she was worrying over nothing. Anyway, no one ever stayed over and now, without any offer of help from the watching Amanda, she grapples with the bed's hefty iron bar.

It's only for one night, Celia reassures herself as the mechanism snaps at her fingers and she manages to haul the thing open. A musty odour escapes and Amanda steps back, flinching, as if she fears being contaminated by it. 'Sorry it's a bit basic,' Celia murmurs as she makes up the bed, trying to plump up the flaccid pillow and smooth out the saggy old duvet in its wrinkled cover.

'This is fine,' Amanda insists. 'This is great. Honestly, it's kind of exotic, with all the plants. I'll pretend I'm in a Kew Gardens glasshouse!'

Later, in her own bed without the snoring bulk of her husband lying beside her, Celia rehearses possible ways to broach the subject of Amanda's plans.

So, what are you up to the next few days?

No, she should be more direct. Be more Terri.

Are you thinking of staying up here for long? Woozily, she considers asking Amanda if she is planning to move on to her Aunt Christine's, a little further out into the suburbs. But now she fears that Aunt Christine is dead.

Maybe the issue will simply resolve itself? Surely Amanda won't put up with sleeping on that lumpy pull-out bed in what Geoff referred to as 'the jungle' for long? And if all else fails, Celia will explain that, sorry, she can't stay any longer – that she isn't up for doing anything 'treaty' right now.

Yes, that's it, she decides as she slips towards a gin-induced sleep. Tomorrow she'll be honest with Amanda – and then she'll start to figure out how to rescue the mess of her life.

18

However, the next day Celia can't bring herself to broach the subject of Amanda moving on – or the day after that. Because now the initial shock has subsided, it's not so terrible having her around the flat.

Amanda has been making sure that Celia showers daily and does not spend the entire day in ratty pyjamas. Frankly, it's been quite a novelty being around someone who notices what she's wearing/doing as, despite Celia's closeness to Logan, he is hardly up to the job of taking care of her.

Meanwhile Amanda has also been out grocery shopping and presented her with poke bowls and exotic salads and fruit platters. Proper lunches to be eaten from bowls and plates, instead of a bland ham sandwich from a Tupperware box. That's what Celia usually takes with her on her shop days, as if to atone for her occasional secret Pret splurges. She has never sat down to such dazzling offerings in her life. But then, she has spent almost a quarter of a century with a man who'll cut the mouldy bit off a tomato and insist that it's 'fine'.

Then on Wednesday afternoon, when Terri has dropped in,

Amanda returns from town brandishing a 'house gift' as she calls it. '"Powerful masticator",' Terri reads from the juicer's packaging while clutching a mug of builder's brew. 'I've met a few of those in my time.'

Amanda laughs dryly and busies herself by unpacking the appliance. She seems a little unsettled whenever Terri drops by, Celia has noticed. As if her self-appointed role as Matron is under threat – even more so, possibly, as Terri is an actual nurse.

'So, what're your plans, Amanda?' Terri asks pleasantly.

'Plans?' Amanda raises a brow.

'Are you up here for long?'

'Oh, I'm kind of playing it by ear right now.' Amanda's smile frosts a little.

Terri nods, and Celia senses the air crackling with tension as Amanda swiftly fits the juicer components together and then loads it with chopped apples, berries and a handful of spinach.

'How's my boy doing?' Terri asks, turning to Celia. Amanda glances up in surprise, as if she'd forgotten that Logan is, in fact, still here. She has given up on offering him food, as he has politely declined her offerings every time. Fair enough, Celia feels. Perhaps, while everything's still pretty raw, it's better to let him fend for himself instead of fussing around him. However, as the days have gone by, her concern has intensified and she's at a loss as to how to reach him.

'Not too good really,' Celia replies, dropping her voice.

'Still hiding away in his room?'

Celia nods. 'I don't know what to do, Terri. It's so unlike him, you know?'

Terri exhales. 'He's probably just trying to make sense of things, hon.' A quick glance at Amanda. 'And I reckon he just needs a bit of space.'

'I think so, yes.'

'I'll go talk to him,' she announces, and Amanda looks startled as if Terri were about to venture into a bear's cave. 'It's okay.' She chuckles. 'I don't think he bites.'

However, when she returns, it's clear that Terri hasn't made much headway either, and Celia is almost relieved when she leaves and the tense atmosphere eases.

As the days go on, Terri drops by in between shifts, and tries again to coax Logan from his lair. Yet it's Amanda who's the constant presence, seemingly with no other obligations right now other than taking care of Celia. The juicer whirrs frequently, as if a steady stream of green liquids will make everything all right.

'You have to look after yourself,' Amanda insists. Celia complies, although it's so unusual to her, to be looked after like this, that she doesn't quite know what to make of it. It's how she imagines staying in an exclusive private hospital and she starts to wonder how it'll feel when Amanda goes home and it's just her and Logan again.

She is only too aware of the huge, steaming pile of difficult decisions to be made and issues to sort, awaiting her just around the corner. What to do about Geoff and how to unpick her life of twenty-four years. How to reconnect with her son somehow and, in a smaller – but still daunting – way, how to break the news to her mum, who adores Geoff. Has a *shrine* to him, actually. A huge photograph of him accepting some pastry manufacturer's award, displayed in a cheap gilt frame on the sideboard next to a picture of their wedding – not the best photo of the day. Logan isn't in the picture and Celia is a little blurry and close to the edge. It's Geoff who's smiling broadly, taking centre stage. She is surprised her mother didn't crop her out of it before framing that one.

So yes, there is a vast mound of stuff awaiting her attention:

emotional, legal, financial. However, while Amanda is here, making decisions for her, Celia is not having to deal with any of that. She is not to contact Geoff yet, her friend has decreed. She must put her own needs first. Fine, she needs to keep her houseplant business going, interacting with customers and tending the plants; Amanda understands that this is good for her. It's *therapeutic*. But she did insist that Celia call Ruth at the boutique to explain that she would need a little time off.

'She can manage without you,' Amanda said firmly. 'If she really needs someone, then I'll do it.'

'You can't work in a shop!'

'Why not? You do.'

'Yes but you're *you*,' Celia insisted.

'So what?'

'You're a TV presenter.'

'Allegedly,' Amanda said with a shrug, and swiftly changed the subject. In fact, Celia has pondered over Amanda's *Look for a Lifestyle* contract coming to an end, but maybe that's how things go in the TV world? She doesn't seem at all worried.

Then on Thursday morning, when her houseguest is out on a bakery run, Celia taps on Logan's bedroom door. Having recoiled at the sight of the cheap sliced white loaf in the bread bin, Amanda has taken to popping out for sourdough and little glass pots of the creamiest yoghurt Celia has ever encountered. It feels almost wasteful to eat the stuff. Celia wants to slather it all over her face.

'Logan?' she calls out, as she's been doing several times daily. 'All okay in there?'

His response is indistinct, and the sudden rush of exasperation hits her by surprise. Why is he hiding away from her? It's making things far worse because now, on top of Geoff's copious lies, her son seems to have turned, if not against her, then *away* from her certainly. It hurts so much.

She pushes the door fully open to see him engrossed in some kind of ragged textbook, propped up by pillows on his bed. 'Hi, love,' she starts.

Logan glances up. 'Hi.' He looks different, Celia thinks. Shifty, almost, in that he won't meet her gaze. He was always an amiable boy – with her at least, they were always a pair – although she was aware that he wasn't like the other kids in his class. Terri reassured Celia that this was a *good* thing; that Logan was unique and wonderful and who cared if he wasn't into football like the other lads? Glasgow is fervently football-focussed, and Geoff had insisted on taking him to a game once. 'He just wanted to read,' he announced on their return. 'He brought a *book* with him.' He never took him again.

Then as Logan progressed through his teens, Terri would insist frequently that Celia had a genius for a son. 'How many people can say that?' Of course Celia accepts that Logan is Logan and she loves every hair on his head. She accepts that he has never wanted to discuss whether he is seeing anyone; if there's a special person in his life (girl or boy, she wouldn't care; she just worries about him being lonely). But now she is desperate to reach him and she can sense him shutting her out.

She perches on the chair at his wonky little desk. He'd left home several times but then came sloping back when courses didn't work out. 'When is he ever going to get his act together?' Geoff complained. Celia found herself defending his choices because wasn't it important to find something he really loved? She wanted everything for Logan that she hadn't had. 'Some of us just have to graft,' Geoff remarked – the 'like I do' remaining unsaid. The implication being that Logan regarded himself as being 'too good' for toiling away in a pastry goods production facility.

'What is it, Mum?' He sets down his book and fixes her with a stare, as if trying to propel her out of his room with the force of his gaze alone.

'I'd just like us to talk,' Celia starts. 'So much has happened, and with Amanda here it's hard for us to get the chance to—'

'Yeah, just a bit,' he cuts in.

She frowns. 'You want me to ask her to leave? I will, you know, if it'll help.'

'No, it's all right,' he says blithely.

'Logan, listen. Let's be honest with each other. Is this why you're hiding away in here? I know she can be a bit full on but she's kind, she's trying to help—'

'I'm fine,' he snaps. She exhales loudly and leaves the room, exasperated and feeling helpless. Of course he isn't 'fine' – he may never be again – but what can Celia do? Soon, of course, Amanda will leave and it'll just be the two of them. And then, come September, Logan will be back off to uni and she'll be truly alone.

Home from the bakery, Amanda sets out the breakfast table and Celia crunches into a slice of toast. My God, it's good. Could this be her life now? Eating toast made from bread that doesn't come in a waxed wrapper? It seems like a small win, all things considered. But she is trying to focus on the here and now, and what needs to be done, and park the bigger, scarier stuff for later.

That afternoon, when she would have been leaving the shop, she cycles to her mother's as if everything is normal and she was never confronted by the sight of her Geoff's hairy arse in a caravan. She watches TV through the fug of her mum's cigarette smoke and she comes home to Amanda's big smiles and Logan's firmly shut bedroom door.

Having pulled off her clothes, she wraps herself in her dressing gown and stuffs them into the wash. Then she sluices off the smoke from her body and hair using a luxury shower gel, lightly scented with almonds and Madagascan vanilla, which Amanda bought. The cheap lemon stuff has disappeared. 'Christ, Celia, did you actually *want* thrush?' Celia had laughed and admitted that, no, it wasn't on her wish list especially.

She has tried to force money on her friend for these distinctly non-Geoff items that keep appearing in the flat, but Amanda won't hear of it. Meanwhile Celia is continuing to tend to the numerous houseplants currently in her care, and when Friday arrives – almost a week since Caravan Day – Amanda decides it's time. Time for Celia to break it to her mother because this pretence is ridiculous, she says. 'By keeping it secret, it's as if you're ashamed or feel guilty or something. Like it's your fault.'

'I'm not ashamed,' Celia protests, but perhaps she is a little, for not spotting the signs.

Amanda hands her a chilled glass of wine. 'Go over and tell your mum what's happened. Do it tomorrow, Celia. Get it all out there in the open.'

'Oh, I don't think so.' Celia shakes her head.

'But you *have* to,' Amanda retorts. 'Remember when we were young? What we always said then?'

Celia looks at her. 'About what?'

'That game we had! Whenever one of us thought of something fun to do, the other *had* to say yes. We made a pact, remember?'

'Oh, yes. Of course I remember.' Celia pictures the days of dressing up and performing, of garden picnics and nights spent dancing upstairs, one floor above all those parties. That precious time before the thing happened that changed everything, and a shy Geoff Bloom appeared at the door with a bunch of carnations.

'So in the spirit of the yes game,' Amanda continues, blue eyes glinting, 'I propose that you go round first thing in the morning—'

'To Mum's? But she doesn't do mornings.' Celia shudders at the thought.

'Lunchtime, then. Whenever.'

'The pact was supposed to be about *fun* things,' Celia reminds her.

'Yes, and when the hard bit's done, we're going straight to the movies and we're having cocktails afterwards—'

'Cocktails in the *day*?' Perhaps this is what Amanda's London life is like all the time, with her handsome young husband and zillions of friends and thrilling job opportunities.

'Yes, why not?' Amanda beams at her. 'You can do these things now. You can do whatever the heck you like. And we made a pact, remember?'

'Yes, we did.' Celia forces a smile. 'But that was a very long time ago.'

Amanda laughs and flaps a hand, dismissing her reticence. 'There's no expiry date on a pact, Celia. It's for life.'

19

Sometimes, Enzo thinks, the thing you weren't remotely worried about – i.e. caring for a cactus for a mere ten days – turns out to be a disaster. And the situation that had been causing you no small degree of stress is actually fine.

In fact, as Hayley ushers everyone to the big oak table in their kitchen, and Nina dishes up, he thinks this is *better* than fine. Wine has been flowing already and, despite their eagerness for him to meet their friend, Nina and Hayley's conviviality is making this feel like any normal fun Friday evening with friends.

Never mind that Nina is serving up some kind of noodle dish so doused in soy sauce it's completely black. Or that – obviously – the seating arrangement has been planned so Enzo is next to Kim. She is friendly and chatty with a dark, glossy fringe that's so sharply cut Enzo wonders if it was trimmed by a machine rather than a human. He can't place her accent, but thinks possibly Midlands; it's not one he's hugely familiar with. But he soon learns that she's an old university friend of Nina's and has her own apparently thriving business.

'What kind of business?' he asks.

'It's embarrassing, really,' she tells him with a smile. 'I'm a coach. Every second person's doing it these days. I realise I'm a walking cliché.'

He chuckles although he knows nothing about the world of coaching – or specifically that there are so many different types.

'Oh God, yeah,' Kim says. 'You've got your wellness coaches and lifestyle coaches, but it gets even more niche than that.'

'Does it?' Sometimes, in between fatherhood and his workload at school, Enzo feels he is failing to keep up with the modern world.

'We had a decluttering coach once,' announces Marianne across the table, and Zain laughs.

'She wanted to throw all my stuff away!'

'No, she didn't,' Marianne retorts. 'She put everything in piles, that's all. "Throw", "Keep", "Undecided"...'

'Everything of mine was in "Throw".' Zain smirks and Enzo turns back to Kim.

'So what kind of coach are you?'

'I kind of cover everything,' she says, 'but really I'm all about making positive change. I'm a reboot coach.' She jabs at her noodles and hesitates, opting for a piece of relatively untainted broccoli instead. 'It's a strip-things-back-to-basics approach. Like, a client comes to me when their life's chugging along and they want a total reset – no messing around...'

'She's tough,' Hayley remarks with a laugh.

'Well, tough gets results.' Kim fixes Enzo with a wide smile. Her eyes are an intense blue, her lips very red. 'Oh, listen to me, going on.' She laughs self-deprecatingly.

'I did ask,' Enzo says with a smile.

'So what about you? You're French, right? Where are you

from?' It turns out she knows the part of Brittany where he grew up.

'I've run retreats on that coast. Rented a beautiful cottage a couple of times. D'you go back often?'

'My sister's still there,' he replies, 'so yes, but not as often as when my parents were around.'

'And you've been in Glasgow a while?'

'Oh, yes. Many years now. This feels like home.'

Kim nods and looks at Nina. 'That accent. You could listen to him reading a fridge-freezer instruction manual, right?'

Everyone laughs at this. 'Oh, I'm sorry.' She plants a hand on Enzo's forearm. 'I didn't mean to embarrass you.'

'No, it's fine.' Enzo chuckles, sensing himself flushing hotly, unused to this kind of direct flirting. Because that's what she's doing, isn't it? It's flattering – of course it is – as Kim is smart and accomplished, as well as being extremely attractive in that slightly intimidating way, with the taut muscles and gleaming white teeth. In fact, he is surprised that she seems so keen to chat to him, and keeps expecting her to direct her attentions elsewhere.

Perhaps he's misreading the situation and she's like this with everyone? Having made a decent effort with Nina's noodles, Enzo becomes aware of Nina transmitting a silent message to him across the table. *See? Didn't I tell you she's great?* Now more wine is poured and Nina and Kim regale the others with anecdotes from the squalid student house-share where they met.

'I can't believe you lived like that, Nina,' Marianne announces, and Enzo can see why. In their early forties, Nina and Hayley are extremely proud of their beautiful flat: all stripped wooden floors and richly patterned rugs with an eclectic array of abstract paintings and vintage prints adorning the walls. On a low table, deep green glossy leaves and assorted cacti sprout from a variety of hand-painted pots.

Enzo turns back to Kim. 'So you live in Glasgow now?'

'Yep, just moved here,' she explains. 'Nina and Hayley have been on at me for years to do it. So if anyone fancies taking me under their wing...' Did Enzo imagine it or did she flash a flirty smile?

'You're going to love it here,' Hayley asserts as Enzo and Marianne get up to clear the table. With a flourish, Nina sets down one of her 'famous' baked cheesecakes. Enzo remembers something similar from last time – it must be her signature dessert – and is bracing himself for its Polyfilla texture when Marianne announces, 'Oh, Zain – we brought cakes, didn't we? Put them out too, would you?'

'And Enzo brought cheeses,' Hayley adds, 'and fancy crackers.' Everything is set out, and as they all tuck in – with everyone risking their digestive tracts with a sliver of cheesecake – Enzo is aware of Kim apparently still not being desperate to move around the room. Even as they all relocate to the two large squashy sofas, she settles at his side.

Now he learns that she has a teenage daughter who lives mainly with her father in the Midlands. 'Her choice, and if it makes her happy, that's fine,' she says, seemingly without a trace of bitterness or sadness. 'So how about you, Enzo? What's your situation?'

'I have a daughter too, Mathilde. Just the one—'

'You're not with her mum?' Enzo suspects his 'situation' has been confirmed with Nina and Hayley already.

'Uh, no, we split up a few years ago.' He glances at the clock on the ornately tiled fireplace. 'It's her birthday tomorrow – Mathilde's, I mean – and we're having the day together, so...' He smiles, placing his wine glass on the coffee table. 'I'd better head off.'

'Oh, which way are you going?' Kim asks as he orders a cab. They confer, and as it transpires that it would make sense to share, they get up to leave together.

'Thanks for a lovely evening,' Enzo says to Nina and Hayley. 'This has been great.'

'Good to see you, Enzo.' Nina gives him a look – a smirk, an eye twinkle – which he chooses not to react to, glad of the distraction of hugs all round, and politely but firmly declining the offer of a slab of dessert to take home.

'Sure you don't need any holes filling?' Kim asks, laughing, as the cab pulls away.

It takes a beat for him to get it. 'Oh, the cheesecake!' He laughs too.

'Sorry.' She grins at him. 'I've drunk way too much tonight.'

'Me too,' he says, thinking, *well, that was fine, wasn't it?* Lots of fun and nothing to get het up about. He's out of practice, he realises, with socialising like this – with meeting new people especially. Laura is always telling him he's become set in his ways. 'Middle-aged cardigan man,' she's called him, which was unjustified, he felt. He doesn't even *own* a cardigan.

During the short journey Kim chatters away about her work, about how she's 'basically there to champion my clients, though not tomorrow, thank God!' And now she's asking the driver to pull up outside a smart modern development. 'This looks nice,' Enzo says, glancing out at the neatly tended gardens.

'Yes, I got lucky.' An expectant pause. 'Fancy coming up?'

Enzo hesitates because he was *not* expecting this – not after a casual black-noodle supper at Nina and Hayley's. This kind of thing never happens to him and he's thinking, *it's an invitation, right?* And not really for coffee (unless she's one of the increasingly rare breed who enjoys late-night caffeinated beverages). It's been over a year since Enzo slept with anyone – a perfectly lovely woman called Heather, an occupational therapist with three cats and the last person he'd met through an app. They'd spent the night together a handful of times. It had been fine – fun, even – yet at the same time somehow empty, as if they were both trying to convince themselves they were really into each other. Something was missing and he couldn't put his finger on what it was.

He looks at Kim and thinks, *well, it wouldn't be like that – maybe it would be amazing* – but he still hears himself saying, 'I'd better not. I really need to get back.'

She nods, smiling. 'Cake to bake?'

'Sorry?'

'Birthday, isn't it?'

'Oh, yes,' he says quickly. 'I'm not a baker. But yeah – early start, so...'

Her clear blue eyes meet his and now her hand is on the door handle. He thinks she's about to open it, but she seems to have a change of heart. Instead, she leans towards Enzo, and the peck on the cheek isn't a cheek peck at all, but a proper kiss on the lips.

She pulls away and smiles broadly, showing her perfect teeth. 'Night, then.'

Enzo is a little stunned. 'Night!'

Kim pauses, seeming to study his face. 'It's been lovely meeting you, Enzo. So maybe a coffee or a drink some other time?'

'That'd be great,' he says, relieved now as, if anything is going to happen with Kim, then he'll have to rev himself up to it. They quickly exchange numbers before she climbs out.

As the taxi pulls away she waves, flashing another big, bright smile, and Enzo replays the words Zain murmured into his ear as they were leaving.

'Keep your wits about you with Kim, mate. I reckon she wants to give you a thorough *reboot*.'

20

Well, you'd think he'd died. You'd think Geoff was Joyce's own flesh and blood – her beloved son – who had carked it in a particularly tragic manner. 'I can't believe this has happened,' she cries, eyes bloodshot and neck mottled pink.

'Mum, please don't be like this.'

'Springing this on me!'

So it's Celia's mother who's the wronged one here? At just gone one o'clock she has been drinking already, Celia suspects – or perhaps this is how she appears at lunchtime these days, still rough from the night before. With her heart in her mouth, on many occasions Celia has tried to broach the subject of her mum's 'relationship with alcohol', as it's termed on any advisory websites she's looked at.

'So I enjoy a drink! Doesn't everyone?'

'No, Mum, not really. Not like you.'

Her mother has flown on to the defensive, then become upset, belligerent and hostile. Celia is at a loss as to how to help her.

Now Joyce has flung open her rickety back door and

marched out to the garden. It's raining lightly and the sky is a blanket of pale grey. She pulls a packet of cigarettes from the pocket of her slim black trousers and lights one.

She's looking awfully thin, Celia notices. Her mum has always kept a tight rein on her calorie input and as a younger woman, had been proud of her neat size. A woman didn't have a 'body' then but a 'figure', implying that numbers – vital statistics – were what mattered. On several occasions Joyce has remarked that Celia could lose a few pounds. However, in recent years, her mum has started to look drawn and undernourished and, judging by the contents of her cupboard and the scatterings of crumbs about the place, Celia suspects that much of her nutrition comes via a steady supply of Ritz crackers.

She watches as her mother paces back and forth on the narrow path that's barely visible among the undergrowth. At seventy, Joyce lives alone in the house Celia grew up in, although there are no traces of her lovingly cultivated garden now. The weeds had already begun to encroach, once Logan arrived. Now almost a quarter-century of neglect has allowed them to run rampant and the abandoned cooker is a rusting hulk. The trailing plants she'd grown to shroud its ugliness have long gone.

A frayed washing line, bearing several laundry items, is strung between two rusty iron poles. Joyce snaps into action and starts tearing down patterned blouses and silky dresses and exotic embroidered underwear – her 'smalls' – sending pegs flying everywhere. She has always loved to dress up and make the best of herself. So many high-end lipsticks are crammed on her dressing table that Celia can't understand how she can afford them all. 'Why buy Maybelline when you can have Dior?' she crowed once. Perfume, too; her mother has gallons of the stuff in sparkling bottles with gleaming gold tops.

'Mum, it's raining,' Celia calls out. 'Leave the washing. It's wet anyway. Please come inside and sit with me.'

Joyce swings round to face her. 'You've given up on a good marriage. What's got into you?'

What should Celia do now? How should she *own* this? 'I've explained, Mum. I've told you what happened. I caught him with someone else and a week's gone by and he hasn't had the decency to contact me to apologise or even try to explain. So how d'you think that makes me feel?'

'You could call him.'

Celia blinks at her. 'Why should I when he—'

'Well, it's only sex, isn't it?' she blasts out across the neighbourhood. 'Just a fling, probably? You know what men are like.'

Celia hates herself for cringing, for wanting to burrow deeply into the earth, like a worm. 'What does *that* mean?'

A sheer burgundy negligee is torn from the line and another peg flies into the weed-strewn rhubarb patch. Celia recognises this behaviour. As a child she'd privately labelled it 'doing furious chores'. Angry washing-up, incensed mopping and demented hoovering; these never seemed to happen at Amanda's house. In her orderly home, housework was undertaken in a normal fashion. Celia often wondered what that must be like.

'I mean,' Joyce announces shrilly, 'it's just a human function. A biological need, especially for men—'

'So you think it's okay that he *needed* to do it with someone else? That was fine, was it?' Celia knows she shouldn't react but she can't stop herself.

'Well, no. Not exactly.' Joyce stops washing-snatching for a moment and shoves back her dishevelled dyed brown hair. 'But men are men, you know?'

'I do know, Mum. I know what men are. I'm forty-three.'

'Your dad had a fling.'

The Woman Who Got Her Spark Back

'And you got divorced!'

'That wasn't the reason, not that silly floosie...'

Out of nowhere Celia wants to run to her mother and take her hand, coax her inside, make her a cup of tea. 'Mum, Dad moved away to *Wales*.'

'Oh, I don't mean her,' she says quickly. 'I mean Sandra Balfour from the paper shop.'

Celia stares at her. 'Dad had a thing with her?' Sandra ran the newsagent in the next street. She always gave Celia a Curly Wurly whenever her mother sent her to buy her cigarettes. Illegal of course, to sell ciggies to a child. But it appears that around here, the line between right and wrong was so blurry it might as well not have existed at all.

'It didn't mean anything,' her mother retorts.

'Well, I think these things *do* mean something. They mean a lot.'

'What I'm saying,' she goes on, 'is that Geoff's a good man. D'you remember how bad things were for you, when he first came round to take you out?'

'I'd just had a baby,' Celia says steadily. 'I know I was young, and it wasn't ideal – but I was happy, you know.'

'Yes, happy being with Geoff. And now look what you've done—'

'Mum, I haven't *done* anything,' she snaps. 'All I did was catch him at it. I haven't said it's over or that I want a divorce or anything, you know?' Her throat catches and she blinks wetness from her eyes. 'And when I said I was happy, I meant happy about being a mum. Happy that I had Logan.'

Joyce purses her lips. 'And Geoff took you on.'

'Can you please stop saying that, like I was a derelict building or something—'

'Raised someone else's child,' she announces. 'Brought up that boy like he was his own—'

'*That boy?*' Celia turns away from her mother and strides back into the house. She plucks her jacket from the kitchen chair and tugs it on roughly.

A few moments later Joyce appears with an armful of wet washing. 'I just meant,' she starts, 'that it can't have been easy for Geoff.'

'Which part is that, then? Which part wasn't easy?'

Her cheeks flush. 'The not knowing who the father was.'

It takes Celia a moment to scrabble together the words to respond to this. 'Geoff knows. I told him.' Of course her mother had wanted to know, when the test had been positive. She'd pleaded and nagged, and then raged, but Celia had stood firm. She wasn't prepared to talk about him to anyone then. Not even Amanda. She wanted his name to disappear from her consciousness.

Now Celia glances out of the open kitchen door to see the pegs scattered all over, tiny glimmers of red and yellow peeping through untended grass. What she wants to do is go out there in the light rain and gather them up, but she will not allow herself to do this. *She will not pick up the pegs!*

Kitchen drawers are being opened now and rummaged through frantically. 'Mum,' Celia says, 'I'm going now.'

'No, don't go.' For a moment Celia imagines that her mum is sorry and wants to make amends. 'I've run out of cigarettes,' she adds. 'Run over to the shop for me, Celia.'

'No, Mum.'

Joyce gusts out air. 'Well, thanks.' She storms through to the living room to delve through the cupboards there. Celia follows her through and watches her from the doorway.

'You haven't even asked about Logan,' she says.

Her mother frowns. 'What about Logan?'

'How he's taking all of this.'

Joyce closes a cupboard. 'Well, he's an adult, isn't he? Not a little boy any more...'

'He's twenty-four. A *young* adult.'

'That's virtually middle-aged!'

'Don't be ridiculous,' Celia exclaims.

'Please, go to the shop for me. I'm tired.'

'Mum, I'm not going out to buy your cigarettes. I'm not eight.'

And that's when it hits her that things have to change, and that perhaps this is what Amanda meant when she said she needed to 'own' a situation. To take control. Because Celia is not eight any more. Not the child who'd wandered into the kitchen to see the terrible mess and her mum howling, 'Our guests are coming and look at the bloody state of the place!'

Already tipsy, Joyce had had a notion to cook a butternut squash for what she'd grandly termed a 'dinner party.' She'd dumped the entire vegetable – unpeeled – into a pan of fiercely boiling water and the thing had burst, splattering orange flesh and seeds all over the kitchen.

Ten years later, when Celia was eighteen and with that man from the park, the image of the splattered squash had filled her mind at a crucial moment.

It informed her decision. It changed everything.

And from then, there was no turning back.

21

TWENTY-FIVE YEARS AGO

Celia has picked up the trowel and is hurrying away from the crocus patch. She is mortified that this man saw her trying to dig up the plants. Is he a park warden or someone from the council? Is she going to be arrested?

He catches up with her and says, 'Hey, it's okay. I was only messing about. You can dig up all the flowers you want.'

Dammit, she is blushing now, radiating a fierce heat. This good-looking man keeps glancing at her and smiling as they walk. Celia isn't used to being the focus of attention like this. She's spent a lifetime keeping her head down, trying to blend in, and now she doesn't know what to do.

'I'm Scott.' She looks round, registering his cool grey-blue eyes and thick wavy hair, dark as treacle. His lips are full and he has a dimple on his chin. He looks like a film star, she thinks. 'What's *your* name?' he asks.

'Celia,' she replies, trying to sound bolder than she feels. And somehow a conversation sparks up. She learns that he's just returned to his home city of Glasgow, having worked abroad for some years.

Gradually, Celia relaxes a little, and is flattered when he asks if she'd like a coffee in a nearby cafe. 'What's your surname?' she asks.

'Chegg,' he replies.

'That's unusual.'

'My dad's from Yorkshire,' he says. 'It's a common Yorkshire name.' She has no reason not to believe him.

They go for coffee and cake in a funny little chintzy cafe. After her initial shyness the conversation starts to flow and she realises she is enjoying his company. It's a novelty to her, chatting to a man like this. She has never had a boyfriend – or even kissed anyone – and her dad didn't have much time for her, even before he left. He'd never been to a school parents' evening, and after her mum had tottered into one fuelled by vodka and intent on flirting with her history teacher, Celia had simply avoided mentioning them. Her mum didn't seem to notice and clearly wasn't interested anyway.

However, this handsome stranger appears to be *extremely* interested. They meet again, and again, always at a pre-arranged time by the pond in the park. Soon, their strolls and cafe visits are exchanged for drinks in the pub. The first time, Celia doesn't know what drink to have, so she says vodka because that's what her mum likes. She enjoys the rush of it, the way it melts away her shyness and makes everything feel so right.

From the start, Celia made the decision not to tell Amanda about Scott. She'd never had secrets from her before but she knew what her reaction would be. *What are you doing, meeting up with someone that old? You don't know anything about him. He could be anybody!* She might even have told her parents – Amanda's family are exceptionally close – and Celia can't bear the thought of adults who aren't her own mum and dad being worried about her. That kind of second-hand caring; she's encountered it before, from neighbours, and it makes her crumple inside with shame. For so long now she has lived virtually self-sufficiently and anyway, she is eighteen years old – legally an adult – and there's nothing dodgy going on. Scott has never tried to kiss her or even hold her hand. He's just bought her copious drinks.

There's a point, Celia believes, when it's too late to share a secret anyway. Because people will only be hurt that you've kept it to yourself for so long. She doesn't want to upset Amanda, whose focus is firmly fixed upon moving to London now.

Anyway, it's Celia's private business and she loves Scott's company, and how he actually listens when she tells him about her plans to study horticulture. Being listened to by an older person is an entirely new and intoxicating experience for Celia.

As the weeks go on she is hardly attending school and is seeing Amanda less and less. Now no one is paying any attention to what Celia might be getting up to.

Then one day Scott kisses her passionately by the lake. She feels as if she is levitating out of her own body.

'Shall we go to my flat?' he murmurs.

'Yes,' she says, without hesitation.

Whenever she thinks back to that day, she sees herself approaching a fork in the road and simply taking the wrong route. Instead of heading home, she goes with Scott. And later that afternoon it is too late to swerve back to how things had been before.

In his flat their kisses are hot and urgent. At least Celia thinks that's what they are. Her only point of reference are her mum's Mills & Boons, stacked up in a raggedy heap on the toilet cistern.

'You're so gorgeous and sexy,' Scott murmurs into her neck. 'You've got me all excited...'

Is this a good thing? Celia is certainly hot now – his two-bar electric fire is blazing – but she doesn't know what to make of this at all. Sex education at school barely covered the basic mechanics, and so much emphasis was placed upon sexually transmitted diseases that intercourse seemed as advisable as plunging a fork into an electrical socket.

Her mum has been no help either. *Never let a boy go too far* has been the only advice ever dispensed. But how far is too far? At what point is it too late to turn back? Amanda has a boyfriend so Celia assumes 'things' have happened there. But she no longer feels as if she can ask her anything personal.

Would what they're doing now count as going too far? Celia needs some kind of guidelines – an instruction manual like the one that came with the not-quite-new but still thrilling black box her mum had acquired from somewhere. But a man is not a video player and it's a lot trickier than pressing the right buttons.

'Uhhhh, my God, baby...' Scott is panting now like Mrs Blakely's German shepherd next door. Could he be asthmatic? He is rummaging for something in his trousers. An inhaler, Celia decides. A puff on his inhaler and he'll be all right.

Ah, that's not an inhaler. 'C'mon, sweetheart,' he wheezes. 'Let's go to bed...'

Bed? Now his jeans are open and he's waggling his thing at her and Celia doesn't know what she's supposed to do. Pat it, like a pet? She has always tried to be a good girl who does the right thing. But she can't remember this happening to any of the heroines in those romance novels.

'I... I don't know,' she mutters, staring down at it in fright.

'But we *have* to do it,' he announces.

'I-I-just—'

'Now! We gotta do it now!'

'But why?' Celia exclaims.

"Cause I'm all excited and if we don't do it, my receptacle will explode—' In the heat of the moment, that's how Celia hears it. She pictures the clear plastic container she'd spied in his off-smelling fridge when he'd told her to fetch herself a Coke.

'Receptacle?' she repeats.

'Not receptacle. *Testicles!* If we don't do it right now they'll explode.'

'What?' Celia gasps. She is not a stupid girl. Although her knowledge of sex is scant, she knows the basics of human biology and has been working hard at school so she can go to college and have a career that will whisk her away from the situation at home. Only then will her adult life truly begin. But now, in this overheated flat, something niggles at her.

She pictures the time that butternut squash had burst all over the kitchen. If there's even the tiniest risk of that happening, Celia doesn't want to be held responsible. And so, because Scott has been kind to her, and she's keen to avoid being in the thick of a medical emergency, she allows herself to be led to his bedroom.

It's her first visit to his flat. She'd felt honoured to be invited until she saw the grimy kitchen with tinned meat pie remains sitting out on a plate. And that plastic tub in the fridge, its lid bulging slightly, presumably with some kind of leftovers fermenting inside.

Now her heart is thumping hard. Celia had always imagined that where sex was concerned, the bolder, prettier Amanda would be the advance party, briefed to come back and report on what it was like. Amanda with the glamorous name – not the oddly old-fashioned one Celia's parents had picked for her. Starting her periods, shaving her legs, drinking alcohol; Amanda has always done everything first. But of course she isn't here now. It's just Celia – pale and naked and wondering what to do.

When it happens, it's not like it is in her mother's novels. Celia doesn't swoon with desire or feel herself being 'swept away'. But Scott wants her and says she is so, so beautiful and that he loves her. 'I love you, my beautiful baby,' he murmurs, kissing her.

And that wintry, gravy-smelling afternoon, as her hair crackles with static on his bobbly nylon sheets, Celia's life changes forever.

22

NOW

Celia leaves her mum pulling up sofa cushions in the hope of locating a squashed packet of Marlboros. 'Bye, Mum,' she calls back from the hallway.

'Bye.' Joyce is preoccupied with the matter in hand.

Celia's chest feels tight as she closes the front door quietly behind her. On the concrete path, between two small overgrown patches of grass, she stands for a moment, aware of light rain landing softly on her face. It's only that. Just rain – not tears. She waits to see if her mother will come out after her but of course she does not.

Normally Celia cycles here after work – her ancient bike is her main mode of transport – but today she chose to walk, to allow herself more time to build herself up to facing her mother. Now she strides away from the house she grew up in. The rain is pleasantly cool against her hot cheeks, and Celia glances up to see a chink in the grey; a break in the clouds, through which sunlight is peeking.

It's only a glimmer but she feels her shoulders relaxing as her breathing returns to something more like normal. She feels stronger now, and somehow lighter too. Her heart is no longer a cold, heavy stone in her chest. Celia fills her lungs with cool spring air and then she stops and pulls out her phone and types a message.

> After what happened I find it even more insulting that you haven't even been in touch with me.

She pauses, wondering what else she wants to tell him. Whether to spill out every furious thought she's had this past week.

But no – today is not the day for that. Maybe that day will never come because really, Celia is not built that way. Instead, she sends the message and lifts her face to the sunlight, and then she messages Amanda to tell her that she's ready now – and that she's told her mum.

> Well done you!

comes the reply.

And Celia feels a tiny flicker of pride at that.

* * *

She delves into a giant carton of popcorn, marvelling at its just-popped freshness. Salty or sweet? Hardly a bevy of choices but she'd found herself dithering as she inhaled the aromas at the snacks kiosk. Now she remembers the last time she and Geoff took Logan to the cinema. Just before Christmas, it was. Logan must have been about twelve – it shocks her to realise how long ago it was – and Geoff had allowed them to have popcorn only if it was bought at the nearby Tesco Metro and smuggled in.

How decadent it feels, to enjoy popcorn without shame or

the fear that someone will march over and shine a torch in your face. Then those thoughts dissipate as the movie starts and immediately Celia is swept away, the popcorn soon devoured. Her head is no longer filled with the image of her mum angrily tearing down washing and barking that it was 'only sex'. For the duration of the film she is laughing and crying and still mopping away tears as they step out into the bright, blue-skied afternoon.

'Oh, that was brilliant,' she announces.

Amanda smiles. 'I loved it too.' She mentions the lead actors by name, but she could be talking about the creative directors of Gucci for all Celia has heard of them.

'But you must go to the cinema all the time,' she says. 'I mean, premieres and things...'

'Sometimes,' Amanda concedes. 'But honestly, they're not as much fun as going with you.'

'Oh, come on!'

'No, really,' she says, linking Celia's arm as they make their way along a narrow side street. 'You were engrossed, almost like you'd been hypnotised. I've never seen anything like it.'

Celia doesn't know quite what to make of this. Is it weird to be so transfixed by a film that you don't want to miss a moment? That you barely want to blink? She wants to explain that it was the *vastness* of it that amazed her. Those faces and feelings and emotions, beaming out at her and pulling her into the big screen. But would that sound silly, as if her normal world were terribly small?

Something's happening to her, Celia reflects, being around Amanda. It may only be a week since she walked in on Geoff and that woman, and of course that's not long enough to get over it – or even to come to terms with what's happened. Yet somehow, Amanda's arrival, with the endless poke bowls and posh bread and being whisked to the pub and the cinema – well, it's certainly shaken her up, and is delaying the terrifying business of facing her new reality. And for the moment, Celia is prepared to go along with Amanda's suggestions, because what else is she going to do? Sit there crying in her plant room?

They are heading for cocktails now, to a place Amanda read about on some list of Glasgow's hippest bars. The only lists Celia encounters are her own shopping lists, or the reminders she jots down in her many houseplant hospital notebooks. She has no concept of what's cool or uncool or anything in between.

Entering the bar feels like stepping from a bright spring day into a dimly lit boudoir. They perch on spindly high stools and Celia watches in awe as Amanda falls instantly into easy conversation with the charming silver-haired barman.

Celia picks up the menu, just a sheet of paper, the lettering resembling that of an old-fashioned manual typewriter. Of the ten cocktails listed she has never heard of any of them. If the popcorn choice was tricky, this is impossible because they may as well be written in Dutch.

'I don't know what to have,' she murmurs.

'What d'you recommend?' Amanda asks the bartender. Clearly happy to chat, he starts on about paprika and seaweed and *'umami* notes'. Celia doesn't know what an *umami* is, let alone what it tastes like – but the talk continues, flirtatiously, as he mixes something he promises will be 'salty and deeply savoury, a really intense flavour hit'. He's recognised Amanda, Celia thinks now. He knows she's a TV person and Amanda knows he knows but they're both too cool to acknowledge it.

With a flourish he hands them their cocktails in small triangular glasses. With all this 'savoury' talk, Celia fears that it will be like drinking a liquidised crisp – but it is delicious and also extremely strong. Instinctively she grabs for the bar's brass rail.

'We're in a *bar,* Celia,' Amanda teases. 'Not on a ship.'

Celia catches herself and laughs off her over-cautiousness, that lurking fear in her that, at any point, things could go very wrong. She takes another sip and a surge of warmth floods her body. 'Mum fell off a bar stool once,' she tells Amanda as the bartender serves another customer. 'We were in a hotel in London when I was a little girl. Remember that time we went on a city break?'

'Yes, I do,' Amanda says. 'That was a big deal back then.'

'I think Dad must've won money on the horses or something.' Celia smiles. 'And poor Mum clonked her head and had to be carried up to our room like a rolled-up carpet.'

'Oh God, darling.' Amanda grimaces, then adds, 'But you're not your mum.'

Celia smiles. 'I'm definitely not.'

'But can I say something?' Amanda's gaze holds hers for a moment. 'You could maybe afford to loosen up a bit.'

Celia takes another sip. 'You think so?'

'I don't mean to your-mum levels,' she clarifies, and Celia smiles wryly before turning serious.

'I don't know what to do about her, Amanda.'

'Look, you knew she was going to be upset about Geoff. But you dealt with it, and that's brilliant—'

'I mean about the way she is,' Celia cuts in. 'I worry about her, you know.'

'Hey,' Amanda says. 'Maybe you can help her at some point, or maybe you can't. You can't make everything right, Celia. She's not like, like a houseplant—'

'Unfortunately not.'

'Yeah.' Amanda smiles kindly. 'That'd be easier, wouldn't it? Regular watering, a sunnier position, a bit of feeding now and then—' She breaks off. 'What am I saying? I can't even keep cress alive!'

'Oh, I'm sure you can.' Celia conjures up an image of how she imagines Amanda's home to be: huge and airy with sunlight streaming in and plants artfully placed around every room. 'I bet your flat's gorgeous,' she announces, this *umami* concoction having rushed to her head. 'I can picture it, like something from a magazine. Maybe I could come and visit sometime?'

'Oh, uh, maybe! You'd be really welcome—'

'And isn't it crazy that I haven't even met Jasper properly?' Celia takes another big sip. 'I'd love to get to know him. He seems so lovely, Amanda. He's obviously crazy about you. I could see that at your wedding, the way he kept looking at you...'

Amanda laughs tightly. 'Well, er, yeah. He's great.'

'So what's *his* life like? Is his art career flourishing?'

'It's, um... He's getting there,' she says quickly.

Celia smiles. 'You're like this golden couple. But you always got it right, y'know? Moving to London so young, I wondered how you'd cope, being away from your mum and dad...' Her lovely mum, she muses, who made Amanda those wonderful packed lunches, all the necessary food groups including fresh fruit (grapes! Kiwi!) and a treat. 'But of course you did brilliantly right from the start,' she adds all in a rush.

'It hasn't *quite* been like that.' Amanda shifts position on the stool.

'Oh, I'm sure you worked hard,' Celia says quickly. 'I didn't mean it's all fallen into your lap...'

'No, it's fine. I didn't take it that way.' Her expression is unreadable now.

'What I mean is, I'm really proud of you, if that doesn't sound patronising,' Celia goes on, carried away by the novelty of drinking in a bar in the day. A beautiful bar, all polished wood and twinkling golden lights, tucked away down an alley that she hadn't even known existed.

'So, shall I come down and visit you sometime?' she prompts her friend.

'Of course, yeah!' There's a catch to Amanda's voice now and suddenly, Celia wonders if she's overstepped it. If mixing her Glasgow life with her London life would be too much for Amanda. *I'm her hometown friend,* she reminds herself. *I'm not like the people she hangs out with normally and I have to remember that.* 'I'd absolutely love you to visit,' Amanda adds, smiling warmly now. As she squeezes her hand, Celia relaxes again.

'You could show me all the London things.'

Amanda laughs, nodding. '*All* of them.' She catches the bartender's eye and he chuckles.

'Hey, that sounds good,' he enthuses. 'If you're doing that, I'm coming too.' Then Amanda falls back into conversation with the handsome twinkly eyed man, and somehow Celia finds herself being part of it too. They learn that his name is Jack and that this is his bar, a new venture; a dream he's had since he was a young man. And by the time they leave, joining the throngs of Saturday afternoon shoppers, Celia feels happy and carefree and not unpleasantly light-headed. She is no longer thinking about her own life, here in Glasgow, as they stroll together along the bustling shopping street.

She is thinking about *all the London things*, which she cannot even start to imagine. She'll buy a picnic for the train! She'll take a brand-new suitcase that doesn't have a busted wheel! She might even go to a classical concert, confident now that she knows not to clap!

Celia's thoughts break off suddenly. Now her attention is caught by a man and a child wandering towards them, hand in hand, up the gradual slope of Buchanan Street. They are chatting animatedly and keep looking around, as if eager to absorb every delightful detail of this sunny afternoon.

The girl says something and the man laughs. It's not a polite *I'm-humouring-you* laugh but a genuine one, unselfconsciously hearty. Then the girl points across the street towards a busker with a guitar and they swerve towards him.

Look at that man with his daughter, Celia thinks. *How relaxed and happy they are together.* He looks like a good dad. Of course, he could be an uncle or a family friend but now she registers the likeness between them.

Briefly, she remembers going to drop some coins into a busker's open clarinet case on this very street and Geoff telling her not to. 'They're just begging,' he'd said. 'Don't encourage it.' Celia has always loved music – the controversial pink CD especially – and is of the opinion that if anything should be encouraged, it's that.

She sees the girl hurrying over to the busker and something lands in the bowl on the pavement. He smiles his thanks.

There's something else about them, Celia decides. Not the girl, whose long dark hair is in plaits, somehow complementing her outfit of red top, black dungaree dress and tights, reminding her of Beryl the Peril. No, she hasn't seen this girl beyond the comics she'd loved as a child. But the man – tall, dark-haired and attractive in a navy-blue shirt and jeans – is somehow familiar to her.

She remembers now. 'Amanda, I know that man,' she says quickly.

'Who?' She looks around.

'Him. That man with the girl there... I mean, I don't know him exactly, but we've definitely met...'

Celia thinks he spots her then. Something like a flicker of recognition crosses his face, and now it's not so relaxed as his expression switches. She can tell, even from some distance, that he is no longer giving the girl his full attention. She is overcome by an urge to run up to him and say it's okay, and that she's sorry. She was just having a very bad day.

You can't make everything right, Celia.

Well, maybe she can't fix the big things but she can make this small thing right. It's being with Amanda, she realises. How easily she chatted with the bartender and how comfortable she is in her own skin. And what else did she say in the bar? *Maybe you could afford to loosen up...*

'Hello!' she calls out, raising a hand. The man's expression switches again. Perhaps she's misread it and he didn't spot her at all. He's in a hurry, she realises. Because now he has bent slightly to say something to the child, and she beams delightedly, nodding as she says something back.

Then together, still hand in hand, they veer suddenly off the busy shopping street and turn the corner out of sight.

23

Enzo knows his daughter very well. As a little girl, Mathilde was never one to accept that the beach was 'closing' when it was time to go home. She believed in Father Christmas, of course, and the tooth fairy, because she was never averse to receiving hard cash. But Enzo knew he wouldn't be able to wriggle out of an awkward scenario like that one.

'I can't decide what to have,' she announces now, hurrying along to keep up with her father's strides. Mathilde is small for her age and slightly built. Today she is wearing a black corduroy dress with a bib, like dungarees, over a sparkly red top, red and black-striped tights and big black DMs. Who's that cartoon character British kids grew up on? The one Laura told him about? Beryl the Peril.

'You can have anything you like,' Enzo tells her. 'Anything at all.'

'Thanks, Dad.' She beams up at him and he readies himself for the unfeasibly cheerful waiting staff and pounding music of Mathilde's favourite restaurant. He hadn't planned to take her there this afternoon. Although it's her birthday – she is ten, quite the milestone – they have already done presents and been out for a fancy brunch involving shakshuka (Enzo didn't encounter such a thing until the age of forty) plus hot chocolate towering with whipped cream. They have seen a movie, as always opting for separate popcorns (Enzo: salty, Mathilde: sweet), and later a bunch of her friends are coming round for a sleepover. He'd planned to order in pizzas. Well, Mathilde will just have to have a double dinner, he decides as they step through the arc of balloons at the entrance to Benji's. Because in panic he couldn't think of anywhere else to hide.

'Can I message Mum?' Mathilde asks as they wait to be shown to a table.

"Course you can.' He hands her his phone – she has asked for one but isn't allowed one yet – and she speedily taps out a message, detailing the day's events so far. Then she forces her dad into a grinning selfie and sends that too. They'd have all been together today if Laura hadn't come down with a dose of flu.

In some ways, Enzo reflects as they're led through the bustling restaurant, it's just as well. It's not that he'd have *wished* a virus on Laura. But if she were here today it would have been a whole lot trickier to make that snap decision and haul them all in here.

Benji's is basically a fast-food restaurant with added streamers and sparklers and wackily named desserts. Laura can't abide it, and understandably so. Several high-spirited birthday gatherings are happening around them and children much younger than Mathilde are charging between tables and clanging against chairs.

'Ooh, careful there!' a young waiter says, cheery demeanour undented. He's probably a philosophy student, Enzo decides, and he spends his Saturdays dodging bread roll missiles and chemical-additive-fuelled kids. And they say Gen Z are allergic to hard graft? As a demographic they're much maligned, Enzo believes. Caring about the planet, wanting a decent work-life balance and being partial to smoothies? What's the problem with that?

In fact, he pities the staff here as the noise level is already making his brain judder against his skull. He thinks back to Kim in the taxi last night and wonders what she'd make of a place like this. Would she have kissed him on the mouth and asked him up to her place if she'd been sober? He has already gathered that she's quite a force to be reckoned with and surmises that, if Kim wants to do something, she'll just do it. And he wonders now whether their coffee/drink will happen and in fact whether *he* wants it to. He's become cautious – not only due to previous dating experiences but also because he'd have to be absolutely sure before introducing anyone into Mathilde's life.

'You overthink it,' Nina has scolded him in the past. 'You're running away with yourself. A drink is just a drink.' Hmm, he'd joked. Wasn't that from *Casablanca*?

'So, what shall we have?' he asks Mathilde as they are seated next to a wall entirely covered with artificial pink flowers. Vertical gardens are everywhere, he's noticed. Mathilde takes a selfie against it with Enzo's phone and then peruses the confusing array of menus, all laminated and cartoonishly illustrated: the set menu, the 'Occasions' menu and 'Nibbles 'n' Bites'. After the speedy dash here, Enzo's pulse seems to have just about normalised. He picks up the 'Occasions' menu, thinking, well, this *is* an occasion, isn't it? Not just Mathilde's birthday but a day when he managed to avoid—

'Hiiii! Hello!'

Enzo looks up with a start. A woman has barged into the

restaurant and she seems to be waving at him. It's the woman he spotted in the street and a sudden wave of dread crashes over him.

He wants nothing to do with her. At least not here, not with Mathilde sitting beside him, wondering whether to opt for the Cajun fried chicken or the crispy haddock goujons. Enzo grips the biggest and most lavishly illustrated menu, hoping that if he focuses hard enough, then the woman will melt into the mayhem around them.

Celia. That's her name: he's remembered it now. He glances up to see her heading towards them, light brown hair pulled back from her delicate face. Why is she here? Has she followed them in? No, he's just being paranoid. She's just come in to eat because *that's what people do in restaurants*, Enzo reminds himself, feeling foolish now. And she must have been waving at someone else.

No, she wasn't. She arrives at their table, pink-cheeked and smiling apologetically and fixing him with her striking green eyes. 'Hi!' She seems to catch her breath.

Mathilde looks up. 'Hi. Please can I order things from different menus?' she asks politely.

Normally Enzo would be proud. Manners were of utmost importance as he was growing up and he tries to encourage the kids at school to at least not be blatantly foul to one another (with limited success). But he's not registering Mathilde's politeness now as Celia is telling her, 'Oh, I don't work here, honey. Sorry.' She turns to Enzo. 'Look, I'm really sorry for chasing you in here. It's just…' She pushes a tendril of hair from her face. 'I'm not sure if you remember me but I do owe you an apology.'

He flushes. 'I'm sorry, I don't think I—'

'The houseplant hospital?' she says brightly. 'Last weekend it was, when you came round with—'

'What's a houseplant hospital?' Mathilde cuts in.

'It's a place where people bring their plants when they're not very well,' Celia explains. 'And I work out a treatment plan for them to make them better.'

'Like an actual hospital?' Mathilde appears to be fascinated by this.

'Yes, sort of.' Celia smiles. 'And you see, your dad – I'm assuming this is your dad...'

'Yes, he's my dad.' *Who else would he be?* her expression says.

'Well, he brought a very sorry-looking cactus round to my house, hoping I'd be able to help. And I'm sorry,' Celia continues, turning back to Enzo now, who is trying to form a calm expression although he is aware that his jaw has set. He does not want a speciality burger now. He wants to ditch this idea and take Mathilde home to get ready for the sleepover.

'I sent you away, saying I couldn't take it in,' Celia reminds him. 'I'd never do that normally. I'd always try to help. But it wasn't normal. I mean it wasn't a normal *day*. But anyway!' She brightens now. Mathilde is staring at her as if she might grab the assortment of menus and juggle with them. 'I hate not being able to help a customer,' she adds. 'So if you'd like to bring your cactus round, I'd be really happy—'

'But he's fine.' Mathilde looks perplexed. 'I mean, our cactus is fine. There's nothing wrong with him at all.'

Celia frowns. 'I'm sorry. It didn't look that way to me. It – *he* – was keeled right over and severely dehydrated.'

Enzo's mind has whirred into action now. He could lie and say he's never seen this woman in his life! *Could someone remove her from the restaurant, please?* But he can't do that. Of course he can't. And nor can he scramble together a lie that Spike *did* in fact take 'a turn' while Mathilde was on her school trip, but then miraculously recovered.

Still gripping the plastic 'Occasions' menu, he seems to be having trouble finding the right words.

'Dad?' Mathilde's laser-gaze is spearing him between the eyes. 'Dad,' she says firmly, 'did something happen when I was away? Did something happen to Spike?'

24

Amanda is picking through the rails in an adorable little vintage shop. Celia's neighbourhood is hardly Fashion Central – there are no designer stores, no high street chains – but in fact this is better. On this crisp Sunday morning the area is buzzing and she is enjoying herself thoroughly with a firm aim in mind.

To see Celia transfixed by that movie – as thrilled as a child – did something peculiar to Amanda's heart. She is aware of having become blasé over the years, of movie premieres in grand venues seeming pretty ordinary to her now. And yesterday's outing gave her something of a mental shake-up.

'I've never tried an *umami*,' Celia had announced in Jack's bar. Amanda had had to stop herself from explaining that it's not a thing, but a *taste* – deep and dark and intensely savoury. A taste that everyone's been aware of for, what, a decade or more? Everyone except Celia, it seems. But then Jack had explained it all in a breezy, friendly way, and she had appeared to be genuinely fascinated. *Wow, really? I never knew there was this 'other' taste. Amazing!*

Celia needs taking in hand, Amanda decides, eager to build on the success of their day out. Not just the film and the drinks but Celia chatting away to Jack, actually losing her guardedness (alcohol helped, of course) for that short time in the cosy bar. And then, out in the street, announcing that she was going to follow that man and the girl, which she did – right into that restaurant choc-full of hyped-up kids!

Amanda wouldn't have dared to venture in there. She doesn't tend to eat in places where rowdy families go. Laminated menus give her the serious ick (she shudders at *anything* wipe-clean) and she has no wish to be confronted by a cream-slathered dessert with a lit sparkler sticking out of it. Yet Celia, clearly on a mission, had marched right in – and no, she did *not* need Amanda to come in with her! She'd wanted to do this alone.

Amanda had loitered on the pavement outside, hardly believing that this was the Celia she'd known since the first day of primary school. The Celia who'd seemed so stiff and uncomfortable at Amanda's wedding, to the point she'd wondered what had possessed her to invite her oldest friend. With that upbringing of hers – boozy mum, dad waltzing off to Wales with some other woman without a backwards glance – she has only ever wanted to blend right in. If only she'd believe it, she has huge potential to change her life, Amanda muses.

Amanda loves a project, something to throw herself into wholeheartedly, especially if it also makes her feel as if she's doing some good and contributing to society instead of 'just' being a fluffy fashion person. That's how many people see her, she's patently aware of that. Her most recent TV slot fulfilled that need in her – especially when she advised brave firefighters and A&E doctors on how to dress properly. And in the absence of any work offers to lure her back to London, she has decided that this will be her project now. *Project Celia.*

As Amanda continues to browse the rails, she toys with the phrase in her mind. Her gaze lights upon a shimmery ivory maxi skirt, and a muscle tweaks in her lower back as she plucks a blue cashmere scarf from a shelf. Thankfully she and Celia are sharing Celia's double bed now (Amanda fears that no amount of Reformer Pilates will undo the damage of having slept on that terrible pull-out bed for three nights). She plans to stay a few more days – another week, max. That should be plenty of time to completely make over Celia's wardrobe: to do a real *Look for a Lifestyle* on her. Amanda also hopes to persuade her to get a decent – *proper* – haircut, having learned that Celia has been trundling round to some woman's flat for a 'dry trim' virtually since the Domesday Book was written.

That sums it up really, she decides. Celia has Domesday hair. Well, not for much longer.

Now Amanda finds a gorgeous angora short-sleeved sweater, so soft to the touch she can barely feel it, and an adorable cream ruffled top. She intends to present her friend with these pieces and show her how to style them. They could even do a little photo shoot with her phone. A video, even. That'd be fun.

When Amanda's career was at its peak she was often asked for style tips for magazine features. 'My wardrobe staples', that kind of thing, and where she liked to shop. Back then, when she was more flush financially – and not propping up her lazy arse of a husband – a small clutch of designer labels were her go-to. But she didn't want to seem elitist or lacking in imagination so she'd fib and say, 'I love picking up vintage pieces on my travels.'

In fact, Amanda's travels amount mainly to holidays at luxury Ibizan resorts, and she's never had the time nor inclination to rake through rails of other people's musty old stuff. Now, however, she is loving her explorations around the various small, thoughtfully curated vintage boutiques around Glasgow's

Southside. So gentrified is this neighbourhood, abundant with independent coffee shops and bakeries, that she could almost imagine living back here. However, she expects Ollie will be lining up lots of work opportunities for her from his South Kensington office and she needs to be in London for that.

There is also the small matter of her potato-printing twit of a husband. Their messages have been curt since she left in a hurry, announcing that she needed to take some time out. 'Fine,' Jasper had said. 'My work's pretty all-consuming right now.'

'Work!' Amanda tried – and failed – not to laugh scathingly at that. At some point she'll have to figure out whether there is anything worth saving, or if she'll have to admit to having made a colossal mistake. However, she doesn't want to dwell on that now, and she certainly doesn't plan to tell Celia any of this. Her friend has enough on her plate – but it's not even that, not really. Amanda is ashamed of what's become of her home, her career, her *life*. She can't stop Celia travelling down to see her – Amanda doesn't own the rail network, nor London – but the thought of her witnessing what's really going on, with her paint-splattering-Laughing-Cow-stabbing husband is more than she can bear.

Project Celia, she hopes, will distract her from all of that for a little bit longer.

At the shop counter she hands several pieces to the young red-haired assistant. 'I think I know your face,' the girl says. 'Yes, I've definitely seen you somewhere before.'

'Just one of those faces, I guess.' Amanda smiles. She leaves the shop, browses in a couple more and buys a box of Syrian pastries, gooey with honey and terribly naughty, but she can't resist. Should she buy a little gift for Logan too? Something to persuade him that she's a nice person, a *good* person – to at least try to bond with him a little before she leaves? Used to making an impression, it bothers her that he has barely acknowledged her presence these past two weeks. As if she were no more significant than a draught gusting in from an open window.

She wanders into a novelty gift shop, wondering if he'd find a squashy fake poo-stress reliever funny or useful (she's certainly sensed stress waves emitting through his closed bedroom door). What about a funny wig? An edible jigsaw? A thing where you press your hand or face or presumably any other bodily part into a Perspex tray of nails to make an impression?

'Oh, they're great,' remarks the neatly stubbled man, pausing from arranging a selection of resin jewellery. 'Everyone loves those.'

'I'll think about it,' she fibs, deciding that Logan is the kind of person who doesn't care about making an impression on anything, nor indeed anyone.

Heading back to Celia's now, laden with bags of vintage clothes and the box of pastries, she stops to check her phone. It's not only Jasper she's cross with right now, but Ollie too. Isn't he supposed to be managing her career? What exactly is he doing to earn his 10 per cent?

She sets down her bags on the pavement. I could call him, she decides. She doesn't care that it's a Sunday because he is always available to her at any time of day or night.

Amanda makes the call. As it rings she pulls her shoulders back and sweeps a hand through her long blonde hair, readying herself.

'Amanda?' He sounds taken aback.

'Ollie, Hi. Hope you don't mind me calling...' *Hope I've interrupted your steaming roast beef lunch,* is what she means.

'No, it's fine! It's great. How are you?'

'Great,' she says. 'I'm up in Scotland, actually. Been here a while.'

'Really! I assumed you must be away...' As if he has been

keenly aware of the lack of communication between them. 'Having a little Highland break?'

'No, I'm in Glasgow,' she says tersely, 'looking after a very dear old friend.'

'Oh. Oh gosh. I hope things aren't too stressful...'

'It's been... pretty bad,' she murmurs.

A pause settles. 'Oh, darling. That must be hard.'

'*So* hard.'

Ollie clears his throat. 'Anything I can do?'

You could get me some work, you goon. 'There's nothing anyone can do for her, unfortunately,' she says, almost relishing her new persona of deathbed companion.

'That's terrible! Can I ask... how old she is?'

'Forty-three.' *Same as me, Ollie. That difficult in-between age.*

'That's awfully sad. Well, I do hope she pulls through.'

'That's all we can do. Hope.' So immersed is Amanda in her role that she's wondering what Celia's last wishes might be, and if she'd prefer burial or cremation. Would Logan know? Then, to fill the pause, as Ollie has clearly run out of things to say to her, 'So, has anything come in for me?'

'What? Oh, uh... couple of packages, I think. I'll ask Millie to send them on...' She doesn't mean gifts, for fuck's sake. Not the stream of outfits and beauty freebies that still come her way via Ollie's office.

'I mean *work* things, Ollie. Jobs. Anything coming up?'

'Um, not at the moment but—' She hears a sipping sound. He is drinking! Quaffing a fine pinot noir, probably, while her career swills down the drain! 'But you'll be the first to know when there *is* something,' he adds in a brisker tone. 'Anyway, darling, I'll let you go. I'm sure you have a lot to get on with. It's so great you can be there at this difficult time...'

'That's what friends are for,' she says tightly.

'Of course.'

'So you will let me know if any jobs—' she starts. But Ollie has ended the call.

25

Celia is prepared to make her usual doorstep diagnosis when Enzo and Mathilde show up with the sickly *cleistocactus strausii*. She has already decided she'll take it in, even if it has a slim chance of survival. She has also decided privately that she won't charge for her services.

'Thanks so much for this,' Enzo says. 'We really appreciate anything you can do.'

Mathilde smiles hopefully. 'D'you think you can help?'

'I'll try my best,' Celia says as Enzo hands the cactus to her. 'I promise you that.'

The late May morning is crisp and bright and an awkward moment hangs as father and daughter stand outside Celia's flat. They are sort of *hovering,* she realises, as if there is something else.

'I have your number,' she adds. 'I'll contact you to let you know how things are going.'

Enzo rakes back his wavy dark hair, looking apologetic. 'Erm, this is probably a bit cheeky, but Mathilde's really interested to see what a houseplant hospital is like.' He glances down at his daughter. 'You were really into growing things, weren't you? At Mamie and Papi's?'

'Yeah.' She nods. 'At their house in France,' she adds by way of explanation.

'Oh, how lovely,' Celia says, picking up on Enzo's use of the past tense. She remembers that pushy woman mentioning grandparents who'd passed away, that first time they'd showed up here. 'What did you grow there?' she asks gently.

'Herbs, mostly,' Mathilde replies. 'Rosemary, thyme, oregano, chervil…'

'Wow, that *is* impressive.' Celia doesn't quite know why this surprises her. At Mathilde's age – she's guessing around nine – Celia had her own garden, and as a child Logan was always keen to help her out in the plant room.

'So at some point,' Enzo starts, 'when you're not busy, would we be able to pop by and have a quick look around?'

'Erm, yes, of course.' Celia glances at Mathilde. Imagine, a child not only knowing, but *growing* chervil! And what a wonderful outfit she's wearing (rainbow-striped polo neck top and embroidered jeans, plus red fake fur jacket). 'You can come in now if you like,' she adds quickly. 'I'm not busy.'

In fact, with Amanda being out for the morning and Logan still mainly holed up in his room, Celia has been at something of a loose end. She beckons them in, and before she's even shown them into the plant room, Terri raps on the door and appears with a thickly iced chocolate sponge.

Introductions follow, and Terri apologises profusely to Enzo for being so abrupt and unhelpful the first time they met. 'We'd had a bit of a morning, hadn't we, Celia?'

'We had,' Celia agrees. She catches Mathilde's dark eyes enlarging at the sight of the cake.

'Freshly baked,' Terri announces. 'Would you like some, hon? Love your look, by the way! You off to a party later?'

'No,' she replies, as if surprised by the question.

'This is Mathilde's normal daywear,' Enzo explains, and his daughter grins.

'Good on you.' Terri nods approvingly. She's not averse to a zingy colour combination herself. 'Cake for you, Enzo?'

'Oh, er, if you're sure...' He smiles.

'That's what it's for!' In the absence of Amanda, Terri slips back into her usual mode of filling the kettle and lifting plates and mugs from the cupboard, making herself at home. Over tea and cake she then sets to work in extracting Enzo's life history. His childhood in Brittany, his love of hillwalking, and life as a French teacher here in Glasgow. Celia finds herself taking it all in, enjoying his light accent, the gentle rhythm of his speech. He has an ease about him that's so refreshing, she decides, as he asks Terri about the hospital where she works (his late mother, too, was a nurse).

Perhaps this comes with teaching, Celia muses. One of the biggest in Glasgow, Enzo's school has something of a reputation, but is highly regarded, nevertheless. The kind of school where Logan would have been eaten for breakfast.

Logan appears briefly, enticed by the chocolate sponge, and is cordial at least. Then Celia suggests to Mathilde, 'Shall I show you the plant room?', and as Terri clears up, Celia takes them through to where – as her friend put it – 'the magic happens.'

'*Wow.*' Mathilde gazes around the room in wonder. From the sturdy rubber plants to delicate trailing ivys, plants of every description fill the workbench and the shelves Celia and Terri built. An enormous *monstera* lives on the floor, and now that the pull-out bed is folded away, Celia has set up a small foldable table on which her tools are laid out neatly and cuttings are growing in jars.

'This is incredible,' Enzo announces. 'It's absolutely crammed but so... *organised.*'

'Like a really organised jungle,' Mathilde suggests.

Celia smiles. 'That's a lovely description.'

'I wish we had a room like this,' she adds wistfully.

'Some, um, people do think it's a bit much,' Celia remarks.

'Oh no,' Enzo says. 'It's wonderful. Terri was right – it is kind of magical.'

Celia is a little taken aback by this. Enzo and Mathilde are so alike, she notes, not just in appearance – the dark brown eyes, strong noses and high cheekbones – but in attitude too. As they chatter together, she finds herself wondering about the woman who'd come round with Enzo that first time. His wife, she'd assumed – or girlfriend – but is she Mathilde's mum? From what Celia remembers she can't detect much of a resemblance, but sometimes, she believes, a child looks very much like one parent and not like the other at all. (She likes to tell herself that this is the case with Logan – although in truth his biological father's face is just a blur to her now).

'What d'you do in here?' Mathilde asks.

Celia laughs, unsure of where to start. 'Everything, really. There's watering, of course...' She points to the small enamel watering can hanging from a hook on the wall.

'It's got your name on it!'

'It has, yes.' She lifts it down. 'This was mine when I was your age. Our next-door neighbour gave it to me for my birthday – she painted my name on it herself. I had a little garden of my own back then.'

'Your *own* garden? You were lucky!'

'I was, yes. I was a really lucky girl.' She hands it to Mathilde, who examines it reverentially before handing it back.

'Would you like me to show you one of the first things I do to help a plant get better?' Celia asks, and as Mathilde nods eagerly, she sets about repotting a silver philodendron.

Houseplant hospital customers often over-think things. They assume their plant has developed a terrible condition due to mites or mould or some other mysterious nasty, when the problem tends to be a very simple one: it's rootbound and needs fresh compost plus a bigger pot. This upsizing seems as obvious to Celia as buying new shoes for children as they grow. You wouldn't expect them to cram their poor feet into last year's outgrown pair and expect them to be happy and thrive. (Buying those ridiculous size fives for Amanda's wedding had been a brief aberration.)

'This is the part I enjoy most,' she explains as Mathilde hovers at her side, watching intently.

'You're *freeing* it,' she observes, and Celia nods, impressed by her perception.

'That's right. It needs room to breathe and grow.' She has eased the roots from the ceramic pot and now, at the workbench, she gently works on them with gloved fingers, detangling them from their spaghetti-like ball.

'What are you doing now?' Mathilde asks.

'I'm sort of *massaging* the roots,' Celia replies.

She senses Mathilde's intense gaze. 'Is that just normal soil like you'd get in a garden?'

'No, it's peat-free compost. I make it myself. I mean, I buy ingredients and blend them to make sure it's absolutely right for each plant.'

'They like different kinds?'

'Yes, they do, just like people feel happiest in different environments. Some like it rich and full of organic matter, and others like it fluffy and light...' Mathilde looks amazed by this. It occurs to Celia that Geoff has never asked her a single question about what she gets up to in here.

'And this is your job?' Enzo says. 'I mean, is it a full-time thing?' He seems to catch himself then. 'I'm sorry, we're bombarding you with questions—'

'Not at all.' She smiles, enjoying their interest. 'I do wish I could do this full time. But no – I also work in a boutique selling occasion wear and fascinators.'

He chuckles and the three settle into a comfortable silence as Celia gently presses down the compost in the philodendron's new pot. Occasionally, she gets to know her customers a little. They might pop in to check on their plant's progress and she's not averse to a cup of tea and a custard cream. And then, as they chat in the kitchen, she sometimes finds herself wondering what their lives are like. Whether in their house there is a Director-in-Chief of the Heating Thermostat and if they are allowed to buy takeaway sandwiches and luxury cookies with chocolate chunks. However, when she'd spotted Enzo and Mathilde in town yesterday, there was no *wondering*. She'd formed an instant impression of the kind of man he is, and the sort of life he leads. It had appeared fully formed in her mind.

That's why she'd followed them into the restaurant. She had to speak to Enzo – to apologise and give him her card with her contact details. Because she could tell he was a good person, a *kind* person – not someone who'd invent a golf weekend so he could shag his lover in a rancid caravan. And she'd remembered when he'd come to her door with the keeled-over cactus that clearly mattered to him. It mattered a *lot* – and to the woman too. That striking, slightly hippyish woman with tons of curly red hair. And she'd decided then that she wanted to make amends and do whatever she could to help them.

'So, d'you have a garden too?' Enzo asks.

'Sadly not,' Celia replies. 'Only this.'

'I wish we had one,' Mathilde announces.

Enzo rests a hand on her shoulder. 'Mamie and Papi's was beautiful, wasn't it?' She nods. 'I probably shouldn't tell you this,' he adds with a smile, turning to Celia, 'but Mathilde smuggled Spike out of France.'

'Did you?' Celia grins. 'That was very... daring of you.'

Mathilde nods. 'No one wanted him so I *had* to bring him home.'

'Of course you did,' Celia agrees, deftly brushing up a spillage of compost now.

'You obviously love your work,' Enzo adds.

'I do,' she tells him. 'It's so satisfying, seeing plants flourish. Almost as much as seeing your child grow.'

'That's a nice way of putting it,' he says as Mathilde explores the room. Celia sees her stopping at the door frame where, every few months, Logan would stand and she'd mark his new height in pencil: 'You've grown a whole inch!' He grew and grew and now he towers over her by a whole foot.

'Shall we mark your height?' Celia asks. And so a new pencil mark is added, and then Celia explains that she'll devise a care plan and keep in touch regarding Spike's progress.

Terri joins them in the hallway. 'Thank you both,' Enzo says, 'for everything.'

'No problem at all,' Celia says as the door opens and Amanda breezes in, clutching carrier bags and a little white box. Amidst more introductions – she too compliments Mathilde's outfit – she plonks the box into Celia's hands and delves into the bags. Various purchases are pulled out with a flourish: a shimmery skirt, two fluffy sweaters and an array of tops and scarves and – what's this? A cape? Mathilde watches, eyes wide.

'*You've* been treating yourself,' Terri observes with a wry smile.

'Oh, these aren't for me,' Amanda explains. 'They're for you, Celia—'

'For me?'

'I thought you could use a few new pieces.'

Pieces? She catches Terri's bemused look and wonders what Enzo and Mathilde are making of this. 'They're lovely,' she starts, 'but I'm not sure they're quite—'

'They're beautiful,' Mathilde enthuses.

'They are,' Amanda agrees. 'We'll see a new Celia soon.' She beams at her friend. 'You won't recognise yourself.'

Celia smiles uncertainly, a little overwhelmed with five people occupying her narrow hallway while Amanda proposes – well, what exactly? That she reinvent herself? She can no more imagine herself in the alligator costume Terri ran up for Logan than the silky maxi skirt Amanda is currently holding up against her.

Finally, Enzo says they must be going and, relieved for air, Celia sees them out. 'Well, thank you,' he says again. 'We really appreciate this and it's been lovely seeing how you work.' He glances at his daughter. 'Hasn't it, Mathilde?'

'It's been great! Thank you.'

'Sorry if it was a bit chaotic there,' Celia says with a grimace.

'Not at all.' Enzo smiles warmly and takes Mathilde by the hand. 'I'm just glad you had time for us. You obviously have a very full and busy life.'

26

Sober Kim is very different to diving-in-for-a-taxi-kiss Kim. Sober Kim is sitting bolt upright across the restaurant table from Enzo – she'd texted to suggest 'a quick bite' – but is also jabbing at her phone and Enzo senses her attention is wavering.

'Sorry,' she says. 'My daughter's having a bit of a meltdown.'

'Nothing serious, I hope?'

'Exams.' She rolls her eyes.

'Oh God.' He nods sympathetically. 'Tough time.'

'Hmm, yes. It's all too much, apparently. But, y'know, she knew they were coming. I mean, they haven't crash-landed on her from outer space. She's had tons of time to prepare and all the support we can all give her...' Kim twirls her fork around her linguine and pops in a neat mouthful.

'Well, that's all you can do,' Enzo offers.

She nods and swallows and sips her sparkling water. 'I was down seeing her a few weeks ago and made sure we had everything in place. I mean, every resource we could possibly offer her. The relaxation apps, the guided meditation practices, the weighted blanket...'

'Weighted blanket?' he says in surprise.

'To calm her nervous system,' she says, as if that should be obvious. 'You're a teacher, Enzo. You know how it's just a matter of sticking to a schedule and applying full focus for the duration.'

He looks at her, aware that he should agree and move the subject on. He really shouldn't get into this, not over pasta on what he supposes is a first date. Yet, all too vividly, he remembers his own chaotic approach to exam revision: the all-nighters spent huddled over textbooks, caffeine juddering through his veins. 'I think it's different for everyone,' he says diplomatically. 'I mean, some kids breeze through it and others find it an awful lot to handle.'

Kim nods, her expression softening, and as Enzo finishes his ravioli he tells himself not to judge her for her tough-love approach. He's met enough mums and dads to know that parenting styles are as varied as people. 'I bet you're a really lovely, supportive teacher,' she adds. 'But don't you agree that it's just about applying themselves?'

'No, not really.' He shakes his head. 'I don't, actually.'

Her eyes widen in surprise. 'Why not?'

'Because people are individuals,' he starts, 'and everyone reacts to pressure in different ways. I mean, some thrive on it. They actually enjoy the challenge. But for many—'

'You mean the kids you teach?' she interjects.

'Well, yeah. A lot of them are managing all kinds of situations and responsibilities and have loads of other stuff to deal with—'

'Yeah, I s'pose at your school it's like that.' She sips more water and he drinks his wine, letting her words settle.

At your school. A school for poor kids, is the implication. Well, yes, he thinks, prickling now, despite trying to let her comment wash over him. Some of his pupils come to school hungry (it's why he keeps a toaster and a sliced loaf in his classroom) and no mum or dad ever shows up at parents' evenings. For these young people it's not as simple as *applying themselves for the duration.*

'I know from Nina and Hayley what those kids' lives are like,' Kim says crisply. 'And you probably think I'm a harsh mother.'

'Of course not,' he says, regretting even getting into this as her gaze flickers back to her phone. 'I'd never judge anyone like that.'

She smiles, red lipstick still perfectly in place after eating. 'You just wait till your little girl hits the teen stage.'

'Yeah.' He nods, raising a smile. 'I'm sure it's not easy.'

'It makes you wonder why you had them!'

'Er, yeah. I bet.' He forces a laugh.

'Don't believe me, do you?' she teases.

'No, I'm sure you're right…' *Why do people do this?* he wonders. *Imply that, while you might be enjoying being a parent now, give it a few years and it'll be hell?* Kim is back to messaging now, frowning as her daughter's replies come thick and fast.

'Sorry,' she says with a sigh. 'This is terribly rude of me.'

'Don't worry about it,' he says. Kim lets out an exasperated groan and goes to shove her phone in her bag when it rings.

'Please, take it if you need to,' Enzo adds quickly.

She frowns apologetically and takes the call. 'Jess, honey, I'm out. It's not a good time… Yes, speak to Dad about that. Do the exercises. Go through your evening routine. Take your supplements…'

Enzo doesn't know what to do with himself while this is going on. He looks around the candle-lit neighbourhood restaurant which is busy for a Wednesday night – around two thirds full – and wonders quite why he is here. 'Because you need to get yourself out there,' Nina has told him. Add in

Laura's gentle cajoling to get back on the apps and the hovering threat of litter pick singles and he wonders if he should have a T-shirt printed with the slogan I AM ABSOLUTELY FINE THANK YOU. And although it's ridiculous – and this is only a casual date – he finds himself wondering what Mathilde would make of Kim if she ever met her. And this leads to him picturing Celia on Sunday, kindly chattering away to Mathilde in her plant room, patiently explaining the things she does there. He shouldn't think this way – viewing any new woman he meets through the eyes of his daughter – but he can't help himself.

'Use your special pillow,' Kim is telling her daughter now, 'and squoosh it with your lavender spray. Have you eaten your almonds?' She grins at Enzo with another eye roll. 'Well, that's good, darling. Nine almonds a day, remember? And your breathing exercises. Don't forget!' Then, meltdown seemingly unmelted, she slips her phone into her bag.

Keen to avoid lurching down the exams route again, Enzo quizzes Kim about her work as a coach, and now the atmosphere eases. 'I love it,' she tells him, 'but at the moment I'm building the business and it's crazy hours. In fact, I'm meeting a client for a session first thing tomorrow morning.'

This, he takes it, is her cue to wind up the evening. 'For a talking session?' he asks, because he still doesn't quite understand what she does.

'A run, actually,' she says, 'with this one. I tailor it to suit the person.' So she does believe that people are individuals and not machines? 'We run together at a pace where we can talk,' she continues. 'It's a great way to work through things – mind and body at the same time. D'you run, Enzo?'

'A bit,' he replies.

She chuckles. 'What does that mean?'

'Well, er...' How should he describe his weekly hoof around the park? 'I guess it's a token effort.'

'You're in decent shape,' she observes, and he reaches for his wine, not quite sure how to react to that.

'I just try not to let things slide too much.' He pauses. 'I really should set up my Garmin watch. Nina and Hayley bought it for me for my fortieth.' He smiles. 'Two years ago, that was.'

'Ah, right.' Her eyes glimmer playfully. 'And it's still sitting there, boxed, in your sock drawer?'

Pant drawer, actually. 'That's about it.' He laughs.

'Haranguing you silently, *"Set-me-up-for-crying-out-loud-it's-not-rocket-science..."'*

'I think you've got CCTV in my flat,' he says, relaxing now.

'Tell you what's the most effective thing,' she says, leaning forward. 'A running buddy. If you ever fancy it, I'd be up for that?'

'You mean, running together?' he asks in surprise.

'Yeah, why not?'

Enzo knows with absolute certainty that she'd be streaking ahead of him and that it would be a humiliating nightmare. But somehow, as they settle the bill – which she absolutely insists on splitting – he tells himself that maybe Nina was right and that he should start getting out there, saying yes to things.

'That was lovely,' he says as they leave the restaurant. 'I'd always wanted to try that place.'

'Yeah.' She sniggers. 'It's finally dislodged the coating of Nina's cheesecake from my mouth lining.'

He laughs and as she catches his eye he thinks, *maybe I was judging her a little back there?* Raising a child is such a personal thing, and he shouldn't have reacted like that, as a teacher with an attitude. He's just out of practice, he decides. Since Janetta-with-the-crisps, he hasn't been on anything remotely resembling a date. And maybe the answer to everything really is a weighted blanket and a handful of almonds?

They hug briefly at the end of the street and Kim smooths down her sleek, dark hair with a hand. Then, with a cheery 'Night, then!' she climbs into her gleaming red Audi and zooms away. Although she'd offered Enzo a lift home, he'd declined politely. Tonight he'd rather walk, and as he strides briskly along the quiet tree-lined streets he tells himself that, as dates go, that wasn't at all terrible. Just a little confusing because what does she think of him really, and he of her?

However, there's one thing he does know. If Kim is planning to put him through his paces, then he'd better up his running game.

27

> I think we should meet up to talk and I propose we do this on neutral ground.

Geoff has messaged, finally. Celia re-reads it several times as if a hidden meaning might float to the surface if she stares at it hard enough. A week after their cinema trip, she is relieved that Amanda is out – on another shopping mission, probably. Because she wants Logan to read it too. With their houseguest here and him hiding away in his room – plus picking up some shifts at a restaurant in the city centre – she feels as if she has barely seen him lately.

'"Neutral ground"?' Logan looks at her and then peers back at the message. 'What does that mean? Switzerland?'

'I assume he means a coffee shop or something,' Celia says.

'God, Mum. Are you going to do that? D'you want to meet up with him?'

'Not really. No, I don't.' She actually wants him to choke on a sausage roll. That would be a fitting end, she thinks. Death by reformed meat product and saturated fat. 'But I'll have to at some point,' she adds. Celia looks at her son, pale as milk, parked at the kitchen table with a slice of uneaten toast in front of him and a knife plunged vertically into an open jar of peanut butter. 'Logan, are you all right, love?' she asks hesitantly.

'Uh-huh.' He shrugs.

Celia studies his face, trying to read his expression. They really do need to have a proper heart-to-heart, but right now she is hardly detecting encouraging vibes. 'I know there's been a lot going on,' she ventures. 'I don't just mean the stuff with Dad. I mean Amanda turning up out of the blue like that. I'm sorry if it's been—'

'Is she staying much longer?' he asks suddenly.

She frowns, startled by his bluntness. 'Erm, I wouldn't imagine so.'

'Haven't you asked her?' His directness is cutting. He doesn't usually speak to her like that.

'Well, no,' she starts. 'At least, not directly. It's difficult.'

'But it's been three weeks now, Mum! Who just turns up and stays with someone for three weeks?'

She opens her mouth to speak but then stops. He's right of course. It's a total imposition. Yet in some ways, for Celia, Amanda's timing was perfect. Although Terri is around, she has a busy work schedule. It's Amanda who's insisted that Celia should still shower and get properly dressed every day, and ask for time off from the shop until she was ready to face customers again.

'I know it's weird,' is all she can say.

'So why can't you just ask her when she's going home?'

Perhaps because I don't want her to just yet? 'I will,' Celia says. 'I promise. But you know, she's actually been a real help...'

'What, by buying you all those clothes?' His mouth sets in a grimace.

Celia winds her hands around her coffee mug. 'In lots of ways, love. But, yes – I have to admit they weren't really me.'

'You wore them, though,' he says – which is true. Dutifully, Celia had allowed herself to be 'styled' for a midweek pub night, and hoped that with each glass of wine her self-consciousness would ebb away a little. Picking up on this, Amanda had promised to 'keep an eye out for pieces that are more you. You're a work in progress,' she'd added with a chuckle.

Celia isn't quite sure how she feels about this. Was Amanda right, in that she won't recognise herself? Surely, after being confronted by Geoff's hairy arse in Ailsa View, the priority is to somehow piece herself back together. But becoming a different person entirely? Celia doesn't know that she's ready for that.

'Amanda's made me a hair appointment,' she adds, trying to lighten the mood.

'What, with that woman you go to?' Sue, he means. She started off as a houseplant customer and for years now she's been giving Celia the same dry cut in a kitchen that always smells of poached fish. As she snips away, she details the current state of her husband's gout.

'No, at a salon,' she replies.

'Why did she do that?'

Celia smiles. 'She said she'd like to see me with a cut with a bit more drama.'

'Haven't you had enough drama lately?'

She laughs, relieved that he can still make a joke, and then turns her attention to the cactus sitting in the middle of the table.

She brought Spike into the kitchen in order to 'get to know him', as she privately terms it. So she can study him in different lights, and at various times of day – because for once, the cause of the problem isn't obvious to her. A week now, she's had him in her care. She has already repotted him but there doesn't seem to be any evidence of under- or overwatering or root rot. Nor can she find any signs of pests or disease. With Enzo and Mathilde due to pop round soon, she was hoping to see a marked improvement and hates to think of Mathilde's disappointment, as if she has failed her somehow.

She needs a flash of inspiration in the form of refined carbs and rummages in the cupboard for biscuits. Syrian pastries aside, Amanda seems to not possess a sweet tooth so there are no fancy treats on that score. Damn, there aren't even any custard creams. Just those cheap pink wafer biscuits that Celia is partial to and which she knows Amanda would recoil from.

She opens the packet and munches several, one after another, then turns her attention to the freezer, tugging open the bottom drawer. 'Oh God. What am I going to do with these?' she says, as much to herself as to Logan.

'With what?' he asks.

She crouches down and peers into the drawer. It's entirely full, packed meticulously to maximise space. 'All these haggis-en-croutes. Remember the luxury snack range they did, trying to tap into a high-end market?'

'No, I don't remember,' Logan says curtly.

'Oh, you must! When they came up with the idea of taking the sausage roll format, re-engineered to encase the hag—'

'Mum, I don't care!' He jumps up, pushing back the chair with a clatter.

Celia stares at him, shocked by his outburst. 'I was only saying...'

'I'm not really into discussing the luxury snack range.'

What's going on here? What is this really about? She shoves the freezer drawer shut. 'Look, I know it's been a terrible time,' she starts. 'I'm sorry that it's your summer, and it's been ruined. Honestly, if I could somehow manage to fix things—'

'You always want to fix everything,' he declares, blue eyes flashing, 'but you can't fix this.'

She blinks at him and tries to steady her breathing. 'I can try, Logan. And I don't want you to worry because I *will* meet Dad and start to sort things out. We need to talk about what we're going to do, to make sure we're secure here in this flat. For the time being, at least. And whatever happens, darling, I promise we'll be all right—'

'Will we though?' he blurts out.

'Of course we will!' And then suddenly his face changes, and from being milky pale, his cheeks flush and she sees that his eyes are wet. 'Oh, Logan. What is it?' She goes to hug him but he shrinks away. 'What's going on, love? What's wrong?'

His mouth twists and he reaches for a pink wafer and snaps it in two. 'This thing with Dad.' The halves of biscuit drop onto the table.

Celia stares at him but he is avoiding her gaze. 'What about Dad?' Now her heart seems to have stopped.

He glances down at the broken wafer, then shoves his outgrown hair from his eyes and, finally, he looks at her. 'I actually thought there was something going on. I mean, I *knew*.'

28

'You knew?' Celia starts.

Logan nods mutely. No further information is forthcoming and now he has turned away.

'How on earth did you know?'

'I'm sorry, Mum. I saw something of Dad's.'

For a moment she can't speak. She doesn't know what to say. All she can think is that he kept something from her. And for how long? 'What was it? What did you see?'

'It doesn't matter. Just forget it.'

'How can I forget it? Tell me, Logan. Tell me now—'

'No!' he snaps and so her brain races to fill the gap. A new tie, she wonders? She mustn't panic. Maybe it's something innocuous like that and Logan spotted the new purchase still in its bag. Geoff still wears one occasionally – he's clinging on to the tradition – whenever he feels the need to emphasise his status and professionalism (for him, the downslide of society began when Tie Rack went bust). Or was it a new shirt, or a pair of fancy underpants? A *date outfit*? A receipt for flowers or a mini shower gel brought home from an illicit encounter at a hotel?

Many years ago, en route to a family holiday in Cornwall, Celia, Geoff and Logan had stayed at a motorway Travelodge. Geoff had gathered up the tiny coffee sachets, the teabags and little packets of oat cookies, stuffing them into his suitcase – stopping short only of wrenching the fixed shower gel dispenser off the bathroom wall.

'Logan, I have to know what it was,' Celia insists. 'Please – just tell me.'

He fiddles with his rumpled dark hair and finally looks at her. She notices a crumb of something caught in it. She often has to restrain from picking bits off him, like a monkey – a speck in an eyebrow, a pillow feather stuck to a sweater sleeve. 'All right,' he murmurs. 'There was, uh… something…'

'What kind of something?'

He stares at the floor. 'Something… in the toilet.'

'What, the toilet here?' she exclaims.

'Yeah?' His look says, *What other toilet would it be?*

'Oh God, Logan,' she murmurs, closing her eyes momentarily. She knows what it was. A used condom. *That's* why Logan hadn't told her; because it could only mean one thing.

Geoff definitely brought that woman here – to their home – while Celia was advising customers on whether a shrug, a capelet or a chiffon bolero would work best with that summer frock. And he'd tried to flush it away – but flushing the loo effectively has never been a particular talent of his. It had bobbed right back up again to laugh at her silly, idiotic face.

Only she hadn't been here, had she? Her son had found it. What has this done to her darling boy?

'When was this?' she asks shakily.

'Erm, a while ago now.'

She winces. 'Can you think when?'

Logan bites his lip. 'February, I think.'

'You *think*?'

'I haven't been making notes, Mum! I don't keep a log!'

She rubs at her face, as if this will help to dissipate the terrible feelings swirling around inside her. 'You were home for a few days then,' she murmurs.

'Yeah, I was.'

'That's four months ago,' she adds. 'And you've known about this all that time.'

Logan shrugs and they slump into a terse silence. So Geoff and that woman must have snuck out from work together during the day, Celia figures. A day when she was working at Elegance and Logan was home from university. She tries to rack her brain as to what he did those few days, and recalls a meet-up with his old friends from the school chess club.

Geoff must get off on the element of danger, she decides, fury surging up inside her now. 'I'm sorry,' she says firmly. 'It sounds like I'm angry with you and I'm not. But I wish you'd told me because that really is disgusting, that you had to see that.'

Now his eyes flicker in confusion. 'I, um... I just fished it out, Mum.'

'You fished it out? What, out of the toilet?'

He nods. 'Yeah.'

'With your *hand*?'

'Yeah!' He looks bewildered now. 'What else would I—'

'You actually touched it? Did you use rubber gloves?'

'No!' he exclaims. Then, in a softer tone, as if she needs careful handling, 'Mum, it was no big deal. I just didn't want you to see it and feel hurt, you know? I didn't know what to do so I decided not to say anything. That's all.'

She looks at her son, trying to make sense of all this, and overcome by an intense rush of love for him. Geoff has often retorted that Logan needs to 'man up' and 'grow a backbone'.

But what had it taken, to do that for her? He'd plunged his hand into the toilet water and disposed of the vile thing in order to protect her feelings. She knows he's an adult, but to Celia he's still a boy. In normal times she loves it when he's home, and not only because it feels as if they're on the same side. She simply enjoys him being around; the way his presence diffuses things as he lopes amiably around the flat. She loves the way Terri comes down and fusses over him, bringing him cake and teasing him about his mycology studies, making terrible mushroom jokes. They are a gang then – a little gang of three – and during those brief periods, Celia feels that she *belongs* here in her own home. That, in fact, there is nowhere else she would rather be.

'Oh honey,' she murmurs. 'I'm so sorry.'

'Mum, really,' Logan says, frowning, 'it was only paper...'

'What d'you mean, it was paper?' Is this what they're made of now? She can't imagine it'd be substantial enough to withstand vigorous activity but then she's never encountered one at close quarters. It was the pill once Geoff came along, and in more recent years, an IUD; he'd never wanted a child of their own together. 'Logan's enough,' he'd insisted, which Celia didn't quite know how to take. Enough in that their little family had felt complete? Or that, secretly, Geoff found him a pain in the arse and didn't want any more like him? Christ, he should count himself lucky if reading a book at a football match is the worst thing he's done!

'It was just something Dad had written down,' Logan says, squashing a pink wafer between finger and thumb. 'And he'd thrown it in the loo.'

She looks at him confusedly. 'What was it?' A list of her failings? A draft letter to a lawyer saying he wanted a divorce? Why hadn't Logan said it was a written thing at the start?

'A poem,' he replies.

'A poem?'

'Yeah.'

'You mean a poem... *Dad* had written?'

He nods, reddening. 'I guess so, yeah...'

'But Dad doesn't write poems!'

'He does, actually,' Logan mutters. 'It was all torn up into pieces but I saw these bits of words—'

'Bits of words? What words?'

'Just *words*, Mum. And I picked them all out and I dried them on my radiator and then I pieced them all together and stuck them—'

'And when you were doing all this *piecing and sticking* you didn't think to tell me?'

'No!'

She stares at him as if he's a stranger to her. Like some imposter Logan who's appeared to mess with her mind. Is this really happening or has all the pink dye in those biscuits altered her brain chemistry? 'D'you still have it?' she barks at him.

He moves away from her, backing up against the fridge. 'No, I don't.'

'You do, Logan! I can tell. Go and get it and show it to me now.'

'Mum, stop this! You're making out it's my fault!'

'No, I'm not,' she cries, feeling wild now. One minute he's telling her it was a condom – hang on, he hadn't actually said that – and now it appears it was romantic verse. 'Was it a love poem?'

'I don't know, I—'

'A limerick?'

'What?'

'You know – "There was a young lady so cute, As tasty as haggis-en-croute—"'

'I can't handle this...'

'Please tell me, Logan. Tell me!' She grabs his arm but he tries to shake her off. She clings on tightly, gripping his hoodie sleeve – 'Get off me!' – and in the scuffle that follows he pulls free and hurries towards the kitchen door. 'You're mad,' he cries out.

'Logan, come back!' It's so shocking to her – that he's about to storm off – that she grabs the nearest object to hand. As Logan is leaving the kitchen she flings the missile at the back of his head.

'Mum!' He whips round to face her, clutching at his scalp as if she'd lobbed a grenade at him. 'You've lost it.'

'Sorry! I'm so sorry,' she cries.

'You *threw* something at me. That's common assault—'

'It was only a biscuit!' *The lightest of biscuits*, she wants to call after him. A flimsy little wafer. But he has rushed off to his room and she knows better than to follow him there.

Instead, she stands in the middle of the kitchen, not knowing what to do next. She is shaking and crying, and when she hears Logan leaving, banging the front door behind him, she feels as if her heart has cracked.

29

"Course you can come,' Enzo tells Laura when she arrives to pick up Mathilde. 'I'm sure she won't mind.' Celia, he means. Their visit to the houseplant hospital last weekend was something of a thrill for Mathilde, and clearly, her mum's interest has been piqued too. Enzo was just relieved that Spike's prognosis wasn't completely hopeless.

He has also been looking forward to seeing Celia again. She's unusual, certainly. On one hand, so bold: the way she'd basically chased them into Benji's, full of apologies after sending him and Saska away that first time. But then at home she seemed sort of reticent, and he'd felt awkward, asking if they could come in. And then again she changed, visibly relaxing as she showed him and Mathilde the magical plant room and demonstrated that thing of massaging the roots. She seemed to open up then, as if she were more comfortable busying herself with a practical task. Happier being around plants than people, perhaps. In truth, Enzo doesn't know what to make of her, apart from that he finds her quite fascinating and unlike anyone he has ever met before.

However, immediately as Enzo, Laura and Mathilde arrive at

Celia's flat, his spirits sink a little. Mathilde has enthused to her mum about the 'organised jungle', not to mention Celia's friendliness and the amazing cake. And this time he senses Mathilde's slight disappointment as Celia beckons them in. Not only in that cake is unforthcoming – she didn't expect it, she knows it's not a cafe – but that Celia's manner is rather brusque.

'Nice to meet you,' she says when Enzo introduces her to Laura. Then it's straight through to the kitchen – seemingly there'll be no plant room visit this time – where Spike is sitting on the kitchen table, still looking somewhat sorry for himself, surrounded by broken pink biscuits.

'Oh dear,' Laura remarks, then looks down at Mathilde. 'Did you think he'd be better by now?'

'Celia said it might take a while,' she says stoically.

'I did say I'd try my best,' Celia says, 'but I can never guarantee that a care plan will work.'

Enzo frowns. 'No, of course not. We do understand that.'

'I'll keep in touch with any progress.' An awkward pause hangs as Celia sets about gathering up the biscuits, dropping them onto a plate and then tipping them into the pedal bin. He catches Mathilde observing this with an inscrutable expression. 'Sorry about the mess in here,' Celia adds. She grabs a cloth and wipes away the scattering of pink crumbs from the table.

He can sense that Laura, too, is surveying the scene, taking it all in. Thinking, *well, this isn't what I expected.* She adjusts her ponytail and glances at the kitchen clock. 'Oh, Mathilde. Your swimming lesson. We really have to dash...'

'Yes, we'd better,' Enzo starts. 'Thanks anyway, Celia—'

'You know what they're like if we're late,' Laura adds, then smiles broadly at Celia. 'Great to meet you and thanks for even trying to help poor old Spike. See what happens when Enzo's left in charge for more than five minutes?' She casts her gaze upwards good-naturedly, and he forces a chuckle as they leave.

Outside the flat, although goodbyes have been said, Enzo is aware of Celia still hovering at the door as if there's something else she wants to tell them. Should they have offered to take Spike off her hands? Or perhaps another customer is due at any moment?

Laura unlocks her car and Enzo hugs his daughter. 'Have a great lesson,' he says.

'Thanks, Dad.' In she hops, and as Laura pulls away, he's already figuring that he'll walk home, and then force himself out for a run in the hope of shaking off the weirdness of that little encounter there. Perhaps they'd built it up too much, he and Mathilde – enthusing about the room in which leaves cascade lushly from shelves stretching up to the ceiling. His daughter's enthusiasm is infectious and sometimes he gets carried away.

No big deal, he tells himself as he starts to stride away down the quiet residential street. Already he's trying to mentally rev himself up for that run.

'Enzo?'

He stops and swivels back. Celia has called him, still standing there in her doorway. 'Yes?' he says.

'D'you have a minute?'

'Um, yes. Of course...' Something's bothering her, he realises – and now it dawns on him what it must be. Why she seemed so uncomfortable in her kitchen today and would hardly look him in the eye.

How dumb of him not to realise, he thinks as he heads back towards her. Of course it's obvious now.

With Mathilde gone, Celia is going to break the news that Spike is officially dead.

30

Everything has a natural lifespan.
Celia tried everything she could, darling.
D'you know, I was thinking we might get another goldfish?

As Celia beckons him back inside, Enzo is already rehearsing how he'll break the news to Mathilde.

'I just wondered if we could have a quick chat.' Celia smiles briefly.

'Yes, of course...' *Here we go*, he thinks with a sinking heart.

Enzo follows her along the hallway and into a neat but rather sparsely furnished living room. Compared to the plant room it feels rather sterile; it's hard to believe that they are part of the same flat. A small, delicate ivy on the bookshelf appears to be the only plant life in here.

Celia motions for him to sit on the pale grey sofa and perches on a high-backed wooden chair. 'I'm just finding it hard to get to the bottom of it,' she starts.

'You mean... the trouble with Spike?'

She nods. 'I've been reading up on it and I feel like I'm not getting any further forward.' A pause, as if right now she's still trying to figure it out. 'D'you know if anything happened? Something to his environment that might have shocked him?'

Enzo frowns, shaking his head. 'Um... no. Not that I know of.'

Celia lets out a sigh, pushing her light brown hair away from her face. When they'd arrived this morning, Enzo had thought she looked a little tired. He'd surmised that she'd probably been out last night – a Saturday night – maybe with the women he'd met on his last visit; the cake baker and the excitable shopper (away from the classroom he's terrible with names). Now, though, he wonders if something has upset her today.

'Erm, I just want you to know there's no pressure,' he starts. 'I mean, I'm sure it's not your top priority anyway. But even so, if you really can't help, then that's totally fine—'

'Oh, no, I didn't say that!' She appears quite taken aback by the suggestion.

'I just meant...' Enzo stops, wondering how to put it now – because somehow this whole cactus situation seems to have spiralled out of all proportion. He should have come clean, the day Mathilde came home from Scarborough, instead of involving Saska, and then Celia, who clearly has a lot on her plate right now.

'Celia,' he starts, 'would you like me just to take him away?'

'Absolutely not,' she exclaims. 'I just need time, that's all. I'm sorry,' she adds distractedly. 'It's just been a bit of a morning...'

He studies her pale, delicately boned face, deciding that what she actually needs is for him to get out of her hair and leave her in peace. But somehow he finds himself asking, 'Are you okay? I'm sorry, I seem to make a habit of showing up at exactly the wrong time...'

'Oh, it's not you,' Celia says quickly, shaking her head. 'It's something else. Logan, my son. We had a bit of an – erm – a thing this morning, that's all. You know how it is.'

'Yes, of course,' Enzo says, although he doesn't know how it is. Not really. He and Mathilde fall out rarely and when they do, it's usually over a silly thing and it blows over quickly. 'Sorry to hear that,' he adds. 'I hope it wasn't anything serious.'

'Well, *he* thinks it was,' she says with some force. 'He stormed out. I don't know where he's gone.'

Enzo shifts forward on the sofa, picturing the tall, gangly young man he'd met briefly. Polite and mild-mannered, he'd thought. Shy with newcomers and possibly only hanging out in the kitchen because there was cake. 'That must be worrying for you,' he suggests.

Celia nods. 'It is.'

'You've tried to contact him, obviously.'

'Yes, lots of times. He won't reply to my texts.'

Now Enzo isn't sure what to do. At school he is pretty adept at helping to unravel the kids' problems and offer support, but this is different. He hardly knows Celia but he *does* know that she is a kind and thoughtful person, from the way she was with Mathilde last Sunday. The way she allowed them into her world like that; he could tell she is used to it being her private space, the way everything is set out meticulously. Yet she seemed in no hurry for them to leave, and that touched him. Now he wants to help.

'D'you think he's gone out for a walk?' he asks. 'Just to clear his head?' Enzo does that himself at school sometimes – just a speedy march around the block following a period with his challenging first years. There's this craze happening right now and he'll be sincerely glad when it's over. The kids are leaning back in their chairs, balancing precariously on the back legs until tipping point happens (this resulted in Toby Watson being rushed to A&E with a cracked head).

'I'm not sure,' Celia says. 'He doesn't really do this, you know? Storm out, I mean. He's not like that. But we had a fight...'

'A fight?' Enzo frowns. 'You mean an *actual* fight?'

'Yes, I suppose it was.' Her gaze meets his and he sees with alarm that her green eyes are glossy with tears.

'Oh God. I am sorry.'

She nods gravely. 'I assaulted him.'

'You assaulted him?' Enzo stares at her. He cannot imagine Celia assaulting an ant.

'Yeah,' she murmurs. 'I just lost it. I've never hit him or anything like that,' she adds quickly. 'I can't remember the last time I even shouted at him. But I just... I just turned into this monster—'

'I'm sure you didn't,' Enzo says firmly.

'I did!' she insists. 'I threw something at his head.'

Enzo looks around the featureless room as he tries to process what she's telling him. 'What did you throw?'

'A pink wafer.'

'A *what*?'

'You know, those biscuits?'

Enzo frowns, shaking his head. He has lived in Scotland for a very long time – fifteen years now – but no, he doesn't know. Now and again the kids at school mention something everyone's intimately familiar with, like some kind of snack they all grew up on, and tease him for not having heard of it. He speaks English so fluently he even *thinks* in English – but maybe he'll never fully belong.

'Those pink wafers,' she reiterates. 'You know, the long rectangular ones?'

Now he pictures the shards of broken biscuit scattered over Celia's kitchen table. 'Uh... yeah. But I can't imagine that hurt him,' he ventures.

'No, but it was the whole thing,' Celia starts, and then it all comes out in a rush: how she and her husband have just broken up. How he's left her for someone – at least she *thinks* he has, there's been no discussion about anything – and how Logan knew about his affair, yet hadn't told her. How he'd been keeping this terrible secret buried inside him for months. Enzo wants to hug her, but of course he doesn't because that would be all wrong. Instead he just listens as confusing details tumble out, about something floating in the loo, and the thing being fished out and pieced back together—

'Celia.' Enzo gets up and touches her arm briefly. 'This all sounds terrible. Really, a horrible ordeal for you and I'm sure it wasn't much fun for Logan either. But we all do things we regret when we're upset.'

He steps back and pushes his hands into his jeans pockets, not sure what else he should do. Celia gets up from her chair, looking around distractedly, as if shocked that she's told him all of this. Regrets it, even. He's not sure. To Enzo, the wellbeing of a cactus no longer seems of any importance of all. 'I'm so sorry,' she says, turning away.

'Please don't be,' Enzo says. 'You have nothing to be sorry for. Honestly.'

'I mean, blurting all that out at you. I don't know what I was thinking...'

'Really, it's fine,' he says truthfully.

She looks at him now and he's struck by how honoured he feels, that she's been able to talk to him. And he doesn't want her to regret that, or to feel embarrassed or bad about it in any way. 'It's good to talk,' he says, realising how feeble that sounds.

'It is.' She nods and then adds, 'Would you have done something like that?'

'Thrown a biscuit at someone? At my child?'

'Not at Mathilde, no,' she exclaims. 'I mean at a fully-grown twenty-four-year-old man, if you were very upset?'

Enzo considers this. 'I guess it depends on what had happened. But if I'd really lost it... then yes. Maybe a *light* biscuit.'

A glimmer of amusement flickers between them. 'Not a Wagon Wheel, then?'

'A Wagon Wheel?' Now he's confused. He doesn't recall his pupils mentioning these.

'It's a large, comparatively hefty chocolate biscuit.'

'Ah.' He smiles.

'I'm sure you think I'm crazy,' Celia adds.

'Of course I don't,' he says genuinely. *Quite the contrary*, he thinks. All of this has been happening to her – whatever it was with the floating thing – yet she's been carrying on, doing her thing, tending her plants. Meanwhile he's been blithely showing up at her flat, expecting her to perform a miracle on a dying cactus that his parents never cared for much anyway. When Mathilde unpacked Spike from her pyjama case, he was fuzzy with dust.

'Things'll get better,' he adds. 'I'm sure of it.'

'I hope so.' She frowns. 'I'm sorry. I haven't even offered you a cup of tea...'

'Or a biscuit,' he says lightly.

She chuckles. 'That could be dangerous.' They look at each other and, although it's not at all awkward, Enzo wonders if he should leave now.

'So, um,' he starts, 'I'm sure you have plenty to get on with—'

'Actually, I think I need to get out of here,' she announces.

He looks at her, confused. 'You mean... move house?'

'Oh no. Nothing quite as dramatic as that. Not yet, anyway. No, I just meant a walk.'

Now she seems more like the Celia who'd shown Mathilde how to massage the roots of a plant. Brighter and warmer and, he suspects, more like the woman she really is.

'Well, I was planning to go for a run,' he starts.

'Oh, you go for your run! Sorry I've kept you by rambling on—'

'You haven't rambled. Not at all. And if you'd like some company on your walk...' He hesitates, wondering if he's overstepped it somehow. 'Then any reason not to run is good enough for me.'

31

'What's mycology?' Enzo asks as they climb the hill towards the flagpole at the top.

'It's the study of fungi and yeasts,' Celia explains, curious to see his reaction. Terri thinks it's funny, Geoff regards it as an affectation – but Enzo just seems genuinely interested.

'Wow. That sounds fascinating. I bet it's applicable to all kinds of careers?' he suggests, and this does surprise her.

'Actually, it is.' She nods. 'It's used in the food business and medicine – obviously that's how penicillin came about – and also in forensic science. You know, by examining fungi on a corpse they can estimate when the person died.' She glances at him, hoping she's not going on, as is her tendency when discussing Logan's field of interest. The two of them can chatter about it happily for hours.

'That's amazing,' Enzo says. 'Does he know what he wants to do after uni?'

Celia smiles at that. They have reached the summit now. The sky is a wash of clear blue and the city is spread out before them, pin-sharp as if carefully drawn in fine pen. She is a little out of breath even though this is her regular walk, her park of choice. The other one, just as close to home, is where crocuses grow in springtime. She stopped going there after the thing happened.

'No, he doesn't know yet,' she says. 'It took him a while to find his feet and a course he loved. But he *does* love it. He was planning to do some volunteering at a mycology study centre in the Lake District this summer, but I'm not sure if that'll work out now.'

'I hope it does.'

Celia looks at Enzo, glad now that he opted to accompany her rather than go for his run. He was right, she does have plenty to get on with at home: a whole bunch of repotting, composts to blend and customers to email with updates. Plus yesterday a fragile orchid was brought to her by an elderly neighbour, a gift from her daughter who now lives in Australia. The fact that it was an ordinary supermarket orchid was irrelevant. It's obviously very special to her, and Celia needs to get to the root of the problem.

'This view's amazing,' Enzo announces.

'It's incredible,' Celia agrees.

'I really should come up here more often.' They find a vacant bench and sit side by side, and the conversation turns back to Logan. 'Would he have gone to a friend's, d'you think?' Enzo asks.

'There's a small group he still keeps in touch with,' Celia replies. 'School friends. Chess club guys. But I'm not sure they're the kind of friends he'd go to if he was upset.'

She pulls out her phone. Still no messages and no missed calls. She has already fired off several:

> Are you okay?

> I'm so sorry, love.

> Please call me.

She slips her phone back into her pocket, keen to turn the conversation towards Enzo and his life. Whatever his situation may be – whether he's with Mathilde's mum, or that auburn-haired woman he first appeared with on her doorstep – she is certain that it is entirely functional while hers is most definitely not.

'So, how about you?' she asks lightly. 'How long have you been in Scotland?'

'Fifteen years,' he replies. 'I met Laura on a walking holiday in France and we ended up back here in her home city.'

'Right.' How wholesome, she thinks. How delightfully normal.

'We're not together now,' he clarifies, 'but we see each other a lot, obviously, with Mathilde.'

She nods, considering this. 'And that works?'

'Oh, yeah, we're pretty good.' His smile is warm and his deep brown eyes, fringed by long dark lashes, catch the morning sun. He really is very handsome, Celia decides – and so easy to be with. And how many men would have been up for a walk together after she'd splurged all that stuff about the pink wafer assault, and the torn-up toilet poem? He genuinely seems to care, which still baffles her a little as she barely knows him. Yet she can tell he's a good dad, and imagines that he's popular with his pupils and fellow teachers and also that he cannot possibly be single. 'I mean, we're mostly good, when I'm not killing plants and pets,' he adds.

'Pets?' she exclaims.

'A goldfish, I'm sorry to say. Mathilde's goldfish.'

'Oh no. But I'm sure that wasn't deliberate.'

Enzo grimaces. 'Still a bit awkward, breaking the news.'

'I'm sure!' They exchange a smile that lifts something in her, and in the easy lull that follows she enjoys the sunshine warming her face. She's wondering again about the woman he was with, that first day he showed up with Spike. Celia seems to have spilled out a huge amount of information to him about her own life, some of it extremely personal – which is totally unlike her. In fact, it's never happened before, apart from with Terri, whom she'd trust with her life. And now she's curious to know more about Enzo.

It takes a few moments for her to rouse the courage to ask. 'And the person you came round with,' she starts, 'that first time you brought Spike to me? I'm sorry, I don't know her name—'

'That was Saska.' She glances at him expectantly. 'She'd heard about you,' he adds. 'I think you're quite famous in plant circles around here. Is that right?'

'Oh, I don't think so,' she says dismissively.

'She said you're a genius with sickly houseplants.' He grins. 'No pressure!'

'I'm terrified now.' She laughs.

'Anyway, it was Saska's idea that we burst in on you like that without an appointment,' Enzo adds.

'There's no need for an appointment,' she says. So they're a couple, she surmises. The way he dropped in the 'we' there. Celia has been a 'we' for a very long time and the realisation that she very well might not be any more triggers a flurry of panic in her. However, it soon subsides as they make their way back down the steep curve of the hill, and now she is readying herself for having a proper talk with Logan. If he's home, that is. It needs to be face-to-face. She's sure he won't be thrilled, but now she feels stronger and also *lighter* somehow, and prepared for it. If Amanda is home, she plans to take him out for a coffee, just to grab a little space. She'll apologise, of course, but then let it go. It was only a wafer, she reminds herself. Not a Wagon Wheel. Nor one of those tins of shortbread petticoat tails that her mum always has in.

'I hope you feel a bit better,' Enzo remarks with a glance.

Celia smiles, grateful now that he's shown up today – not at a bad time, after all. The perfect time, actually. 'Thanks. I do – much better.' She pauses, then adds, 'It can feel quite claustrophobic sometimes. Being in the flat, I mean. Since it happened.'

They stop and Enzo seems to be studying her face. 'Since your fight with Logan?'

'No, since...' She stops. It's ridiculous, even thinking of going into all this. 'Since I caught my husband with his other woman.'

He gasps at this. 'You actually caught him?'

'Yes, I did.'

His mouth twists. 'At your flat?'

'No, in a caravan he's inherited from his dad.'

Enzo exhales slowly, shaking his head. 'I am sorry, Celia...'

She shrugs, trying to normalise herself, like all of these people enjoying the park on a sunny Sunday morning. Dog walkers, runners, young families with kids. 'The worst thing is, you feel like such an idiot for not knowing. Isn't that weird, when there are so many bigger things to worry about?'

Enzo's kind brown eyes are full of concern. 'You're right. That really is the hardest part.'

Celia catches a look then, gone in an instant. He gets it, she realises. He understands. Because something – not as dramatic, perhaps, but something all the same – has happened to him too.

'When you *know*,' she continues as they stroll on, 'you realise how obvious it's all been. And what a colossal fool you've been not to see it. Because anyone else would have – I mean, anyone with their eyes open and their wits about them.'

'Hey, you're not the one at fault here.' A tennis ball rolls towards them. Enzo picks it up and throws it in an impressive arc towards an excitable terrier. 'And surely,' he adds, 'you shouldn't need to have your wits about you with someone you love?'

She laughs dryly as they leave the park and head down one of the grander roads in the neighbourhood. The tenement flats have small, neatly tended front gardens and Celia catches the scent of rosemary as they pass. This isn't her usual route home, and within minutes they've found themselves amidst the vibrancy of the main shopping street. There are numerous bustling coffee shops and vintage boutiques. A record shop's window is filled with seventies-inspired T-shirts, embellished with sequins and the slogan DISCO.

She should come here more often. Somehow her life has become terribly small. Celia thinks of Terri and their beloved pink CD, the one Geoff has banned her from playing at home. Geoff who doesn't enjoy music especially. Not pop nor rock nor anything at all. It's bizarre. To Celia, that would be akin to not liking food or air. Her love of an exuberant disco track kicked off with Amanda, back when they were kids, dancing at night in her bedroom. It filled her head, drowning out the sounds of her mum stumbling into the nest of tables or trying to coax Barry the car salesman into the cupboard under the stairs.

Having reached the end of the street, Celia and Enzo prepare to part ways. 'Thank you,' she says warmly. 'That was great. You've really helped to clear my head.'

'No, thank *you*,' he says lightly.

Celia smiles. For what, she's not sure. For getting him out of going for a run? 'It was really good to talk,' she adds.

'Any time,' Enzo says lightly.

'Same for you. I mean, if you'd like to bring Mathilde round to my place again—'

'She'd love that. Thank you.'

'I'll get in a better class of biscuit next time.'

Enzo laughs, and then Celia notices a tall, athletic-looking woman jogging on the opposite side of the street. *How do some women manage to look so good while they're running?* she muses briefly. Celia runs for a bus and feels like her face is going to explode. Yet this woman looks perfectly poised in a turquoise vest and matching shorts as she crosses the road towards them.

Now Celia realises Enzo's demeanour has switched, and that the woman has raised a hand in greeting. 'Hey!' She stops and beams at Enzo. 'How are you?'

'I'm good,' he says, seeming a little flustered. Celia takes in the woman's healthy flush, her sinewy arms and straight-cut fringe which appears entirely unruffled by running. She tugs out her earbuds and looks expectantly at Celia. 'Erm, Celia, this is Kim,' Enzo adds.

'Hi.' Celia smiles.

'Hi.' Kim looks back at Enzo with a smirk. 'Lovely day for a run, Enzo. Perfect conditions, I'd say!'

It's as if she's teasing him, Celia thinks. Is she a friend, a neighbour, or what? 'It's perfect,' he agrees with a nod.

'Unleashed the Garmin yet?'

'I'm building up to it.' He chuckles at what's obviously a private joke, and Celia is still wondering what their connection might be.

'It won't do you any good stuck in the drawer,' Kim chastises him.

'No. No, I'm aware of that.' He smiles awkwardly.

What's a Garmin and what's it doing in a drawer? Celia realises she should know about these things.

'Well, good to see you.' Kim beams. 'And nice to meet you, Celia. Enjoy the sunshine!' And with that she's off, bounding lightly along the street.

Now Celia is aware of an uneasiness between them. 'D'you know, I really should get back,' she says quickly.

'Oh, okay. Well, good luck with everything,' Enzo says.

'Thanks.' She smiles briefly as they part ways, suddenly relieved to be on her own again, instead of thrust into awkward situations with strangers.

Her plant room is calling – *that's* her comfort zone – and now Celia wants to be there more than anything.

And if Logan is home, that really will be the icing on the cake.

32

There's no Logan at home. Just Amanda busily unpacking more new purchases at the kitchen table. 'Hey, where've you been?' she asks.

'Out for a walk,' Celia replies.

Amanda gives her a curious look. 'Just a *walk*-walk?'

'Yes,' she says with emphasis. 'What other kind is there?'

'Just...' She smiles. 'Just... you look like something's happened.'

They've barely seen each other for twenty-five years and Amanda can read her mind now? 'Nothing's happened,' Celia says breezily, peering closely at Spike in the hope of detecting an improvement. Tea, she's thinking. She has a plethora of tea therapies up her sleeve that she's still experimenting with, having noted encouraging results with other more amenable succulents. She turns back to Amanda. 'Okay, I went for a walk with Enzo.'

'With *Enzo?* Cactus-Enzo?'

'Yes.' Celia smiles. 'Just up to the flagpole and back.'

'Right!' Her brows rise and she looks quite delighted by this news. Celia, out walking with a man! Taking the air! 'Did he just... come round? Or what?'

'Yes, with Mathilde and Laura this time. That's Mathilde's mum...'

'Oh, so you all went together?'

'No, just me and Enzo,' Celia replies, filling the kettle now as if there is nothing notable about that. And there isn't, she tells herself. It was just a walk and a chat and it was lovely, and she'd started to think she might have made a new friend until he seemed a bit awkward when they ran into sporty Kim. Now all Celia is concerned about is the whereabouts of her son.

'So just the two of you?' Amanda reiterates.

'Yes.' Celia shrugs.

'Is he with Mathilde's mum? I mean, are they together?'

'No, they're not.' Celia is keen to veer off the subject now. 'They're good friends, I think.' She pauses and adds, 'The first time he came round he was with this other woman, Saska. And then today we ran into this *other* woman called Kim, who seemed to, I don't know...' She blows out air. 'It just felt a bit funny. That's all.'

Amanda seems to be studying her. 'So he has women friends? That's allowed, isn't it?'

'Of course it is! Amanda, I don't even know him. I'm just saying.' Celia doesn't actually know *what* she's saying. Just that her senses are up and she wants to move the subject on to something else.

'You think he's a bit of a player?' Amanda ventures. 'I don't get that feeling...'

'Well, who knows? I don't really care,' Celia says firmly.

Amanda gives her an exasperated look, and then seems to catch herself, and her expression softens. 'Anyway, was he upset about the cactus?'

'He was okay, actually.'

'Oh, that's good. He seems nice,' she adds lightly, which Celia chooses to ignore. 'So, what d'you think?' Amanda is holding up a dress now; one of her new purchases that's notably out of place in the shabby kitchen. 'Don't you just love it?'

'Oh, that's gorgeous,' Celia enthuses. The fabric is floaty and patterned with tiny flecks of greens and blues – like water, she thinks. Water with sunlight dancing on its surface. It's knee-length and sort of flippy – possibly slightly twenties-style? – and bias-cut. She's picked up the terminology from the boutique. 'You'll look amazing in it,' she adds.

Amanda beams at her. 'It's not for me. It's for you.'

'Oh no,' Celia exclaims. 'I can't have that.'

'Celia's, it's yours,' Amanda says firmly. 'Go and try it on. I need to see you in it.'

Celia's heart sinks. She's not up to this right now – being Amanda's pet project. 'It *is* lovely,' she starts, 'but—'

'I promise, it wasn't expensive,' Amanda insists.

Now Celia feels guilty and is yearning to hide away and tend to her baby spider plants. They're ready to be potted up now. 'You're incredibly generous,' she says, 'but honestly, you have to stop buying me so many things. I don't expect it, you know.'

Amanda regards her steadily. 'I know you don't. But you've put me up here, all this time—'

'You don't need to *pay* me for that.' Without thinking Celia crosses the kitchen towards Amanda and hugs her. 'You don't think that, do you?'

'Of course I don't.' They pull apart and Celia is taken aback to see how emotional her friend looks.

'It just feels like a fair exchange, that's all.' Amanda raises a bright smile, a *TV smile*, and Celia wonders – if it really feels like an 'exchange' to her, then what is Amanda gaining by being here? Because when she'd shown up on her doorstep, she'd claimed she just needed 'a little break' – and by anyone's standards, three weeks is a lengthy stay.

It's not that Celia minds any more, or even that she did at the start, once she'd recovered from the shock. And they have settled into a rhythm now. Amanda has found a Pilates class and her rampant shopping habit often lures her out of the flat. So they're not exactly under each other's feet. What Logan feels about her being here is another matter, but who knows what he really feels about anything? Celia tried to talk to him and look what happened there.

'So you like the dress?' Amanda prompts her.

'Of course I do. It's gorgeous.'

'I've got it right this time, then?'

Guiltily, Celia had given her the previous purchases back.

'I love it,' she says. 'But where would I wear it?'

'That's not the point.' Amanda smiles. 'You know what I always used to say to my ladies?'

'Your ladies?'

'My ladies on *Look for a Lifestyle*,' Amanda confirms. 'Those timid ladies who were terrified about appearing on live TV. You know what I'd always tell them? That if you have the outfit, then the occasion presents itself.'

Celia smiles. 'D'you really think it works like that?'

'I do! You look in someone's wardrobe and it tells you *everything* about their life. C'mon – let's have a look through yours.'

Celia hesitates. All she really wants to do is make contact with Logan, and brew a pot of strong Darjeeling tea for plant-resuscitating purposes. 'Okay then,' she says with some reluctance.

As they go through to her bedroom, she fills Amanda in on

the pink wafer assault. 'Celia,' she says firmly, 'that was *not* assault.'

'What was it then?'

'That was just you losing your shit for one *minuscule* moment – and it's about time, if you don't mind me saying. It was high time for your shit to be lost. You've spent your whole life keeping your feelings battened down, not letting anything out.'

'Have I?' Celia exclaims. What does Amanda know about her life?

'I shouldn't have said that,' she says quickly, cheeks flushing now. 'But yes. I think what you did was totally justified.'

Still somewhat stunned, Celia opens her flimsy wardrobe that leans slightly to the left. She steps back and Amanda grins at her before delving in.

Although Celia doesn't understand the point of this, she is curious to discover precisely what Amanda is looking for and whether she'll announce that its entire contents should be burnt. She's certainly *fiery* today as she flips through trousers and skirts, and then moves to the shelves where there are neatly folded sweaters, sweatshirts and tops.

Finally, Amanda stands back. 'There's a lack of colour here,' she announces. 'In fact, I don't see any colour at all.'

Celia thinks of the shameful red shoes, stashed away at the bottom of the wardrobe in their box. 'Grey is a colour,' Celia says. 'So are black and navy—'

'I mean *colour*-colour,' Amanda scoffs. 'And I'm getting the feeling of everything being a bit... basic. Practical, I mean. Worn for doing a job.'

'Well, that's exactly what it is,' Celia points out. 'I'm either tending the plants or working at the shop. That's my life.' Her statement seems to shimmer between then. 'It's the look for my lifestyle,' she adds, forcing a smile.

Amanda smiles too, and then goes to fetch the flippy dress from the kitchen and again orders her to try it on.

Celia picks up the fragile, beautiful thing, about to take it through to the bathroom. She is a communal changing-room avoider, not a fan of stripping off in public. On the rare occasions when Geoff seemed to notice her body, he seemed somehow disappointed, as if it had fallen short of his expectations now the wrapping was off. But Amanda isn't 'the public' and she's certainly not Geoff. So, as her friend continues her inventory of her wardrobe, Celia pulls off her trousers and top and slips the dress on, and before she's even glanced in the mirror she can tell that it's not just a dress, but *the* dress – for an occasion that has yet to happen.

Amanda springs around to face her and gasps. 'Oh, Celia. My God. I wish you'd worn that to my wedding—' Her hand flies to her mouth. 'Not that you didn't look *great* that day…'

'I wish I had too.' Celia smiles.

Amanda appraises the dress, stepping back and studying Celia from all angles, approvingly. 'I love it. This is so you, y'know – this silhouette.'

Celia has never thought of herself as having a silhouette.

'Would you have put me in this on *Look for a Lifestyle*?' she asks.

'Definitely!' Amanda throws her arms around her and grins. 'Because I can tell you something, Celia Bloom. Your lifestyle is going to change.'

33

'Feeling all right there?' Kim asks.

'Fine!' Enzo replies with as much enthusiasm as he can muster.

'You're doing great!'

He supposes he must be, if not collapsing onto the ground counts as 'great.' 'A little light jog', she'd promised when they'd been messaging. They'd start gently – nothing too strenuous. 'Don't want to put you off!' Enzo reckons this definitely contravenes Advertising Standards because they are *hill* running. Actually running – not jogging – up the steepest hill for miles around. To Enzo this seems unnecessary as the park has plenty of flat bits too. Flat bits that typically suffice whenever he runs normally.

'It's so much more beneficial than running on the flat,' Kim announces.

'I'm sure it is,' he agrees, although Enzo wonders whether the science backs this up. He was wrong to imagine that she'd streak ahead, a dot in the distance, laughing to herself about his shoddy performance. What she's doing is *slowing* her pace with much deliberation – in the way that Zain and Marianne do whenever they're walking their little dachshund (Enzo has accompanied them on some of these walks. While he's not stopping to sniff every tree and pee against it, he's aware that he's the sausage dog in this scenario).

Briefly, with the flagpole in view, he visualises his cosy living room where he'd normally be on a Thursday evening, lesson planning or marking probably, if he weren't 'utilising the muscle groups that flat running doesn't reach.'

It's not once that they're doing this circuit but *three times*. To Enzo that feels overly harsh – especially as some weird geographical shift appears to be happening, in that the hill seems about ten times longer when they're going up it than when they're heading back down. *It's the same fucking hill! How can this be?*

'A lighter step,' Kim instructs him. 'Lean *into* the hill—' hang on, if he does that much more, won't he topple over? '—and let your body weight roll over the entire length of your sole.' To think he'd assumed that running was a matter of simply putting one foot after the other. 'You're doing really well!' she reiterates, flashing a teeth-baring smile and hardly breaking a sweat while Enzo is conscious of his ancient running top adhering claggily to his torso. '*Really* well done,' Kim announces as, finally, they reach the top.

'Thanks.' He forces a grin as they circuit the hilltop and then make their way back down to the bottom again. That's better, the downwards bit – as long as his knees don't crumble.

'What we'll do,' Kim tells him as they canter onwards, 'is increase the number of circuits each time we come out.' Like, do more than three? Is he really up to this again, let alone an extended version? 'Because with all your flat running,' she continues, 'you haven't been building all-round stamina. So that's what we're going to focus on, all right?'

'Right,' is all he can say to that. He's aware that he should be grateful for her having hauled him out – that her clients pay good money for this – yet Enzo notices that Kim is talking about 'all your flat running' in the way that she might say 'all your beer drinking' or 'all that cocaine you stuff up your nose.' As if it were a *vice*. Surely flat running is better than no running at all?

They're heading for the park exit now, passing normal runners jogging on horizontal ground. Last time Enzo was here was with Celia, and how different that had felt, even though it had ended rather awkwardly. His fault, of course. That stark introduction: 'Celia, this is Kim.' It's been niggling him and he's not entirely sure why. Celia probably hasn't given it a second thought – not with all that stuff going on in her life. Yet the way she'd shared it all, about her unfaithful husband, the caravan, the biscuit-flinging – there had definitely been a feeling of trust there. And he knows now that he wants to see her again to check she's okay; that *they're* okay as friends. But what can he do? He can't keep popping round to check on Spike's progress. If there isn't any, that'll wear pretty thin.

Now he and Kim have left the park and are running along a residential street. His spirits sink as he spots a couple of his pupils ambling towards them; one smoking, one vaping. If it weren't too late he'd have pulled his running top up over his head but the boys have seen him too. 'Keep going, Monsieur Fontaine!' There are loud, barking laughs – the kind of laughs that only ever shoot out of teenagers' mouths – and only when he sees the end of his street do his cringes subside.

'Slow down to a brisk walk,' Kim instructs. 'Let your heart rate return to normal.'

'I'm not sure that'll ever happen,' he jokes.

She smiles and stops, checking her sports watch. 'Remember to get yours set up for next time.'

He hesitates and she catches this. 'That is, if you want to go out again? I was thinking Saturday morning. I have a slot then, nine-thirty—'

'Oh, there's this thing then.' It has sprung into his mind like a gift. 'This community thing I help with sometimes,' he explains.

'What's that?'

'Just the weekly litter pick to tidy up the streets.'

'Oh, you do that, do you?' Kim grins. 'Good for you!'

'Mathilde likes it,' he says truthfully.

'Right!' She nods. 'Well, enjoy yourself. And if you change your mind, you know where I am.' And with that she scampers off at twice the speed of their run together. In fact, Enzo would describe it as a sprint.

* * *

By the time Saturday comes he has decided that the worst that could happen is that Celia won't be persuaded to join them. But that's fine, he figures, as he and Mathilde stop off at the corner shop. He's aware that grappling bin bags of rubbish isn't everyone's idea of a fun weekend activity, and actually he just wants to see her.

'What d'you think she'd like?' he asks as he and Mathilde browse the packets of Super Noodles and a rather wizened selection of vegetables.

'Biscuits?' she suggests. 'Or a cake?'

His gaze rests upon the packets of pink wafers and he smiles. 'You choose.' And so, with a distinctly corner-shop variety biscuit box, they head towards Celia's place.

On the street corner an elderly woman is playing a wheezy

old accordion. They stop to listen, and as he fishes for change – Mathilde always wants to give buskers money – he wonders if this is a mistake, and that it'll seem weird to Celia, them showing up out of the blue when he could have texted. But he shakes this off and tries to assume a breezy demeanour as he presses her doorbell.

However, it's not Celia who answers the door but Amanda, her TV presenter friend whom he's gathered from Mathilde is pretty famous. 'Oh, hi!' She is all big bright smiles and pleasantries. 'I'm sorry, you've just missed Celia. She's in town having her hair done.'

'Oh, no problem.' Enzo smiles. 'We're just off to the litter pick and wondered if she might like to join us sometime.' He hands her the box of biscuits. 'And we wanted to drop this in to say thanks…'

'For taking care of Spike,' Mathilde offers.

'Oh, thank you.' Amanda takes the box and glances down at it briefly as if unsure of what it is.

Enzo clears his throat. 'I just, erm, wondered how Celia's doing?' he says, adding, 'We had a chat last weekend. I just, er—'

'She's doing great,' Amanda assures him. 'She's been back working at the shop this week so that's a good sign, don't you think?'

'Definitely. That's good to hear,' he says.

'Yeah.' She nods, glancing down at the biscuit box again. 'This is very sweet of you. I'll tell her—' She breaks off at the sound of a trilling mobile somewhere in the flat. 'Sorry, better get that—'

'No, of course. Thanks anyway,' Enzo says quickly, feeling a little silly now at having expected Celia to be there. She's busy, he reminds himself. She doesn't have space in her life for cleansing the neighbourhood with Saska's gang.

34

'I told you, Jasper,' Amanda announces, pacing around with her phone clamped to her ear. 'I'm taking care of Celia.'

'But how long for?'

'I'm not sure. There's no set timescale on grief, you know? Or on recovery after being cheated on. So I'm just taking things as they come—'

'Three weeks you've been away now—'

'Not *quite* three weeks—'

'Let's not quibble,' he snaps. 'You keep saying you'll be a little bit longer and on it goes. What's really going on here, Amanda?'

Her jaw tightens as he continues in this vein: about how she took off to Scotland with virtually no warning and how he was barely aware of 'this Celia' before her trip. Amanda can understand that he'd forgotten she'd been at their wedding – their introduction had been hurried – but really! Celia is her oldest friend, and Jasper expects her to be fascinated with the minutiae of *his* friends' lives.

Amanda's right ear is throbbing with it all as she moves to

Celia's living room window. A bunch of people are out there now, milling around in fluorescent yellow tops. At first she thinks it must be workmen, or people doing community service. As far as she's concerned, having to wear a hi-vis waistcoat-type thingie would be punishment enough for any crime. Seeing them en masse like this is really hurting her eyes. But then she realises it's the litter pick crew, and now she spots Enzo, actually looking quite *fetching* in his, if such a thing were possible.

'The thing is,' she tells Jasper in her most patient voice, 'when I came up here I didn't know Celia's husband had been shagging someone else.'

'Well, no, obviously,' Jasper huffs.

Amanda continues to watch the litter gang, specifically Enzo. She knows Celia has been through hell lately. But surely, making a new friend like him has to be a tiny compensation for catching Geoff with his pants down? Shame there aren't men like that in *her* life, accompanying her on walks and popping round with funny little boxes of biscuits. Men who happily spend their Saturday mornings picking up filthy rubbish rather than moaning about how 'abandoned' they feel.

'I'm sorry if you're miserable,' she says, trying to dredge up some sympathy now. 'Honestly, I promise I won't be here for much longer.' There's a pause, which Jasper is supposed to fill by saying, *Good, because I miss you so much, darling.*

'Good. So you'll be back in plenty of time for the install? I could do with your help.'

'The install?' she repeats. 'What d'you mean?'

'Installing my exhibition.' *Obviously* is the implication.

'You're having an exhibition?' she exclaims.

'Yeah!' He sounds excited now, and she's conscious of a tiny prickle of guilt.

'Wow. That's brilliant. How did that come about?'

'There's just been growing interest,' he says, affecting a blasé tone now.

'So...' she starts, still taken aback. 'You mean it's a solo show?'

'Yep, just little me, with gallery representation!'

'An *actual* gallery?'

'Yes!' A dry laugh. 'Don't sound so shocked.'

Amanda exhales and sweeps back her hair with a hand. 'A London gallery?'

'Of course. Where else?' As far as Jasper is concerned, no other UK city is worth bothering with.

This new information is a little overwhelming and now she wonders if she should have been more tolerant of Jasper's 'work'. Perhaps those potato prints are actually really good, and she was showing her ignorance in not appreciating them?

'Well, I'm really happy for you,' she says truthfully.

'Thanks, babe.' She can sense him smiling and this triggers another guilty twinge. 'It's a really great location,' he adds. 'It's going to be a real breakthrough for me...'

'So when does it open?'

'July the fourth,' he announces. 'Private view, 7 p.m.'

'Independence Day,' Amanda remarks.

'Yeah.' He chuckles. 'The start of my new career as a fully independent artist. I'm cutting ties with Ollie,' he adds.

'Really?' she exclaims. In recent times, Ollie has been her husband's agent too. Naturally, Amanda made the introduction, employing maximum charm in order to persuade him to take Jasper on. However, whenever she speaks to Ollie, Jasper's name never comes up. It just lurks there on the periphery – the great unmentionable – like an embarrassing stain.

'Yep, I don't need him,' he says breezily. 'Time for a whole new chapter, darling. I'm ready to make that leap.'

Amanda turns this over in her mind: the fact that he no longer considers himself an actor (and it was Jasper-the-actor whom she'd fallen in love with) but a fully-fledged artist now. Reluctantly, she decides that this is probably a wise move. After all, he was only really cast for his pretty-boy looks. She can admit to herself now that, on that cop show, he displayed all the acting ability of a bedside cabinet.

Conversely, being offered a solo exhibition in London is a *huge* deal, and she should be there with him, praising his splodgy vegetable prints and ensuring that he has an endless supply of Maris Pipers. Although distinctly unkeen on being involved in the 'install' of the exhibition (she envisages hammers, nails, manicure ruined), she is not averse to being there at the opening night, glass of wine in hand. Is there time to have her highlights done, she wonders? Already she is mentally appraising her wardrobe back home, figuring out what she might wear. Then she catches herself because of course, this will be *Jasper's* big night – not hers.

Perhaps finally she can be proud of him. Does this mean there may be hope for their marriage after all?

She glances out again and sees Enzo's daughter, grabbing at a drinks can with her litter picker stick. What's her name again? Something pretty and French, she remembers now. Mathilde, that's it. And here comes Enzo again with a rubbish sack. It strikes her again how terribly handsome he is. Not in a great-angles-for-camera way, just naturally attractive *in real life*. She gets the feeling that it's never occurred to him how good-looking he is.

Jasper is still chattering on about his art but Amanda's attention has wandered. Now Enzo is in conversation with a striking-looking woman with long crinkly reddish hair. She hennas it, Amanda reckons. That trailing cheesecloth skirt too, and possibly her patterned shirt worn open over a vest. She's 98 per cent henna, Amanda estimates. If she'd had her on *Look for a Lifestyle* she'd have advised her to ease off on the plant dyes.

'I feel terrible,' Jasper announces.

'Huh? What about?' Amanda's attention snaps back to her husband.

'I haven't asked how Celia is.'

'She's doing okay,' she replies. 'I mean, she's a lot better than when I arrived.'

'Glad to hear it.' Jasper seems to be considering this – that Amanda really has been needed here. 'It might sound harsh,' he adds, 'but she will need to stand on her own two feet at some point. I mean, I think it's amazing, how supportive you've been...'

Celia senses a small glow of pride. 'I'm just doing what any friend would—' She breaks off as her phone bleeps with an incoming call. She checks it quickly and sees her agent's name. 'Sorry, hon. Ollie's calling me—'

'Just before you go. You will come back for my opening night, won't you? *Please*, babe?'

Amanda bites her lip. "Course I will.' Then she accepts the call and clicks on her professional voice. 'Ollie, hey!'

'Hi, darling. Still in Scotland?'

'Yep, I am. Why, has something come up?' *Please say yes,* she wills him. She's hoping that the people who'd approached her some months ago have come back to him again, hoping for a yes. She'd dismissed the new show on which people would confess their 'crimes' – such as using a housemate's toothbrush to shift a stubborn mark off the loo – and to whom she would administer a 'punishment.' Disgusting bathroom behaviour? That wasn't her world at all. Now, though, she'd bite their hand off for that job.

'There is something, actually,' Ollie says.

'"Crime and Punishment"?'

'No, they've got someone else for that now.'

Ouch, that stings – but still, he said there's something. 'So, what is it?' she prompts him.

'A commercial,' Ollie replies.

'Oh, great!' Adverts are generally extremely well-paid. She did a couple back in the day, at her career peak, for hair products and a skincare line. On top of the fee, she didn't have to buy moisturiser for a year. 'What's it for?' she asks.

'It's, er...' Ollie clears his throat repeatedly, as if he has something stuck in it. 'It's for a funeral plan,' he says with artificial brightness.

'*What?*'

'Listen, before you react, before you go off on one—'

'A funeral plan?' Amanda splutters. 'You mean to pay for a funeral before you're dead?'

'Er, I believe that's the idea, yes.'

'And you're sure it's *me* they want?' Ollie must be losing it, she decides. He has dozens of clients on his books, many way older than she is – from steel-haired gazelles to cuddly nana-types. One particular twinkly octogenarian nabs all the best granny roles in the Christmas ads. Rent-a-Nan. Is this Amanda's future? With the money they pay she wouldn't knock it.

'Yeah, they really want you,' he says.

'But I'm forty-three,' she reminds him snappily. Virtually a millennial in a good light!

'Yes, but you fit their profile, darling.'

'The *funeral* profile? How come, Ollie? I thought I was at that difficult in-between age!'

'You are! I mean, you're not. You're not anything—'

'I'm not anything?' With his gallery representation and one-man show, suddenly Jasper seems to be the one with the stellar career.

'I didn't mean it like that,' Ollie says hastily. 'I just meant you're not in any particular box these days. And that's a good thing, darling. Who wants to be boxed in? It means you can stretch in any direction, which is all the better for your career. It means we can put you forward for anything!' *Why aren't you, then?* she fumes. 'And this job...' he goes on.

'This coffin advert,' she snaps.

'*Funeral plan.* Oh, cheer up, sweetie. It's a great market to be in. Trends come and go but we're all going to cark it someday!'

'Ha.' Amanda emits a mirthless laugh. 'Well, there's a cheering thought.'

He sighs audibly. 'Will you at least think about it?'

'I s'pose I'll have to,' she mutters.

'Don't take too long.'

'I won't.'

'Oh, and I do hope things are... y'know.' He affects a caring tone. 'Not so critical up there.'

'What d'you mean?' Amanda frowns.

'Your friend. Your friend who's, uh...'

'She's fine,' Amanda says quickly. 'I mean, she's getting better. Much better—' She breaks off as Mathilde looks round in the street and spots her at the window. She grins and waves, seemingly untraumatized by having that hi-vis waistcoat forced upon her, the poor child.

'Well, that's great,' Ollie enthuses. 'Her treatment's been successful then?'

'It has,' Amanda says, waving back and flashing a big smile. 'She's responded to it incredibly well.'

'Modern medicine really is amazing,' he marvels as the entire litter pick crew seems to pass Celia's window now, all chattering loudly and full of the joys. Maybe that's a job Ollie could put her up for? As a street cleaner? 'Anyway, you're obviously busy there,' he says brightly. 'Sounds like it's all going on. Are you still on the ward?'

'The ward?'

'At the hospital,' he clarifies.

'Um, no, they've let her come home.' In fact, pretty soon she'll be sitting in Glasgow's coolest hair salon, being transformed. Amanda wishes she'd gone with her instead of mooching around here to receive the shittiest job offer of her life. If she were there now, her hair covered in foils, she'd have missed Ollie's call and wouldn't be feeling about ninety years old and a complete has-been.

She stomps through to the kitchen, fills a glass with water and gulps half of it down. *Maybe I'm not drinking enough water,* she muses. *Maybe that's why I've slipped effortlessly into the funeral market.*

Something has switched around here, Amanda realises now. When she'd arrived it was clear that she was needed very much. And that had made her feel good – that she had a purpose again – because back home in London it had started to feel as if she weren't needed very much at all.

Here she has thrown herself into being supportive in the only ways she knows how: by shopping for treats, and encouraging Celia to ditch those terrible sub-Primark drawstring trousers and nana slippers she was sloping about in – convalescence wear – in the aftermath of Caravan Day. But now Celia seems to have made, if not a *full* recovery, then shown more obvious signs of gaining strength than the sorry-looking cactus that's still sitting there on the kitchen table.

'I'm glad things are going so well,' Ollie enthuses. 'So, about the commercial? What shall I say?'

Amanda slugs more tepid tap water, wondering if that press-for-champagne button will ever materialise in her life again, and bangs down the glass on Celia's worktop. 'Tell them I'll think about it,' she says.

35

Celia has decided to walk into town, to settle herself really. She passes the park she never goes to, and then takes the back streets to avoid the main roads. She wants fresh, cool air on this bright summer's day, not traffic rumbling past her.

Crossing the river, she stops part-way over the bridge and looks across the Clyde, at the wide expanse of still water and old and new buildings all jumbled together. At the waterside, a bunch of skateboarders have congregated. She sees a girl doing impressive flips – or whatever they're called – who looks like a slightly older Mathilde.

Celia has thought about Enzo a lot these past few days. How safe she felt with him, even though it's utterly out of character for her to blurt out such personal stuff to a near stranger. However, it's occurred to her that he only suggested that walk out of pity for her, and that makes her shrivel a little inside. And was that sporty Kim person someone he's dating, or has dated in the past? There was definitely a frisson there. Celia doesn't quite understand the situation with Saska either, but one thing she does know is that – adding in Laura, Mathilde's mum – his life appears to be filled with extremely self-assured, not to mention *beautiful* women, and her instinct is to step away and to regard him as just another houseplant hospital customer. Which, of course, he is. A man who happened to show up for a doorstep diagnosis and whom, so far at least, she has been unable to help.

Celia is in the thick of the city centre now, making her way through the busy shopping streets. As a girl she imagined she would leave Glasgow one day, as Amanda planned to. Amanda always did everything first. Off she went to London, for a college course that was swiftly abandoned in favour of a thrilling career in TV. After having her baby, Celia had never again thought of leaving her hometown.

Now she remembers Scott in his living room with the electric fire radiating an intense heat, and what felt like an even fiercer heat coming from inside his unattractive mustard underpants. She hadn't touched him at that point. But she could sense the heat – a man's heat – and then his thing twitched like a hamster in a paper bag and she'd leapt back.

Scott had laughed softly. 'Nothing to be scared of, love.' The kissing had started again and soon, in his bedroom, Celia had remembered her mum's warning about 'never going too far'. When he'd mentioned being infertile he must have assumed – wrongly – that getting pregnant had been her only concern. In fact, it was *all* of it. The whole thing. 'It's all right, love,' Scott had assured her again. 'I can't have kids. No need to worry about that.'

Later, as she'd left Scott's flat, she'd tried to imagine how she would have described it to Amanda, if they'd still been close. Would she have glossed it up, and said it was wonderful? Or told her the truth? Perhaps it was best that they were no longer inseparable as Celia wouldn't have been able to lie.

That afternoon, Celia and Scott hadn't made an arrangement

for their next meeting as they usually did. But still, over the next few weeks, she patrolled the park, expecting to see him, and then one afternoon she took herself back to his street, to his flat.

When she peered into the bleak little kitchen she saw that it looked empty. Scott must have moved out. And a few weeks later she began to feel queasy, and everything seemed to trigger nausea: food frying, the smell of tinned soup, her mum smoking in the kitchen. Yet as her bump grew, Celia also started to experience a sense of peace that she'd never experienced before. Now it was no longer her and her mum and the still-tangible void where her dad had once been. It was Celia and her baby, whom she couldn't wait to meet – because things would be different then.

She remembers how neighbours had descended with gifts of velour sleepsuits and tiny hand-knitted outfits when Logan was born. 'Oh, he's such a beauty!' 'You're going to be such a good mum, Celia. I can see that already.' 'He's a wee darling, and the image of you.'

Logan did look like her – she was thrilled about that – and he still does. They have similar slightly elongated greenish eyes and full lips. Maybe that grated on Geoff, and he felt like the odd one out? Celia strides on purposefully now. As she passes the skateboarders, she pulls out her phone and types a message.

> Hey love I spoke to Gran this morning. Think I might've woken her up. She says you've been staying there? Thanks for keeping in touch btw. Good to know you were OK even if you wouldn't say where you were. Fair enough. We all need a bit of space sometimes.

She pauses, wondering what else to say. She doesn't want to give him a hard time for storming out like that, and he did have the decency to let her know he was all right. Strange that he's at her mum's – they've never been close – but she is his grandma and at least he's close by.

> Hope you'll be home soon. Call me anytime you want to.

She's about to leave it there because Logan teases her about her long, rambling messages when two words are usually his max. But no – she has to share this.

> Just wanted to let you know I'm doing it today. I'm going to Switzerland. Will report back. Xxx

* * *

Celia has to use Google Maps to find the salon where she's booked in for 1 p.m. How funny, she thinks, that Amanda knew about this place when she lives 400 miles away and yet Celia had never heard of it.

As she approaches, she glimpses the young stylists moving around in the bright, airy space and is seized by an urge to turn right back and hurry home again. Because this is definitely a 'space' – not Sue's fishy-smelling kitchen – and Celia doesn't belong in a salon like this. She stops, feeling as sick as the peace lily that was brought to her for emergency care, teetering towards death.

However, she also cannot face the prospect of returning home to Amanda with her hair uncut – not to mention being a no-show at the salon. So she forces herself in through the door, in the way that she has to mentally propel herself up the path towards her mother's house sometimes. And once inside she is greeted warmly, her faded old jacket whisked off her, and shown to a chair.

The place definitely has a buzz, which is how Amanda described it. Striking black and white photographs of modern urban buildings adorn the walls, and Celia's spirits lift at the sight of several *anthurium clarinervium* on a shelf, seemingly in excellent health. She doesn't recognise the music that's playing, but she likes it. It's at once relaxing and invigorating and now she experiences a tiny flurry of excitement as she is led to a basin and her hair is shampooed by a person other than herself.

Celia can't remember the last time this was done for her, what with her and Sue's arrangement spanning a decade or more. Conditioner is applied, and as the young man's hands swirl rhythmically across her scalp, Celia almost forgets that Caravan Day ever happened.

Now she wonders if he has gone into something of a reverie himself, and forgotten to stop swirling, in the way that you can easily forget to stop posting Kettle Chips into your mouth once the big sack's open. However, it's so heavenly that she's happy for it to go on for as long as he's prepared to do it. No part of Celia's body has ever been massaged before – not even by Geoff. Now she realises that this is what it is. In places like this, instead of gouty feet talk you're treated to *a head massage*.

'Thank you,' she says, almost weeping with gratitude when it ends. Amanda has paid for all this upfront. 'An early birthday present,' she insisted. How can Celia ever repay her?

Celia's stylist, Jenna, is from Orkney. She's young and pretty with a choppy dark bob and a silver nose ring, dressed casually in baggy denim dungarees and a white vest. She chats away about growing up on an island while Celia nods and chips in occasionally, thoroughly enjoying herself now.

Eventually they fall into a comfortable silence, and Celia watches through the mirror as Jenna snips deftly. And as the drab locks fall away and she sees a new person emerging.

You won't recognise yourself.

Now much of her hair is lying on the salon floor and what's left is a soft elfin crop. When she came in here she'd felt a little reckless and said, 'Honestly, I'm happy for you to do whatever you think.'

Jenna had looked surprised, but pleased, as if readying herself for the challenge. She'd probably assessed her as a bit mumsy, Celia realised. Someone who normally has her hair cut in someone's kitchen. 'If you're sure?' Jenna asked. 'Okay then. Let's go for it!' And now, having finished, she is holding the hand mirror so Celia can see the back.

She doesn't really care about the back. But she beams a huge smile and says, 'I love it! I really do.'

'I do too,' another stylist calls over. Cropped hair, tattoos covering his muscly upper arms; from what she's noticed of his demeanour she assumes he's the owner. 'That is such a cute cut. You look a million dollars,' he adds.

Celia blushes and smiles and checks her reflection again. Jenna's cut has worked magic, lifting away not just the weight from her but also *brightening* her somehow. She looks almost filtered – but real.

She thanks Jenna profusely and leaves a generous tip, aware of what Geoff would have to say about that. Then she steps out into the cool, breezy summer's afternoon, feeling as if she is ready for anything.

With a little time to spare she wanders through the back streets, stopping off at a funny little shop she pops into occasionally when she wants to try out a new treatment for a plant. She supposes it's a health food shop, a little unkempt and dusty, and she wouldn't like to study the use-by dates on some of the products too closely. However, she selects a few packets and tubs, going on nothing but instinct with a rising sense of optimism filling her heart.

A little farther down the street she is surprised to see that the comic shop Logan loved as a child is still in business. It was always the American superhero comics that he wanted. She'd treat him occasionally, safe in the knowledge that Geoff would have no idea that it had been as pricy as a book. Actually, she didn't care if he found out. It was only a comic, for God's sake.

Celia has read that you take cues on how to raise your kids from your own parents. That you either follow their lead, mining your own upbringing for clues on how to do things, or you go the opposite way, which is what Celia has done – rejecting the example her own parents set. She didn't want Logan to experience things in the way that she had: discovering his mum lying on the floor the morning after a party, surrounded by shattered vol-au-vents. Or mentioning the school trip to Blackpool, knowing deep in his gut that the two steps needed for him to go were insurmountable.

Step One was getting the form signed. Celia could do that; she'd forged her mum's signature plenty of times. But then would come the paying for the trip, and money was always tight. At her primary school there was this club that no one wanted to be a member of: the 'not on the school trip club.' The two or three kids spending the day in a classroom, allowed to play board games in lieu of a day at Blackpool Pleasure Beach, with a resentful teacher keeping an eye on them.

Right from the start, from the moment Logan was placed in her arms, Celia knew she would do things differently. She'd be loving of course, and kind and caring – but also actively involved. She would be part of his life, as much as he'd let her. And so she didn't resent the fact that she was the hands-on parent, the one pushing the swing in the drizzly park, accommodating his numerous food fads and helping him to learn to read and write and just *loving* him.

Her phone rings. She pulls it from her bag, expecting it to be Amanda, demanding a photo of Celia with her new haircut. But it's not Amanda and when she sees Logan's name displayed, her heart soars. 'Hello, love!'

'Hey, Mum,' he says.

All at once she feels choked and yearns to hug him. 'Darling, I've really missed you. Are you okay at Gran's?'

'It's all right.'

She runs a hand back over her hair, still surprised at how different it feels, and manages not to ping questions at him. *Why are you there? Are you still mad at me? When are you coming home?*

'It's nice to hear your voice,' she says, adding, 'You got my message then, about meeting Dad?'

'Yeah, I did.' She can tell he's smiling now. 'That's why I'm calling. I just wanted to wish you luck.'

36

'What did you do to your hair?' Geoff asks.

'I've had it cut,' Celia replies. What does he think? That the sighting of his naked arse caused it to shrink back into her head? She takes the seat opposite him in the rather functional, no-frills cafe.

'Hmm. It's very short.'

'It is, yes.' She turns when the girl comes over, and asks for an Americano. Geoff has a coffee already and a half-eaten plain croissant sits on a plate. *Whoo, buying cafe food,* Celia muses.

It was his choice to meet here. She'd never noticed the place before and right now they are the only customers. She catches him assessing her new look; the feathery crop that shows off what the hairdresser described as her 'lovely neck.' In all of her forty-three years no one has never mentioned Celia's *neck* before. It reminded her that she has one. That, and a silhouette too! Whatever next?

'So,' Geoff says, fingers laced together, 'how have you been?'

'Oh, you know.' Celia observes him coldly, telling herself to stay calm, to be neutral, to not rise to him. 'Fine, really,' she adds. 'Getting on with things.'

'That's good.' He sips his coffee, making the familiar slurping noise that's always made her wince. 'How's Logan?'

'Staying at Mum's at the moment.'

'What?' His brows shoot up. They're different, Celia notices now. Tidier and perhaps a little darker? Has he had them *laminated*? He's definitely done something to them.

'We had a silly tiff,' she says, not wanting to go into it now. 'I think he just needs a bit of space—'

'Must've been desperate to go there.'

'She *is* his gran,' she reminds him.

'Yes, I know, but...' *We know what your mum's like*, his expression says, and the surge of loyalty that rises up in her takes Celia by surprise.

'They're getting along fine,' she says firmly. In fact she'd been relieved, when she'd spoken to her mum, to hear how well they were rubbing along together. Celia suspected she was enjoying having someone around the place.

Now she stirs her coffee unnecessarily and looks at Geoff. All the anger she's been harbouring, all those fantasies about him choking to death on a pastry product – a cheesy bake, the crusty edge of a pie – have dissipated. She doesn't feel any of that now.

She feels nothing, she realises. However, she does want to know the bare facts, in order to piece things together and figure out whereabouts she scores on the idiot-ometer. 'So how long have you been seeing her?' she asks. 'Just out of interest.'

Geoff reddens, and she pictures him as the nineteen-year-old boy who'd shown up to take her out that first time. The petrol station carnations. The fluffy upper lip and troublesome complexion. How her heart had leapt then, that he'd wanted to see her so much, he'd summoned the courage to come round.

She can just about picture him further back, too: the quiet boy in the too-small blazer whom she had barely noticed. Until that time, when Amanda had been given the role of Rizzo in the school production of *Grease*, and she'd caught him staring longingly at her from the front row of the audience. Of course he'd fancied Amanda all along – but then everyone did.

'A while,' he replies, looking down at the croissant. 'I suppose about a year or so.' His gaze rises to meet hers. 'I'm sorry, Celia. I'm not proud of it – I have to tell you that. It just sort of... happened.'

She nods, letting this information form a sort of skin over the surface of her emotions. *About a year.* Wow. So he was seeing her as far back as last summer, when Logan was home, doing his summer job at PPP. Over Christmas, too, when her mum had come over as usual and Celia had tried to trick her with alcohol-free wine: 'What *is* this stuff?' As if she'd served her water from the drains.

Celia is on the verge of winding up this conversation already. Of saying, *Well, that's that then. We've met on neutral ground and I'll quickly have this coffee – actually, no, I think I'll leave it and go home, even though it cost £3.50!* But Geoff leans towards her, forearms on the table. 'I really am sorry, Celia. I'm sorry I've put you through this.'

She clears her throat. 'Can I ask you something, Geoff?'

He nods.

'Is there... a reason why it happened?'

'Well,' he starts, 'I suppose there is, really.'

'And what's that?'

He chews on his bottom lip. 'You've always had your own thing, haven't you? For years now, it's totally dominated your time...'

'What are you talking about?' she exclaims.

'Your plants,' he announces. 'You were always so *busy*.'

'That's not true!'

'Yes it is,' he says firmly. 'You were either wiping down leaves or repotting something, or making up some kind of horrible oil—'

'It's not horrible oil. It's *leaf* oil.'

'Or there were people coming round, your customers, in and out the whole time—'

'There weren't, Geoff! There aren't. You can't say that. You know I've always tried to keep them out of the flat.' This is true, at least when Geoff's been at home. She's tried to shield him from her customers – or actually, she realises, shield them from *him*. That's why she came up with the idea of the doorstep diagnosis. More often than not she can figure out precisely what's wrong there and then. Geoff barely saw anyone at all.

'I'm just saying,' he says with exaggerated patience that makes her want to crack her coffee cup over his head, 'that for a lot of our time together I've felt like I've been at the bottom of the pile.'

She stares at him. 'What pile?'

'*Our* pile! The pile of me and you and Logan. That's what it's been like for me, Celia. With your shop job and the flat being turned into a jungle—'

'But I keep it all in one room!' Well, not quite, but she tries...

'And right from the start,' he goes on, 'Logan was always your priority.'

She gasps at this. 'At the start, Geoff – he was a *baby*.'

'A toddler—'

'Less than one year old! He wasn't even walking. Not even *toddling*. What was I supposed to do? Stick him in a cupboard?'

'The way you've pandered to him...' Geoff shakes his head, as if the time has come to assess her parenting and find it lacking.

Sudden tears sting Celia's eyes. 'Pandered to him? I don't know what you mean! I just wanted to do what was best for him. I honestly don't know what else I was supposed to do.'

Geoff posts the remaining piece of croissant into his mouth and chews it gamely as if it were a tough cut of meat. Has he always eaten like this? She is aware of bile rising, and something simmering unpleasantly in her stomach, heightened by a faint smell of bleach in this otherwise deserted cafe.

'I just want to be honest,' he goes on. 'It's felt like you haven't had a lot of time for me, especially this last year or so.'

Celia is genuinely bewildered. 'I don't know what you mean.'

'Well, what about when my dad died?'

'What?' she exclaims. 'I'm sorry, I thought I was supportive through all that. I was there for you, wasn't I—'

'All those weeks when he was in hospital?'

'I went with you!' she cries. 'Every visit, I was there...'

'Yes, upsetting him,' he snaps. 'Very helpful.'

'Upsetting him?'

'Saying that women aren't a minority—'

Celia splutters. 'Well, they're not, Geoff. Women are *not* a minority. That's just a fact.'

'Yes, but did you have to say that? Jump on your feminist high horse and finish him off—'

'You're saying I *killed* your dad?'

He fiddles with his coffee cup. 'Not exactly, but—'

'And what d'you mean, my feminist high horse?' She is a feminist at heart, of course she is, in that she believes wholeheartedly that women are equal to men. But she's hardly acted like one, has she? She hasn't exactly spearheaded the movement by allowing Geoff to control whatever they did and didn't do, what kind of shower gel they used, and God forbid she bought anything other than the cheapest rancid-tasting orange juice!

'Just what I said,' he mutters.

Celia looks at him dispassionately. The tears that were threatening to spill over have miraculously evaporated, or been sucked back into her eye sockets or wherever it is they go. To think she was so worried about the practicalities; the colossal task of untangling lives that have been tightly bound together. She can liberate an African fig, gently separating its compressed roots – and although this is somewhat trickier, she knows she can handle it.

'What are you doing?' Geoff stares up at her.

'I'm going.' Having jumped up from her seat she delves into her old, worn tote bag, rummaging among her purchases from the health food shop, and pulls out her purse. 'Here.' She slaps down a ten-pound note. 'Don't want you to be out of pocket.'

She turns and marches away, between vacant tables, aware of the woman behind the counter staring at her in surprise. 'It's not that much!' Geoff calls after her.

At the door now she glances back briefly. 'Keep the change,' she says.

37

Suddenly it's as if Enzo isn't in Celia's kitchen but in the house he grew up in on the coast. His parents' house, with the old range cooker and the ceramic food storage jars lined up on the shelf and Mathilde announcing, 'There's a flower! A pink flower!' He remembers his mother's enthusiastic response, before she moved on to more pressing matters as Mathilde cooed over the cactus.

'What did you do?' she asks Celia.

Celia laughs, shaking her head. 'I should probably tell you I made up some kind of magic potion but it was a bit random, really. I just mixed up what I thought might work as a particularly nutritious fertiliser, and then he started perking up and this morning, well—' She breaks off, eyes shining. 'The flower appeared.'

'I can't believe it,' Enzo says as they all gaze at what is a perfectly ordinary cactus, standing fully upright now, on which a single tiny pink bloom has appeared. He thinks it's the most beautiful flower he's ever seen in his life. When Celia had texted him earlier, he hadn't even dared to tell Mathilde what she'd said, in case it had been some kind of mix-up (one of the many other succulents currently residing in Celia's plant room, perhaps? But he can't imagine she'd confuse one plant for another). Anyway, he hadn't wanted to give her false hope.

'Celia is a miracle worker,' Amanda announces with a note of pride.

'Oh, stop that.' Celia grins, shaking her head.

'You are,' Mathilde insists. 'And I love your short hair. It really suits you!'

'Thank you!' She blushes.

'It really does,' Enzo agrees and now he catches Celia's flush intensifying, and he checks his watch. 'Well, we'd better get going, Mathilde. You know Saska's keen on a prompt start.'

Celia looks at him, seeming to hesitate.

'Still want to come?' Enzo asks, not wanting to push it.

'Yes, of course. And you're coming too, Amanda, aren't you? You did promise...' Amanda pulls a face as if she's had a change of heart. 'Come on,' Celia urges her. 'It's only an hour and a half, and we're given rubber gloves.'

'Oh, that's all right then,' she says with a wry laugh. So they all head out to meet the cluster of good citizens who have already gathered outside the library. They are handed picker sticks and hi-vis vests – Enzo catches Amanda dangling hers at arm's length, as if it had been found lying in the gutter – and off they go.

While Mathilde and Amanda are swept off by Saska and Honey, Enzo and Celia find themselves working their way along a narrow side street. 'So, does Saska sort of run this thing?' Celia asks, jabbing at a Mars bar wrapper in the gutter.

'There's no "sort of" about it,' Enzo replies. 'Saska basically runs the neighbourhood. And I should warn you – she set up a litter pick singles thing at her place afterwards.'

'What's that?' Celia looks quizzical.

Enzo delves under a car in order to access a flattened plastic water bottle. Then – thrillingly – he spots one of those Sylvanian Families rabbits that Mathilde used to love. Filthy, though – so into the rubbish bag it goes. 'The things you find!' Celia smiles.

'Never a dull moment,' he says with a grin. 'So, yeah – litter pick singles is a kind of mingling thing once the streets have been tidied. Y'know, while she has us all captive.'

Celia's eyes widen. 'You mean, like a dating thing?'

'That's right.' He pulls a mock-terrified face. 'She reckons there's this common link. People who care about the state of the neighbourhood, who'd rather spend their Saturday mornings picking up crisp packets than having coffee in bed.'

'Wow.' Celia laughs. 'You mean mad people like us?'

'Exactly.'

He senses her studying him as, clutching their rubbish bags, they make their way farther up the street. 'And have you been that?' she asks.

'I have not.' He chuckles, aware of her considering this and possibly building up to her next question. 'I'm single,' he clarifies, 'but not a *litter pick* single.'

'Right!' She laughs. 'Why not?'

'Well, apart from how horribly awkward I imagine it'd be...'

'Maybe it'd be fine?' she offers with a shrug.

'You think so?' He smiles.

'I... I really don't know.'

Enzo jabs at a discarded Chupa Chups lollipop – these things are a devil to pick up – and drops it into his bag. 'Well, I think we should skip it.'

'Oh, me too.' She chuckles, seeming relieved, and then they settle into easy chatter about Celia's days at the shop, and Enzo's week at school, until they glimpse Amanda, Saska and Mathilde in the distance. 'So you and Amanda have been close since your schooldays?' he says.

She seems to hesitate and they stop. 'Not exactly. It's quite... well, it's a bit odd, actually.' And she tells him how, late last year, the invitation to Amanda's wedding had dropped into her inbox and she'd been surprised to be invited at all. 'Geoff wouldn't come,' she explains, 'and of course now I know why. And I was so nervous, you know? It sounds silly, I realise that—'

'It doesn't at all,' he cuts in. 'Walking into a big event on my own isn't my favourite thing either.'

'Really?' She seems surprised.

'Not at all,' Enzo says. 'No one enjoys that, do they? At least, that's what I always tell myself...'

'And it was in London,' Celia continues. 'Honestly, the way I'd studied the Tube map beforehand, you'd have thought I was going to be tested on it.'

'It's complicated!' he agrees. 'When I took Mathilde to Paris, she was better at navigating the system than I was.'

'She's a smart girl,' Celia says with a smile.

'She is.' He nods. 'But she was only seven then.'

Celia chuckles, and her green eyes glint in the cool morning sun. 'I'd actually thought about making an excuse,' she adds, 'not to go to the wedding. You know, feigning an illness or a domestic disaster. An exploding boiler or plumbing emergency or something like that.'

Enzo laughs. There's many a social situation he's been at pains to wriggle out of.

'I must've been the only person in Glasgow willing the pipes to freeze last winter,' Celia adds.

'It never happens when you want it to.' He smiles, wanting this conversation to continue, but is then summonsed by Mathilde calling from the end of the street.

'Dad, we're all done!'

How quickly time has sped by, he thinks as they join Mathilde and Amanda and make their way back to the meeting point. Hi-vis jackets and picker sticks are gathered efficiently by Claire, whom Enzo thinks of as Saska's second-in-command. 'Fancy coming back for a coffee?' Celia asks him.

Enzo smiles, surprised but pleased. 'Yes, that'd be lovely.' How different Celia seems now, he decides. More relaxed and at ease as they all make their way back to her flat.

'I think Mathilde won the prize for the most bizarre litter item today,' Amanda announces as Celia lets them in.

'Oh, what was that?' Enzo asks.

Mathilde looks at him and grins. 'False teeth!'

'What, a whole set?' Celia asks.

'Yep, upper and lower,' Amanda announces, then busies herself making coffee. She's clearly at home here, Enzo notices, in the way that she flits about, knowing where everything is.

'I like what you said to Saska,' Mathilde announces, fixing her dad with a grin.

'That you had something to go to?' Celia says, seeming unsure whether she should elaborate. But Mathilde knows about the singles thing and, although she's agreed with her mother that Enzo should 'meet someone', she found the concept hilarious.

'Well, I did,' Enzo says with a shrug. He looks around Celia's neat and tidy kitchen, deciding that she obviously likes things this way. Calm and orderly and just so. Then Celia's phone pings with a notification and she checks it and smiles.

'Terri's coming down,' she says.

'The cake lady?' Mathilde looks delighted by this.

'That's right,' Celia tells her. 'So if you're not in a hurry to get to that something you've got to go to...'

Enzo laughs, shaking his head. Right now he's in no hurry to go anywhere at all.

38

A kitchen filled with people and chatter. Not just people but *friends,* all happily drinking coffee and munching on biscuits from a variety box. It's something Celia imagines is so ordinary to people like Saska, with her gatherings. But to Celia it's still something of a novelty and she isn't quite sure why she feels so at ease with all of this going on around her.

Perhaps because Geoff isn't here? It still triggers a sudden pain in her, that all of those years together seem to have crumbled to dust. But still, it's liberating, to have friends here – with the heating on, if she wants to! Celia can hardly believe she can behave in this way in her own home.

Now Terri is unboxing home-made brownies. They've been short-staffed at the hospital recently and Celia is aware that, whenever she can, Terri grabs at the chance of extra shifts. But it hasn't just been that. She also suspects that, since Amanda seemed to settle herself in here, she's been keeping her distance a little, and preferring to offer her support through daily texts. 'I love your hair, by the way,' Terri announces, giving it a ruffle.

'Thanks.' Celia smiles. 'I kind of like it too!'

'You look like a different person,' Terri adds. 'I mean, you're still *you*, obviously—'

'But better,' Amanda chips in.

Terri shakes her head. 'Not better. Just... lighter. Like a younger version of you...'

Celia is so taken aback by the compliment that she spins towards the cupboard and lifts out a plate for the brownies. Blushing at forty-three years old? Ridiculous.

'So, my favourite boy hasn't come home yet?' Terri perches on a kitchen chair.

'Nope.' Celia shakes her head. 'I'd love him to be here but I can't force him. I think it's all been a bit too much, and he needed a change of scene...' She breaks off, not wanting to delve into it all in front of Enzo and Mathilde.

'He'll be home again,' Amanda says reassuringly, 'when I'm out of your hair.'

'I'm sure it's nothing to do with that,' Celia says quickly.

Amanda pulls a face. 'It might be soon, actually. Or soon-ish. My agent called. A job offer's come up and I'm still not sure whether to go for it...'

'Oh, when did you hear about this?' Celia asks.

'A week ago,' she admits.

'A week ago? Why didn't you say?'

Amanda nibbles a brownie, as if she needs to build up to sharing the news. 'Mmm, this is delicious, Terri.'

'Amanda, what's the job offer?' Celia prompts her.

She exhales forcefully, and then she describes the funeral plan commercial. How it would involve her strolling dreamily along a riverbank.

'That doesn't sound so bad,' Enzo offers, at which Amanda splutters.

'That's my demographic now. Maybe they'll want me to topple into the river in a sudden tragic accident—'

'Ridiculous,' Terri retorts. 'You look thirty-five if you're a day.'

'It's true,' Celia insists.

Amanda smiles. 'You're both very kind.'

Terri shrugs. 'Well, honestly. The world's gone mad. Will you do it, d'you think?'

'Honestly, I don't know.' Amanda shrugs. 'There's not an awful lot else going on at the moment...'

'You're not on morning TV any more,' Mathilde announces suddenly.

Amanda blinks in surprise and then smiles stoically. 'No, I'm not, sweetheart. That came to an end, unfortunately.'

'Why?' she asks, and Celia catches Enzo giving her a quick look, as if warning her that this might be a sensitive issue.

'They didn't want me any more,' Amanda says lightly.

'But why not?' Mathilde asks, frowning.

'Mathilde,' Enzo starts.

Amanda dismisses his concern with a flap of her hand. 'It's fine, really.' She turns back towards Mathilde. 'They actually wanted someone younger.'

'I liked you,' Mathilde announces, reaching for a second brownie. 'I used to watch you in the school holidays or if I was off sick.' She glances at her dad. 'At Mum's, I mean.'

'Oh, right!' Amanda beams at her. 'Well, thank you, darling. So, not long till the summer holidays now, is it?' Celia suspects she wants to swerve the topic away from her career.

'Just two weeks to go,' Mathilde replies.

'What're you up to this summer?' Celia asks her, remembering those glorious days when the long holidays began – late June in Scotland, she was always delighted that it was so early in the summer. Logan would burst into the flat and fling his bag down, all smiles.

'My Auntie Valérie's coming over from France,' Mathilde tells her. 'She's bringing her campervan.'

'Oh, I bet that's fun, honey,' Terri says. 'Are you going away on a trip?'

'Yes, we are!' Mathilde says.

'Just a night away,' Enzo says. 'There's this beach we love, isn't there, Mathilde?'

'Yeah. No one ever goes there but us.'

'Well, hardly anyone.' Enzo smiles. 'Just the odd dog walker and one time there was a bunch of students in a tent, remember?'

Mathilde nods. 'There's a cave as well. A hermit's cave—'

'That sounds magical,' Amanda enthuses.

'You could come too!' Mathilde announces. 'All of you, I mean—'

'Oh, I think it's *your* trip,' Celia says quickly. 'With your dad and auntie, I mean.' She turns her attention to Spike, allowing herself a moment's pleasure at the sight of his perky erectness and the single pink flower blooming there. She doesn't know which – if any – component of her tea leaf fertiliser blend did the trick. But it seems like something of a tiny miracle.

Now it occurs to her that, all those summers when Geoff didn't want to go away with her – well, things can be different now. She can do whatever she wants. The thought is at once thrilling and faintly terrifying because actually, she doesn't know what she wants to do.

Having asked for her dad's phone, Mathilde shows Celia their beloved beach on the map. They pore over photos together and indeed it looks beautiful. Celia has lived in Scotland her whole life and had never heard of this secluded spot on the west coast.

'Honestly,' Enzo says, catching her eye, 'you'd be very welcome to come if you'd like to. All of you, I mean,' he adds quickly.

'But this is your family time,' Celia reiterates.

He looks expectantly at Mathilde. 'You'd be fine with that, wouldn't you?'

'I'd love it,' she says with a huge smile. 'You'd *all* love it. It's my favourite place.'

Celia shakes her head. 'Space-wise, it'd be impossible. In a campervan, I mean...'

'Mathilde and I can camp.' Enzo turns to his daughter. 'We've done that before, haven't we? That time we brought Honey and Kizzy with us?'

Mathilde nods. 'There'll be room for all of us.' She looks around the kitchen as if that's the matter settled. Panicking now, Celia doesn't know what to do. Obviously they can't all butt in on their family trip. Mathilde is just being carried away in a burst of enthusiasm – and Enzo is being polite.

'I'm sure you'll want time with your sister,' Celia ventures as she wipes up table crumbs.

Enzo shrugs. 'Val's over for three weeks. We'll have plenty of time and there's only so much I can handle, one to one.' He smiles wryly. 'Big sister, little brother. Those roles are hard to shift.'

'She bosses Dad,' Mathilde says, and they exchange a conspiratorial grin.

'Well, maybe we could join you,' Amanda announces now. 'When are you going?'

'Weekend after next, if that'd work for everyone,' Enzo replies.

'The start of the holidays,' Mathilde enthuses.

'Of course,' Enzo adds, 'you might have commitments—'

'I'm really not sure,' Celia starts, but Amanda jumps in.

'I don't have anything happening, unless my agent comes up with a better offer. Also, that'll be my last weekend here...'

'Will it?' Celia stares at her.

Amanda nods. 'It's time to go home. Jasper needs me there. He's got a big art exhibition coming up and...' She pauses, pushing back her hair. 'So wouldn't that be great, to do something fun together before I go?'

Celia frowns. The news of Amanda leaving has hit her with something of a thud. 'So you should go!' Terri announces.

'What about you?' Enzo asks her.

Terri shakes her head. 'I'm full-on with work at the moment. Need the money.' She grimaces and touches Celia's arm. 'I can keep an eye on things here, if you like? Before you start rolling that out as an excuse. "Oh, I can't go, I need to look after my plants..."'

'Are you good with plants, Terri?' Amanda asks.

'Terrible.' She sniggers. 'But we're only talking a couple of days, right? I mean, what could possibly go wrong?'

Celia laughs dryly, her gaze skimming her kitchen that feels more full of life than she's ever known it. And now Amanda has wound an arm around her shoulders.

'C'mon!' she urges her. 'Remember the yes game?'

'What's that?' Mathilde asks.

It's Amanda who answers. 'It's from way back when me and Celia were kids. This thing the two of us came up with. Whenever one of us thought of something fun or exciting to do, the other had to say yes. Isn't that right, Celia?'

'Er, yes,' she replies, feeling horribly in the spotlight.

'Sounds like a good game,' Enzo remarks with a smile.

'So will you come?' Mathilde grins.

Celia hesitates. Her brain is telling her, *Yes, but you were young then and you're not any more.* But somehow, despite that, she catches Enzo's smile and she finds herself saying, 'Okay then. If you're up for it too, Amanda?'

'Of course I am!'

'Then yes,' Celia says. 'Yes, we'll come.'

39

The shop is quiet on this damp and grey-skied Wednesday afternoon. As Celia straightens hangers on the rails she tells herself how delicious it will feel to plunge into clear, cool water.

She likes the sound of the yellow iris Enzo described, growing wild on the remote beach, and sheep pottering down to where the pasture meets the shore. Yet still, she can hardly believe she's agreed to this. A camping trip. Enzo has assured her that wild camping is allowed at the beach. That he and Mathilde do it every summer and between his tent and the campervan, everything'll be fine. But will it really? The only time she's ever slept in a tent was with Amanda in her garden as kids – but that's not the point. She and Amanda and Enzo and Mathilde, plus Enzo's sister, whom she hasn't even met... How will they all get along? The yes game has a lot to answer for, she decides.

Now the shop door opens and Celia recognises the stylish woman with the silvery bob who'd been in a few weeks before. 'Hi,' she says brightly, noticing that she is clutching one of the shop's rope-handled paper carriers. 'Did you have a nice time in the Highlands?'

'You remembered! Yes, I did, thank you. It was perfect.'

'And did you wear the dress? The oyster brocade, wasn't it?'

The woman smiles a little bashfully. 'I didn't, actually. It, um...' Now Celia remembers that she'd planned to slim into it. Never a wise move, in her experience. 'It was a bit on the tight side,' she admits. 'Would I be able to exchange it? I'm sorry, it was a while ago now but I haven't worn it—'

'Oh, that's absolutely fine.' Celia smiles reassuringly, taking the bag from her and lifting out the dress. At this point she should offer a credit note but she doesn't have the heart. Occasionally she oversteps the rules. 'Would you prefer a refund?' she asks.

'No, I think I'll exchange it for something that actually fits me.' The woman seems to relax now. Her grey eyes meet Celia's as she laughs. 'Why do we do this? Why do we kid ourselves?'

'It's what we want to believe.' Celia smiles. 'Like the shoes will stretch—'

'And they never do, do they?' The woman shakes her head at the madness of it, and starts to flick through the rails, stopping at a simple knee-length navy dress. 'Now this is elegant.'

'I do love that,' Celia says truthfully, and the woman goes to try it on.

While she's behind the curtain Celia quickly runs a feather duster over the shelves, and when the door dings again she spins around, expecting to see another potential customer.

'Hi, Mum. Is it all right to come in?'

'Logan,' she exclaims, beaming at him. 'Of course it's all right.' Then the woman emerges wearing the chic navy dress, and Celia wants her to have it so much that she would almost buy it for her herself.

'That really was made for you,' she says.

The woman chuckles. 'I feel terribly grown-up in it.' Celia

catches Logan looking confused for a moment because the customer must be around his grandma's age.

'You can definitely carry it off,' Celia says.

Now the woman glances at Logan who's perched on the chaise longue. 'Is this your son?'

'He is, yes.'

'What a handsome boy!' Logan laughs awkwardly and blushes, and she looks at him fondly before turning to Celia. 'I'll take the dress,' she says.

When she leaves, Celia is relieved to be able to give Logan her full attention. 'So, how are things at Gran's?' she asks. Rather than visiting while he's been staying there, she has kept in touch by text instead. It's not that she hasn't wanted to see him. More that she's been wary of upsetting the balance of their living together – their delicate eco-system – by showing up.

They are sitting side by side on the chaise longue now, and Celia is willing no more customers to come in. 'It's been all right,' Logan says. 'I actually wanted to come back sooner, Mum. But I know Gran likes me being there.'

'I'm sure she does.' Celia's heart seems to twist.

'It's been kind of difficult getting away,' he adds. 'She always wants me to watch the soaps—'

'What a treat.' Celia smiles.

He chuckles but his eyes look tired, she thinks. 'I worry about her, Mum.'

She reaches for his hand and squeezes it. 'I know, love. I do too.'

Logan inhales, and then adds, 'But I can't be there any longer. I'm coming home, Mum—'

'Oh, honey, are you?' She turns and hugs him. 'I'm so glad. And I'm sorry about things being so weird and awful…'

He tries for a smile. 'I overreacted over the biscuit.'

'The wafer,' she says.

'*Wafergate*.' He laughs and then she looks at him, overcome with happiness that he's here with her today.

'Was it Amanda, love?' she asks. 'I know she's quite... dominant. A big presence around the flat. Was it too much?'

Logan shrugs. 'Actually... not really.'

She studies his face, searching his expression for clues. 'What was it then? What made you stay away?'

He looks down at his feet. 'I s'pose it was... well, y'know. Dad not being there.'

'Oh, was it?' Something sinks inside her.

'Yeah.' Logan nods. 'I know he was always a bit...' The pause says it all. A bit miserly. Hardly emitting joy.

'He was, yes,' she says softly. 'But he was – and is – still Dad.'

Logan looks away now and the air seems to shimmer between them. *Of course he's not your real dad and you know that. I've never lied.* And now the dust has settled, she reflects that, having been thrown headlong into parenthood – much as she was – Geoff did his best. In his own way, he was always there for them: attending parents' evenings, sitting on a damp beach towel on that Cornish beach while Logan built a castle with an extensive network of moats.

'Logan?' She touches his arm. 'You know, if there's anything you ever want to ask, about your—'

'Oh God, Mum. No.' He shakes his head decisively. 'It was just a thing, wasn't it?'

Celia nods.

'I've figured that you haven't told me any more because there's nothing else to tell.' She presses a hand to her cheek, afraid that if she does say anything, she'll lose it. 'Mum, it's all right,' Logan adds, concern filling his blue eyes now. 'We're all right, you and me.'

'You think so?' She smiles.

He nods and delves into his jeans pocket, extracting a piece of paper. She can see that it was torn into pieces, and that those pieces have been sellotaped together, and that something is handwritten on it.

He hands it to her and her gaze falls upon it. 'This is... Dad's writing, isn't it?'

'Yeah,' he murmurs.

'It's... Dad's poem?'

'That's right. Sure you want to read it?'

She nods, allowing her focus to settle on the tidy forward slope of his script, and she reads:

> *Your breasts are breathless.*
> *Your luscious curves*
> *Set me wild with desire,*
> *Your lips, your tits,*
> *Your vulva of fire—*

And there it stops. Perhaps that was the end of the poem – or he ran out of steam at that point. Celia re-reads it, aware of a bubble of mirth deep inside of her, rising up. She clears her throat, and as she catches Logan's eye she sees his mouth quivering. Now she starts laughing and he is laughing too. And she can't stop herself. 'Oh God, darling,' she manages finally. 'Not very good, is it?'

Logan shakes his head, seemingly unable to speak for a moment. It occurs to Celia that she can't remember the last time she's seen him laugh like this. 'You know, love,' she says eventually, 'whenever I feel like I've been a colossal idiot, then I'll read this and feel a whole lot better.'

'You're not an idiot,' he says firmly. 'That's the last thing you are, okay?' He pauses. 'But there's something else.'

Now her heart seems to clang. 'What?' she asks.

He shifts awkwardly on the chaise longue. 'You know my biological dad's name?'

She nods. Of course she does – and Logan does too because she told him the first time he asked. Although she's never been temped to do it herself, she's pretty certain that he'll have tried googling him. 'Didn't you realise?' he says with a frown.

'Realise what?' she asks.

'Scott Chegg.' Logan's mouth compresses into a line and his gaze seems to bore into hers.

'What about him, love? What d'you mean?'

A mouth corner twitches. 'Scott Chegg. *Scotch Egg*, Mum! Didn't you ever say it out loud?'

She blinks at him and blows out air as the information settles. *Scotch Egg.* All these years and she'd never got it. 'Oh, Logan. No, I never realised...' A joke name. How gullible she'd been.

'So my biological dad also has a sausage meat connection,' Logan adds gently. 'There's a theme there.'

Celia shakes her head, relieved that no more customers have come in. 'I can't believe I fell for that. I mean, I thought it was just a *name*—'

'Mum, it's okay!' Logan grins and winds an arm around her shoulders.

She looks at him, surrounded by occasion wear and fancy hats. 'I'm the biggest idiot,' she adds.

'No, you're not.'

'What am I then?' she blurts out.

'You're just *you*, Mum.'

'What does that mean?'

'Just... I dunno!' He laughs. 'Just my mum. And I love you!'

'I love you too.' She rubs at her face, overcome by emotion. How lucky she is to have Logan in her life. 'You don't think I'm mad, do you?' she asks.

'Oh, I totally do.' He gets up from the chaise longue as the door opens and a rather tentative-looking woman comes in.

'Hi, can I help you?' Celia jumps up too.

'Just having a look,' the woman says pleasantly as Logan makes for the door.

'See you at home, Mum,' he says. 'But I won't be back for long, okay? Just a few days...'

'What d'you mean?'

'That volunteer programme. At the mycology centre?'

'So you're going to do it?' she asks.

He shrugs, a gesture that they've laughed about because it's been his default since he was about fourteen years old. There's even an emoji for it: the shruggie. ''Course I am,' he says. 'I'm not giving up an opportunity like that. Terri would never forgive me.' He laughs, and then he's gone, and the woman plucks a dress from the rail: an explosion of orange and pink, like a beautiful flower.

'That's lovely,' Celia says.

'It really is, isn't it?' The woman studies it at arm's length. 'But I have no idea where I'd wear it...'

Celia smiles, having switched fully into shop-lady mode now. How easily it comes when she needs it. She pictures this woman wearing the dress, as she always does when a customer picks out the perfect thing.

'I always think, if you love something enough, then the occasion will present itself,' she says.

40

NINE DAYS LATER

It'll be fine, Celia tells herself as she pulls on her jacket – even though she has never done a trip like this before. It's just a jaunt to the coast with her new friends. What's the big deal? And isn't Amanda always saying that she should be open to new things? First thing tomorrow, Enzo will be picking her up. She thinks back to that giddy day out with Amanda – cinema and *umami* cocktails, that was new! – and reminds herself that this is her life now.

That she can do whatever she wants.

Actually, she could do with an *umami* cocktail right now at 8.20 a.m., even though she's about to cycle to work. *Don't be such a coward*, she tells herself.

Logan was all for it, during their five-minute chat. 'It sounds great, Mum. One night at the beach? What are you so worried about? It'll be fun!' Then she was aware of chatter in the background, and someone calling his name. Already he seemed to have made a bunch of new friends at the mycology centre. Names have been mentioned – Jonno and Ella and Ben – and she's relieved to know that he's happy and settled there. *Of course he is*, she tells herself. He doesn't need her fretting about him, and it was clear that he was in a hurry to wrap up the call. 'Amanda's going too, isn't she?' he asked.

'Yes,' she replied.

Then just as Celia is about to leave for the shop, Amanda emerges from the bathroom, wrapped in a towel. 'So you're off to your mum's after work?' she says.

'That's right.' Celia manages a smile. 'Just a quick visit to check she's not missing Logan too much.'

Amanda nods, her expression inscrutable. 'I'll cook us a nice dinner when you're back.'

'That'd be lovely. Thanks.' Celia quickly runs through everything she's packed in Logan's old rucksack, trying to figure out if there's anything she's forgotten. *Relax. It's only a couple of days by the sea!*

'Erm...' Amanda looks down now. Her hair is wet and tangled, streaking over her bare shoulders. No one else Celia knows would look as good like that – all glowing and pink and gorgeous. 'I, uh... I hope you don't mind,' she starts, looking up at Celia now. 'But I'm not going to go on this weekend.'

'What?' Celia stares at her. 'Why not?'

'Because...' She pauses. 'I think it'd be good for you to go on your own.'

'No, it wouldn't! Why d'you say that?'

'I just think it would,' Amanda says firmly.

Celia stands there, knowing she should leave for work – she is never late – but also unable to move from this spot in the hallway. When was the last time someone said this to her? That she'd have to go somewhere alone? It was Geoff – when they'd been invited to Amanda's wedding. *You'll have a lot more fun on your own.* 'If you're not going, then I'm not,' Celia says firmly. 'You have to come.'

'Celia, listen.' Amanda's forehead crinkles as she touches her shoulder. 'I'm leaving soon and, well, I just think you can get to know Enzo properly without me being there.'

Suspicion rises up in her. 'What d'you mean, get to know him properly?'

'Well, just have time together!'

Celia looks at her, trying to make sense of this. 'You think I'm actually hoping something's going to happen? Like, this weekend? So soon after Geoff? I don't think—'

'No, of course not,' Amanda cuts in. 'I just meant—'

'As if he'd be interested anyway!' she blasts out.

Amanda's cheeks redden and her mouth crumples. 'Celia, honestly. Why are you being like this?'

'I'm not being like anything!'

With a loud sigh, Amanda strides straight past her to the bedroom.

Celia stares after her. 'There'll be loads of us, anyway. Enzo, Mathilde, his sister...' She presses her hands to her face, feeling stranded now in her own hallway. Amanda has left a speckling of water droplets in her wake. What should she do now? Exasperated, she calls out a curt goodbye and fetches her bike from where it's chained at the back door, and cycles off to work.

The shop is unusually busy on this warm and sunny Friday, which helps to distract her from Amanda's announcement. Perhaps she'll change her mind, Celia decides. If Amanda agrees to go with her, then it'll be okay. She catches herself having these childish thoughts, and wonders what is wrong with her. Why she cannot manage to do things easily on her own, as everyone else appears to do. Even Logan who seems to be thriving at the mycology centre. What is she so afraid of?

She shuts up the shop and cycles, tired and scratchy-eyed, to her mum's. Amanda was probably just testing her, she decides – trying to encourage her to do this thing on her own.

Well, no way is Celia being pushed *that* far out of her comfort zone.

At her mum's, instead of pressing the buzzer and waiting patiently, she raps sharply on the door and marches right in.

'Oh, Celia!' Her mum scuttles out of the living room towards her.

'Hi, Mum.'

'Hi.' Her mum looks different; Celia sees this at once. Brighter, somehow. More together. Her brown hair is neatly combed and her eyes are clearer, Celia thinks. Not so puffy and tired.

'You look well,' Celia says with a smile. 'So how was it, having your grandson here?'

'Extra work, of course,' her mum says, making for the kitchen, 'and he ate me out of house and home. But it was fine. Nice, actually, having the company.'

Celia watches as she fills the kettle and switches it on. 'That's good to hear. I think he enjoyed it too,' she adds. 'Thanks for having him. I appreciate that, Mum.'

She nods. 'Like some tea?'

'Er, yes, please.' Her mum doesn't usually offer her anything. She makes their tea, and instead of the TV blaring they sit together in the quiet of the living room.

'I've been thinking,' her mum says.

Celia looks at her. She is definitely sober – there's not a trace of the familiar flush, the glassy eyes. 'What about?' Celia prompts her.

'About the garden,' she says. 'I think I'd like to make a start on it out there.'

'You mean... sort it all out?' Celia asks in amazement.

'Well, not all of it,' her mum says quickly. 'I couldn't manage that all on my own—'

'But I could help you,' Celia cuts in. 'I think it's a great idea. Such a waste really, leaving it all wild like that—'

'I've had a lot on my mind!' her mum exclaims, eyes flashing now.

Celia leans towards her, clutching the chipped mug. 'I know, Mum. I know it's a lot. But honestly, I'd love to help...'

Her mother nods, her face softening. 'I was wondering about this weekend, if you're not busy?'

'Oh, this weekend's tricky,' Celia says. 'But as soon as I can—'

'What're you up to this weekend?'

Celia hesitates. She could make something up – that she's having to work in the shop, or has too much to do with the plant hospital. In fact, until she'd arrived here she'd still been unsure about this trip – especially with Amanda announcing that she wasn't going. But then she'd given herself a mental shake, and told herself not to be so silly. After all, she is an independent adult woman who's weathered a break-up. And of course she's perfectly capable of enjoying an overnight trip with friends.

'I'm actually going up north,' she starts, 'to this place on the coast.'

'Oh, with Amanda?' Her mum knows all about her oldest friend bowling up for an extended stay.

'Erm, actually with a couple of other friends.'

'Other friends?' As if she were amazed that Celia has any.

'That's right.'

Her mum is scrutinising her now, and Celia knows she can't leave it like that. 'There's this new friend, Enzo—'

'Enzo?' She frowns. 'Who's that?'

'Just someone I've got to know, Mum.'

Her mother's eyes widen. 'Is that a man?'

'Yes, it's a man.'

'You mean you're carrying on with someone else already?'

'I'm not carrying on!' Celia stares at her. 'Like I said, he's just a friend.'

'Fast work, that!'

Celia sits there, frozen for a moment. Then she gets up and takes her mug through to the kitchen with her mum in pursuit. 'You're going away with a *man*?'

'Yes, and with his daughter and sister too...' As she says this it dawns on Celia how utterly crazy this is. The way she'd agreed to the trip, only because Amanda had urged her to. And right now, Celia is sick of having her life managed, and going along with what every other person wants her to do. Secretly, she'd hoped that Amanda would change her mind and agree to join them after all. However, whether she comes or not is irrelevant now, as Celia's mind is made up.

She washes her mug at the sink and tries to switch the subject to her mother's garden: how they can hack down the weeds and she can dig it over – perhaps Logan will help, when he's back from volunteering?

However, her mum won't take the bait. 'No sooner is Geoff out the door than you've shipped another one in!'

'Mum, that's ridiculous!' Celia storms out to the hallway where she grabs her jacket from the hook. She pulls it on, her head spinning.

'Celia, I'm sorry.' Her mum grabs at her arm and suddenly she is crying, tears spilling down her cheeks. Celia cannot remember the last time she saw her mother cry.

'Mum, it's okay! Please don't cry.'

Her mum pulls away, looking at her imploringly. 'I'm sorry. I really am trying, you know.'

'Oh, I know you are. And that's great.' They hug then, tightly and properly. And finally Celia pulls away and her mother virtually pushes her out of the door.

'Please, forget what I said. You enjoy your weekend away at the beach, all right? We can do the garden together whenever you have time.'

Celia doesn't want to go. It's cracking her heart, to leave her mum like this. But she needs to leave now, to be alone and try to figure things out. She hugs her mum again – it's so unfamiliar and weird – and instead of cycling home, she wheels her bike, blinking away tears as the steady rain hits her face.

Almost home now, she pulls out her phone and scrolls for Enzo's name.

> Really sorry but there's a change of plan. We can't make it this weekend. Hope you all have a brilliant time. Love Celia.

41
———

The wild irises are still in flower. Enzo was hoping they would be as they drove, the three of them, in his sister's campervan. And now, as they make their way in single file along the rocky path, the swathe of butter-yellow blooms is there to greet them, fringing the beach.

'Oh, Enz, this is beautiful!' Valérie has always had to be first at everything. Now she's powered ahead with her cool box and a rucksack filled with provisions. She flatly refused to let Enzo carry either of these. 'I can manage, Enz. Anyway, you've got the tent.' And now she's swung around and is calling back, 'Does no one come here? I can't believe it!'

'It is something of a secret,' Enzo replies. He's trying to be happy and positive about the trip, but Celia's messages took the wind out of his sails and he still feels deflated as he steps over the rocks.

However, of course he understands. She's had so much going on, and when he messaged back, asking why she'd had a change of heart, she explained that Amanda had decided not to come, and that she really wasn't up to it either.

'I think we'll just have a quiet weekend,' she'd said.

Well, that's fine, of course. Better to be honest rather than hauling herself along if she wasn't in the right frame of mind. Just as he'd been with Kim, a couple of days ago, when he'd messaged her.

> Kim, it was great meeting you. Thanks for our run. I'll bear all that in mind, about hill running.

How feeble that had sounded.

> Thanks too for your offer of going out again, but I don't think it's for me right now.

He'd pressed 'Send' quickly before there was time to dither or waffle on.

> Hey, no problem. But get that watch sorted! Track your progress!

'Enz?' his sister calls out. 'If this were back home it'd be full of people. Oh, it's going to be great staying here!' Like Enzo, Valérie is a natural at languages – and she's always keen to boost her skills. So whenever she visits him, and Mathilde is around, they always speak English.

Now Mathilde is running ahead, eager to reach the sea as always. It's a beautiful summer's day: a clear, bright blue sky, the water sparkling. Enzo wonders if he was pushing it now, asking Celia to come. He's probably blown it, he thinks – jumping in too soon. But he can't stop thinking about her and the times they've spent together.

It's probably for the best, he decides as they find a perfect spot, in a slight hollow in the soft silver sand, and spread out Valérie's blanket. He knows his sister can be something of a powerhouse. She has a high-ranking job in HR and is extremely competitive. It was always that way between them, growing up. Valérie was – is – the smartest academically, as well as being a fantastic aunt to Mathilde. Divorced and child-free, she has always run on adrenaline.

Now she is assuming the role of Director of Operations, deciding precisely where the fire will be built. Soon she has it glowing hotly, and has unpacked a tub of chicken in her own special marinade from the cool box. Coffee is poured from her big industrial flask into enamel mugs and handed around. The plan is that, after their overnight stay here, Valérie will drop Enzo and Mathilde at the train station, and then carry on solo on the NC500 route. 'There's something magical about driving right round the northern edge of a country,' she announces. 'Sure you don't want to do it with me, Enz? You and Mathilde?'

'I'm going away with Mum,' Mathilde reminds her.

'Yeah, of course.' She grins. 'Sardinia, isn't it?' Mathilde nods, beaming.

'The NC500 can't compete with that, can it, Mathilde?' Enzo asks, chuckling.

He knows his daughter, and that she wouldn't want to hurt her aunt's feelings. So instead of answering she says, 'Can we swim?' This, he knows, is one of the very few things his sister cannot do, and that it's a source of embarrassment to her, having grown up so close to the sea. So he pulls off his jeans and sweatshirt, having had the forethought to wear swimming shorts underneath.

The sun is high and bright, a silver-white ball in a searing blue sky, and yet the water is bracing cold as he and Mathilde wade in. 'It's freezing!' she cries out, laughing, and splashes her dad.

He retaliates, and as his daughter shrieks with laughter, Enzo looks towards the beach. Now he sees that someone is making their way down the path towards the sandy cove. A lone figure, he thinks. Perhaps a dog walker? Mathilde is swimming now – Enzo knows her feet can still touch the bottom – but he is standing still.

The person has reached the beach and is looking around, as if searching for someone. At first he thinks he must be mistaken because how can this be possible?

'Dad?'

He sees the woman stepping across the sand towards Valérie, and them seeming to strike up a conversation.

'Dad... is that Celia?' Mathilde stops swimming.

'I, uh... I think so, yes.' He knows Mathilde was disappointed that she – and possibly Amanda too, but mainly Celia, he thinks – had decided not to come.

'It is!' Mathilde announces, pushing through the water towards the shore. Enzo follows her, wading through the shallows until he is out of the water and running across the warm sand.

'Celia!' He laughs. 'What happened? You changed your mind?'

She laughs too, and then pushes back her short choppy hair. 'I did.'

'But... how did you get here?'

'I hired a car,' she says with a grimace. 'I know it's a bit mad...'

'No, not at all,' he says, and quickly introduces her to Valérie, even though they have already introduced themselves.

'Lovely to meet you, Celia,' his sister says with a smile.

'You too.' Celia presses her lips together and looks around the beach, as if still unsure that she should be here. 'I hope I'm not gatecrashing,' she adds.

'Of course you're not,' Enzo exclaims.

Celia, smiles, seeming to relax now. 'D'you think you'll have room for me? If you don't, I can sleep in the car—'

'Don't be crazy,' Valérie insists.

'No, we have the tent,' Enzo says quickly. 'So there's plenty of room for all of us.' And then his sister and daughter go off in search of more wood for the fire, and Celia changes – with some difficulty, shrouded in one of their beach towels – into her swimsuit.

'I'm so glad you came,' Enzo tells her.

'Amanda made me.' Celia smiles awkwardly. 'Actually, that's not true. I wanted to come. But she figured out how I could get here.'

'Driving's the only way.' Enzo nods, taking in the green of her eyes in the bright sunshine. He can still hardly believe she's here.

'Yes, she was on to car hire companies, bossing me around...' Celia tails off and laughs. 'I *can* take care of myself, you know.'

'I'm sure you can.' Enzo truly believes this. She's incredible, he thinks. He has never known anyone like her.

Valérie and Mathilde are coming back now, armed with firewood. 'Shall we swim, then?' he suggests. 'D'you like to swim?'

'Yes, I love it!' she announces. And so they make their way across the sand, towards the clear, glistening sea. Celia's swimsuit is black, plain and sporty and there's no hesitation as she wades into the cool water. 'This is lovely!' she announces.

Enzo looks at her with her new short cut, her cheeks pink from the sun, and a huge smile on her finely boned face. 'It is, isn't it?' he says. 'You're glad you came, then?'

She nods and smiles and something peculiar seems to be happening, Enzo realises. He and Mathilde have been here many times – it's *their* place – but it feels different today. As if he is seeing the beautiful cove for the very first time. 'I'm so glad,'

Celia says, pushing back her hair. Then they swim side by side, and he can tell she's loving this as much as he is. The cool, clear water, the sunshine beaming down on them.

Now Valérie is waving from the beach and calling out that lunch is ready. As they swim back to shore Enzo looks at Celia. He wants to tell her something but he doesn't quite know how to say it. That she seems different now; that in the short time he's known her she seems to have, well, *blossomed* is the only way he can put it. But that would sound ridiculous and anyway, it's hardly his place to comment on how Celia seems these days, after everything she's been through.

'Enzo?' Her voice cuts into his thoughts as they wade through the shallows. 'It was really good of you to invite me here.'

'Oh, you're welcome,' he says quickly. And then a look passes between them, and it lifts his heart as they make their way across the sand and sit down to lunch.

42

Two in the campervan and two in the tent. That's how Valérie organised everyone last night, with Enzo and Mathilde opting happily for the tent option. At just gone 7 a.m., dawn is breaking as Celia steps quietly out of the van. She left Valérie snoring softly in the other berth, and presumably Enzo and Mathilde are still asleep.

Celia's swimsuit was still damp but she pulled it on anyway, and as soon as she is in the sea, she no longer cares. She plunges forward, gasping as the chill of the water takes her breath away. Then she is swimming with all sense of coldness gone, and as she glides through the water her thoughts seem to unspool, one by one.

She knows there'll be wrangles with Geoff over money – the flat in particular – but for now it is her home, and she runs it her way. If it's chilly, the heating goes on, no question. Every morning she showers with the deliciously scented almond gel contributed by Amanda. In her kitchen there are posh herbal teabags, each one in its own little envelope which – she has to admit – are especially pleasing. 'These have been around for about thirty years,' Amanda teased her.

So, life is good. Celia no longer has to sleep next to a man who always smelt faintly of sausage rolls, or worry about the fate of a decrepit caravan – although she does wonder what'll happen when it reaches the end of its life. Will it be compressed into a cube like a knackered old car? Not her problem, she reminds herself as she swims parallel to the beach. That's for Geoff and his sister to figure out. Celia is out of the picture now, swimming on a beautiful summer's morning, with not a sound in the air apart from the occasional squawk of a gull.

Now a sudden movement at the little tent catches her attention. Enzo has emerged in tracksuit bottoms and a sweatshirt, dark hair attractively mussed. As he gazes around, shielding his eyes from the bright sunshine, she knows what it is that he's looking for. Or rather, *who*.

He spots her then and waves. 'Come in!' she mouths, waving back, and knowing that he won't hear her. But she doesn't want to wake the others, not yet.

Celia sees the smile light up his face, and briefly he's back in the tent, emerging now in swimming shorts, looking fit and toned and, she has to admit, quite delicious. She watches him as he comes nearer, unable to drag her gaze away as he wades towards her. Something surges up in her that she's never experienced before. It quickens her heart and almost takes her breath away.

'Morning,' he calls out, swimming towards her.

She smiles, and that's when it happens, before his sister and daughter have even emerged to greet the day. Right now, it's just the two of them – Enzo and Celia in the sparkling sea, his arms suddenly around her. This is how it feels, she realises, to be held. She had almost forgotten – and yet it seems so right. She feels as if her head is exploding and yet she is completely calm and happy. They stand there, with the waves swishing gently and the morning sun beaming down on them.

And then they kiss. As Celia closes her eyes, she feels herself dissolving into the sea as his lips caress hers. She feels like she might cry because it's been so long since she has been kissed like that.

Actually, she has *never* been kissed, so tenderly, like that.

It is entirely new and engulfing and wonderful.

And when they pull apart, with Enzo's arms still around her, she cannot think of anything other to say than, 'Morning.'

He smiles, and then they start to swim back to shore, just as Mathilde emerges from the tent, already in her swimsuit.

'Dad! Celia!' she yells.

'Hey, honey!' Enzo calls out. He turns to Celia and grins. 'Well, that was lovely.'

'It was,' she says, beaming as Mathilde calls out, 'I'm coming in!'

43

'Drinking hot water? What's that all about?' Terri rounds on Logan as he fills a mug from the kettle, adding a squoosh from the cold tap to bring it down to a drinkable temperature.

'I just like it,' he offers.

'It's weird!'

'It's cleansing,' he states, and she splutters, looking across to where Amanda is installed at Celia's kitchen table with her laptop. The three have been hanging out together on this bright and sunny Sunday morning. They have had breakfast together – bacon rolls made by Terri – and now they are on a second pot of coffee and enjoying the fact that no one has any pressing commitments today.

Logan is back home on a brief visit – to check up on his mum, Amanda suspects.

'*Cleansing?*' Terri sniggers now. 'My God, Amanda. What's up with the youth of today? Why aren't they smashing up phone boxes?'

'Phone boxes?' Logan splutters.

Amanda smiles dryly. 'I think Terri's stuck in 1986.'

He smirks. 'And I'm hardly *the youth* any more. I'm nearly twenty-five.'

'Virtually middle-aged,' Terri agrees with a nod. 'You'll be in funeral plan adverts next.'

She catches Amanda's eye and they laugh. They're close, Logan and Terri; that's obvious to Amanda, and she's conscious of a tiny kernel of what she can only label as envy. Of course, living upstairs, Terri has witnessed him growing from being a little boy to a fine, handsome young man.

Terri isn't at all what Amanda thought her to be at the start. She is kind and warm, and incredibly hard-working – there's a lot to look up to, Amanda decides. So she has given up on maintaining a front that everything about her own life is perfect. Now both Terri and Celia are aware that being married to Jasper isn't quite what she'd envisaged. They know about the potato printing and the gradual trashing of her flat.

Amanda picks up her phone, seeing that Celia has sent her a bunch of photos from the beach. 'Oh, look at these,' she enthuses, and Logan and Terri gather around to see. There are bright yellow irises, something cooking in a pan over an open fire, and an attractive, dark-haired woman with strong features who can only be Enzo's sister.

A photo of Celia too, sun-kissed and laughing to the camera. Amanda can't help comparing this Celia to the version who'd turned up at her wedding, stressed and alone, with a busted wheelie case, just six months ago. She looks so happy now; the opposite of how you'd expect someone to be after they'd been lied to and cheated on.

'Why didn't you two go?' Logan asks, clutching his mug.

'Too busy with work, love,' Terri replies.

'And I just thought...' Amanda starts, then hesitates. 'I just thought your mum might like to hang out with them.' She shrugs. 'Without me around, I mean. She's had an awful lot of me over the past few weeks.'

She catches Logan giving her an inscrutable look, and she sees Terri registering this too. Nothing needs to be said, Amanda feels. Celia just needed a bit of time away from this flat.

The morning passes pleasantly, with Logan having retired to his room, presumably to enjoy further mugs of hot water without ridicule. Amanda checks her emails and Terri rummages in her bag and pulls out a CD. 'That's old school,' Amanda remarks.

'It's a favourite of mine and Celia's,' she says, popping it into the antiquated CD player on the shelf.

'Oh, Celia and I always loved this music,' Amanda enthuses as the first track fills the kitchen.

'We do too.' Terri grins. 'But it was banned from the flat, so we only ever got to play it at my place, or in the car...'

'Banned?' Amanda stares at her. 'By who?'

'Who d'you think?'

A look is exchanged. 'What did you think of him really?' Amanda asks. 'Before Caravan Day, I mean?'

Terri shrugs, hesitating, as if being careful how she puts it. 'I think Celia felt as if she didn't have much choice, back in the day.'

Amanda frowns. 'I wish I'd known what was happening. I wasn't a very good friend to Celia back then.'

'You were in London,' Terri reminds her, 'living your life. And you're here now, aren't you? That's what matters.'

'I hope so,' she murmurs.

Terri pats her arm. 'Celia's going to really miss you, you know.'

'I'll miss her. And you too.' They hug, and Terri slings her bag over her shoulder, ready to head back upstairs. 'You coming up?'

Amanda nods. 'I will, yes. Leave Logan in peace for a bit...' Terri smiles, and then she indicates the space on the table once occupied by Spike.

'How d'you think she revived it? The cactus, I mean?'

Amanda laughs. 'Honestly, I have no idea.'

Terri's gaze meets hers. 'She's pretty amazing, isn't she?'

'Yes, she is,' Amanda agrees with a smile. 'She's always had the magic touch.'

44

Celia looks at the bathroom shelf that was crammed with Amanda's numerous pots and jars, and which is now empty. Unlike her friend she has never adhered to any kind of beauty routine. She is a soap-and-water type, very low maintenance. Working with plants would make manicures impractical and really, she can't see the point.

In the living room, she waters those that now populate the shelves in here. She no longer feels she has to keep them all in the plant room, with a small overspill allowed in Logan's room. In fact, the word 'allowed' doesn't even feature any more. Celia does whatever she likes.

She is repositioning Spike on the shelf when Amanda appears. Soon he'll be going home with Enzo and Mathilde. Celia just wants to make sure her tea 'cure' wasn't a fluke, and that he really is back to full health. 'He's looking a lot perkier, isn't he?' Amanda remarks.

'Yes, he is.' Celia nods, though it's still baffling to her. 'Weird, isn't it?'

Amanda laughs. 'D'you think he was putting it on? By flopping over like that, I mean?'

'To get attention, maybe?' Celia grins.

'Yeah, to keep Enzo on his toes,' Amanda suggests.

'God knows. Honestly, I always liked to think I had all the answers. But really, what do I know?'

'A lot, Celia. You know a heck of a lot.' She senses Amanda assessing her for a moment. 'So, anyway, you've got a date tonight?'

'A *date*.' Celia laughs, scoffing at the word. But if it's not a date, then what is it? Last Sunday, on the beach, she and Enzo had taken a walk together while Valérie and Mathilde tended the fire. 'I was wondering,' he'd said, 'if you'd like to go out to dinner sometime?' Of course she had said yes, but then perhaps it's just a friends thing he's looking for? Unaccustomed to dating in any form, Celia has no idea.

She sees Amanda checking her watch. Celia knows she's leaving within the hour and now her friend is hugging her, minty-breathed and smelling of her colossally expensive moisturiser from the hefty glass jar. 'You promise me you'll look after yourself, won't you?' Amanda says.

'Yes, of course I will.'

'As well as you look after your plants?'

Celia nods, aware of tears prickling her eyes as she studies Amanda's face.

Amanda was always beautiful, she reflects. At her wedding she seemed different – jawline taut, lips a little plumped, something off-kilter, she'd thought. But now those features have softened and she looks like the Amanda she always knew.

'Before I go,' Amanda says, 'can we do something?'

'Sure, what?'

Amanda beckons her through to the kitchen where she bobs down to pull open the bottom freezer drawer. She looks up, grinning. 'Celia, what is all this shit?'

Celia laughs. 'A load of haggis-en-croutes.'

'Please enlighten me,' Amanda teases.

'Um... Geoff's company wanted to do a premium range. He was convinced this would be it – the big seller, the game changer in premium snack foods...'

Amanda is laughing now. 'And no one tried to persuade him it was a bad idea?'

'Oh, you know what he's like.' Celia chuckles. 'When his mind's made up, there's no reasoning with him.' It's true; you could show him a lemon, and if he decided it was a cabbage, you could argue until you were crying hot, frustrated tears and it'd still be a cabbage in Geoff's eyes.

'Well, it's time to clear the decks,' Amanda announces. 'Give me a bin bag.'

Celia hesitates. Would it be wasteful to throw them away? She hates waste. But really, what else could be done with them? So she hands Amanda a bag, and they start to pull out all of those haggis-en-croutes that filled the entire drawer, and which always made a little more of Celia's lifeblood seep away every time she saw them there.

And now, with the job done and Amanda's taxi on its way, Celia ties up the bag of failed pastry products and carries it out to the bin.

* * *

Celia doesn't quite know what to do with herself on this cool and breezy Tuesday afternoon now Amanda has gone. Logan is out, meeting his old chess club friends, and soon he'll be away volunteering again and she will be quite alone.

Switching her attention to tonight's date with Enzo, and needing to clear her head a little, she heads out on a walk. At the park she follows the path that snakes up the hillside, past runners and dog walkers and young parents with gaggles of toddlers and kids. A black spaniel runs to her and she stoops to ruffle its head. Then finally she reaches the flagpole at the top and she can see for miles.

For a few minutes Celia sits on a bench and she breathes it all in. Then she starts to make her way back home, figuring that perhaps she'll wear *that* dress tonight. The beautiful blue and green one, the gift from Amanda. Perhaps this is the occasion it's been waiting for.

She is wondering which shoes to wear as she approaches her flat. Those block-heeled red shoes really have to go, she decides, having concluded that they will never miraculously fit her. Next time she's out, she'll drop them at the charity shop. That terrible shift dress, too; the one she felt so uncomfortable in at Amanda's wedding. She knows she'll never wear that again.

Now Celia pokes her key into the lock and realises with a start that her front door is unlocked. Her heart thuds. Has Logan come back unexpectedly?

Tentatively, she pushes it open. 'Hello?' she calls out into the hallway.

'It's me,' comes a male voice, and he steps out of the living room, into the hallway, looking sheepish and tired.

Geoff. A sudden fury rises up in her. 'What are you doing here?'

'I... I just wanted to see you.' He looks down at his feet.

'You can't do this,' she exclaims. 'Geoff, you don't live here any more. You can't just march in here whenever you feel like it!'

'I know, I'm sorry...' He fishes keys from his trouser pocket and hands them to her. 'I should've called,' he adds. 'I need to talk to you, Celia. That's all.'

She looks at the man she thought she knew so intimately. Now he seems like a stranger to her. A stranger she almost feels sorry for, standing there in his beige sweatshirt and jeans. She'd loved him once, and Logan had too. He will always be Logan's father – the one who was there for him, albeit in his somewhat remote, Geoff-ish way.

'What d'you want to talk about?' she asks. *Please, not the legal stuff*, she wills him. She's not quite ready for that yet.

His gaze meets hers and his cheeks redden. 'I want you to know it's all over,' he murmurs. 'The thing, I mean. It's finished now. It was all a mistake...' He clears his throat and looks distractedly around the hallway, his gaze resting briefly on the trailing variegated ivy than now tumbles prettily from the shelf. 'Celia, I'd like to come back,' he adds, 'and try to make things right again.'

Celia regards him steadily. 'You mean she's kicked you out.'

'No, no. It just wasn't working.' He blushes hotly. 'And actually—'

'Geoff, admit it. You have nowhere to go, do you?'

'Well, there are friends, of course,' he blusters. Then he gazes at her with an expression of what she can only interpret as hope.

She looks at him, considering what he's just told her. Then she strides through to the living room, opens the shallow drawer beneath the coffee table, the drawer where all kinds of random bits are kept. She pulls out the key with the paper label attached. His mum's writing: *Caravan spare*.

'Here you go,' she says calmly, 'in case you've lost your set.'

'Oh. Um... thanks,' he murmurs.

'I know you have friends,' she adds, not unkindly. 'But I don't need it, and you might one day.'

'Yeah, good to have it,' he mutters.

Celia raises a smile. 'And it does have an *incredible* view.'

45

Everything looks normal, Amanda decides as the cab pulls up outside her flat. Well, of course it does. Even a klutz like Jasper was unlikely to burn the place down, and he'd hardly cause a kitchen fire surviving on crackers and triangle cheese.

She thanks the driver and drags her enormous suitcase along the short, tiled pathway to the front door. July the fourth, she muses as she steps into the beautiful Victorian building. Independence Day. She decided, on the train down, that she'd step back into her life with an open mind and see how things pan out. *Be more Celia*, she told herself as she sipped a gin and tonic at her table seat in the quiet coach.

Be more Celia. She turns the phrase over in her mind as she starts to lug the suitcase upstairs. Celia who, just before Amanda left this morning, announced that she had a plan. That is, a plan that might just help her mum. Celia will overhaul her garden, she explained. Enzo has offered to help, and Mathilde wants to be a part of it too.

'It's worth a try,' Celia had told Amanda, 'even if it just shows Mum that she's cared about and that anything is possible.'

Amanda knows the garden is overrun with weeds and marvels at Celia's appetite for that kind of manual work. She also knows that Celia is hoping her mother might even get involved, and that somehow, they can work together to help her change the way she lives – the way she *is*. 'It has to come from Mum, though,' Celia said.

Amanda hugged her. She's learnt from Celia that working with plants is a wonderful healer, but will it help her mum? 'If nothing else,' Celia added, 'she'll have a beautiful garden to look out on again.'

'Like it used to be,' Amanda said, her eyes filling with sudden tears, 'when it was yours.' She'd quickly blinked them away because Celia did not need her getting all emotional about her own mum.

Now Amanda stops on the half landing and rotates her stiff shoulder. She will do that funeral plan ad, she's decided. The money is great, and Ollie hinted that it'll only be shown on daytime TV, in the ad breaks on quiz shows. So what's the harm? It's not as if anyone she knows will see it.

She is about to haul her case up the remaining stairs when she becomes aware of a hubbub coming from above. Not just above in a vague way, but directly above where she is standing now – *in her flat*. Voices and laughter and the clinking of glasses. A loud guffaw and someone announcing, 'It's looking fantastic, Jasper. Well done!'

Amanda blinks slowly and rubs at her tired eyes. Then from out of nowhere comes a surge of energy as she lifts her case and storms up to her front door – which is wide open – and bursts in.

Her flat is full of people. Artsy people and actorly people – everywhere she looks there are chunky spectacles and little beards and scarves worn like cravats. Several of the women present are wearing brightly coloured snug-fitting tops and dark-wash jeans the size of sails. Her fashion-eye also picks out graphic prints from the Uniqlo x Marimekko collab, and a Stella McCartney pinafore.

Amanda stops in her tasteful hallway with the warm grey walls and tiny spotlights. When she'd left for Scotland, her favourite picture had hung here. A beautiful, stylised image of her head in profile, turned into a chic graphic, created for her fortieth birthday by an old friend on a TV job.

The picture has gone. Now the walls are displaying what look like Jasper's fucking potato prints, framed simply under glass. She stands there, looking through to her living room, taking it all in like a stranger who has walked into a party alone and doesn't know who to talk to.

'Hi.' A man with ginger hair and a tiny moustache has appeared at her side and smiles at her. 'Red or white?'

Amanda stares at him. 'Sorry?'

'Red or white wine, or a soft?'

'Er... nothing, thank you.' *I do not need to be offered a drink in my own home!*

He sips from his own glass and gazes around at the artwork in the hallway. 'Exhibition looks great, doesn't it?'

She nods, tight-lipped, momentarily feeling as if she might cry. With some effort she manages to calm herself with a huge, deep breath, and then somehow, miraculously – like a floppy cactus springing back to erectness – anger rises up in her. 'It's quite powerful, yes.' *As powerful as the punch I feel like giving him.*

'It's very bold,' the man remarks. 'So how d'you know Jasper?'

She senses her nostrils flaring as she looks at him. 'Excuse me.' Leaving her suitcase in the hall and the man hovering beside it, she marches through to her crowded living room.

Amanda has thrown wildly successful parties that were less populated than this.

'Ooh, sorry!' A woman in baggy black dungarees has clonked into her shoulder but Amanda barely notices. Instead, she is looking around at yet more prints, and paintings too – all Jasper's art entirely filling the walls.

'Honey, you're here!' Having spotted her across the room he wends his way between a woman in a denim boiler suit and a cluster of tall, interchangeable braying men, and he stops in front of her. There's a tight hug which causes Amanda to compress her arms to her sides, and when he pulls away he looks quizzical. 'I thought you'd be here earlier!'

'Train was delayed,' she says.

'Oh, really? Well, never mind because you're here now—'

'Jasper, what are all these paintings doing on my walls?'

He frowns now as if she's a child who's just sworn in front of his mother. 'Your walls? I thought I lived here too!' He emits a barking laugh and glances fretfully around the room, and then looks back at her as if to say, *Don't be difficult, darling. Not tonight with all these people here.*

'But you said you had an exhibition?' she says carefully. *Keep calm*, she tells herself. *Look what Celia's dealt with. Don't lose your shit now.*

'I do,' Jasper says.

'A London gallery, you said?'

'Yeah, this is it! It's the thing now, didn't you know? Showing work in a home environment? Much more relaxed, seeing the work like this, showing how the work can work in a normal living room...' If he says 'work' again she will slap him across the head. 'In a space where people live,' he concludes.

'Yes, where *I* live!' It comes out louder than she'd intended and she catches the boiler suit woman shooting her a surprised glance.

Jasper forces a tight smile. 'Shall we talk about this later, sweetie?'

'What about gallery representation?' Amanda asks. 'You said—'

'Yes, I'm representing myself,' he announces. 'Who needs a middleman taking a cut? Please, darling. Settle down and get yourself a drink. Mingle a bit – there are some fun people here. You've had a long, tiring journey. I'd better mingle myself, people want to talk to me...'

'Don't let me keep you,' she says, in as bright a voice as she can muster. As she leaves the room for the sanctuary of her cool, chalky white bedroom, she tells herself again: *don't lose it. Be more Celia.* She sits heavily on the edge of the unmade bed – he hadn't even bothered to make it – telling herself that it's fine, this is her place, and her bed, and pretty soon it will really feel like hers again.

Back to the way she had it, when she loved her home, and being alone, just doing her own thing. In the days when her vegetables remained, unmolested, in her vegetable rack.

I can have all that again, she decides, and this realisation brings about a new sense of calm in her – that it *will* be okay, that she can take control of her life again.

Just like Celia does, Amanda reflects as she pulls her phone from her jacket pocket and calls her oldest friend.

46

EIGHT MONTHS LATER

The crocuses are out. Great drifts of yellow and purple cover the grass. There must be thousands, Celia thinks. She has never seen anything quite like it.

It's not *that park* that Celia has brought Enzo to – the one where 'Scott Chegg' first found her, alone as a teenage girl. They are not even in Glasgow. Celia and Enzo are staying at Amanda's in east London and this is Kew Gardens. Although Geoff is occupying less of Celia's brain space with every passing day, she couldn't ignore her frisson of pleasure when they bought tickets.

Full price tickets, that is. Not the cheaper post-4 p.m. option. Feeling reckless and wild, she took Enzo's hand as they strode in through the gates. Now they have walked for hours, chatting constantly, marvelling at the beautiful Victorian Temperate House, filled with lush ferns and tender species. They have explored the kitchen gardens, wandered through the wild expanse of untamed woodland and climbed to the top of the pagoda.

'Oh, this is amazing,' Celia exclaims, catching her breath.

'It feels like we can see the whole of London,' Enzo agrees.

They fall into an easy silence, drinking it all in. And then Celia turns and catches his look of bemusement.

'What is it?' She smiles.

'Just...' He winds an arm around her shoulders, pulling her close. 'Who'd have thought we'd be here together? That first time, when I came round with Spike—'

'When Terri shooed you away?'

He laughs. 'I thought she seemed quite ferocious.'

'And what did you think of me?'

'I thought...' Enzo pauses. 'I thought you seemed fascinating. And also sad.' He smiles and then kisses her lightly on the lips.

'I'm not sad any more,' she says.

'I can tell, and I'm glad about that...' They make their way back down the pagoda and, at ground level now, they are soon back among the crocuses. It's not their first trip together – they have been to the Highlands with Mathilde – but it is their first with just the two of them.

'I love it here,' Celia announces happily.

'Me too.' Enzo squeezes her hand.

'It's so inspiring,' she adds, pausing to take photos with her phone.

'Bet you can't wait to start your course,' he says, and she nods. It'll be busy, she realises, studying garden design while going all out to promote her houseplant hospital, bringing in more business to keep herself afloat. But she'll cut down on her shop hours and hopefully quit before too long. Meanwhile, Logan will help out once he's graduated. He'll be home for the summer and has offered to build her a website. Until he flies the nest again, they can work together as a team.

That's how it feels as Celia and Enzo wander towards the Palm House and step into its steamy warmth. That they, too, are a team. How easy he is to be with and how good he makes her feel.

Inside the vast glasshouse, her senses are fizzling with the sights and smells all around her. Celia scribbles away in her notebook, jotting down descriptions of rare plant species to make sure she doesn't forget a thing. Not that she will, because this is one of those golden days you remember forever.

Today she is wearing that dress again – the green and blue patterned one, gauzy and light against her bare legs, now with a soft angora sweater worn on top, at Amanda's suggestion. 'Really?' Celia had said this morning. 'A dress, for going to the gardens?'

'Why not?' Amanda said.

She was right, Celia thinks. It's the perfect dress for a day like this.

As Enzo's hand folds around hers, she stops and looks at his handsome face, taking in the deep brown eyes, the mouth she loves to kiss.

They kiss now and her heart seems to soar with happiness. Then together they step out of the glasshouse and into the beautiful spring day.

* * *

MORE FROM FIONA GIBSON

Another book from Fiona Gibson, *'Tis the Damn Season*, is available to order now here:

www.mybook.to/FionaBackAd

ACKNOWLEDGEMENTS

Huge thanks to my brilliant agent, Caroline Sheldon, and to all at RCW. Thank you to Rachel Faulkner-Willcocks, Claire Fenby, Jenna Houston and the fantastic Boldwood team. Thanks to Gary Jukes for excellent copyediting, to Christina de Caix-Curtis for fantastic proofreading, and to Rachel Gilbey for blog tour wizardry. Book ideas spring from funny places sometimes. This one grew from a late-night chat over dinner with Hazel and Jack Henderson – did I know there was a houseplant hospital nearby? As an accidental houseplant killer, I loved this idea. Huge thanks to Helen at foxbotanics.co.uk for the tour around her gorgeous plant-filled house and garden, and to Emma at glasgowplantmama.com for her fascinating plant care class. These women can rescue your desiccated aspidistra! Thanks to my ever-brilliant friends: Jen, Kath, Wendy R, Susan, Ellie, Marie, Tania, Cathy and Liam, Michelle, Jackie B, Maggie, Wendy V, Lisa, Adele, Jennifer, Mickey and the Currie clan. Last but not least, thank you to Jimmy for keeping me (mostly) calm, and to Sam, Dexter and Erin.

ABOUT THE AUTHOR

Fiona Gibson writes bestselling and brilliantly funny novels about the craziness and messiness of family life.

Sign up to Fiona Gibson's mailing list for news, competitions and updates on future books.

Visit Fiona's website: www.fionagibson.com

Follow Fiona on social media here:

- facebook.com/fionagibsonauthor
- instagram.com/fiona_gib
- bookbub.com/profile/fiona-gibson
- x.com/FionaGibson

ALSO BY FIONA GIBSON

'Tis the Damn Season

The Woman Who Got Her Spark Back

BECOME A MEMBER OF

THE SHELF CARE CLUB

The home of Boldwood's book club reads.

Find uplifting reads, sunny escapes, cosy romances, family dramas and more!

Sign up to the newsletter
https://bit.ly/theshelfcareclub

Boldwood

Boldwood Books is an award-winning fiction publishing company seeking out the best stories from around the world.

Find out more at www.boldwoodbooks.com

Join our reader community for brilliant books, competitions and offers!

Follow us
@BoldwoodBooks
@TheBoldBookClub

Sign up to our weekly deals newsletter

https://bit.ly/BoldwoodBNewsletter

Printed in Great Britain
by Amazon